In the Tunnel

by JULIE LEE

HOLIDAY HOUSE   NEW YORK

HOLIDAY HOUSE is registered in the U.S. Patent and Trademark Office.

Printed and bound in March 2023 at Maple Press, York, PA, USA

www.holidayhouse.com

First Edition

1 3 5 7 9 10 8 6 4 2

Library of Congress Cataloging-in-Publication Data

Names: Lee, Julie (Children's fiction writer), author.
Title: In the tunnel / by Julie Lee.
Description: First edition. | New York : Holiday House, [2023]
Audience: Ages 8–12. | Audience: Grades 4–6. | Summary: Fourteen-year-old
Myung-gi flees North Korea with his family during the height of the devastating Korean
War, beginning an epic struggle for survival that pushes them to the brink.
Identifiers: LCCN 2022043532 (print) | LCCN 2022043533 (ebook)
ISBN 9780823450398 (hardcover) | ISBN 9780823455294 (ebook)
Subjects: LCSH: Korea (North)—History—20th century—Juvenile fiction.
CYAC: Korea (North)—History—20th century—Fiction. | Refugees—Fiction.
Survival—Fiction. | Korean War, 1950–1953—Fiction.
LCGFT: Historical fiction. | Novels.
Classification: LCC PZ7.1.L417262 In 2023 (print)
LCC PZ7.1.L417262 (ebook) | DDC [Fic]—dc23
LC record available at https://lccn.loc.gov/2022043532
LC ebook record available at https://lccn.loc.gov/2022043533

ISBN: 978-0-8234-5039-8 (hardcover)

For my father, the scholar

CHAPTER 1

October 1952: Myung-gi, Age 16

> I am determined, unstoppable,
> body-flinging-down determined
> on this thousand, ten thousand ri I shall go.
> Leap quick as an arrow up
> this road and go, and let
> the burning mountain, the mountain burning
> raise its columns of smoke.
>
> —Kim Sowol, *Thousand, Ten Thousand Ri*

This is the end.

Myung-gi knows this because everything is in slow motion—bodies flying, mortar shells dropping, the lieutenant's mouth moving. And all he can see is his father—sitting in his office, wearing his principal's suit jacket. *Sorry, Ahpa*, he tries to say, but his father's face disappears in gun smoke.

Advance forward! To the top! Go, go, go!

It's the lieutenant. Lit up by searchlights. His arm thrusting wildly toward the top of the hill. But in the autumn dark, the enemy crawl out of hidden foxholes—right behind the line of advancing South Korean soldiers.

"Watch out! Lieutenant!" Myung-gi runs up the rocky slope, carrying his rifle on his back like a satchel of books. Because he barely got training, never fired at anyone. He didn't sign up to be a front-line soldier. He signed up to find his father.

Bullets whiz past his ear. He ducks, dodges, prays for dumb luck.

But still he roars, joining the chorus of others. Louder than he's ever shouted. Harder than he's ever pushed. And for a second, it feels right.

Until a grenade flashes before Myung-gi's eyes, blinding him.

He trips, rolls, drops his weapon, loses his helmet. His ankle snaps.

"No! Myung-gi!" someone shouts. It sounds like Gum Boy—the only other recruit who never knows what's going on. All he does is chew gum all day and hop onto the Americans' Patton tank to gawk at all the moving parts. Why so much worry in his voice?

Myung-gi is falling.

Down the hill. The mountainside jabbing, pounding, scraping him raw.

He lands in an opening—a gigantic rabbit hole—and crawls in deep. He pictures himself in a cross-section of the earth, positioned on all fours, pink and hairless. But no, this is no animal burrow—this is a tunnel, an enemy tunnel. A dusty wind blows in his face, stifles his breathing, narrows the walls. He coughs and sputters.

A terrible crash slams the hillside. Myung-gi flattens himself, covers his head. Bits of rock and dirt rain down on him. Parts of the tunnel are collapsing. He can no longer see the way he came in. And it's not just because of his glasses, which are now cracked. Walls are caving—

Until it stops.

It's quieter now. The blasts are muffled. And the absurdity hits him. He's fighting people who look like him, who eat rice like him, who celebrate Lunar New Year like him—North Korean soldiers and their Chinese allies. How did he even end up here in the middle of a war, at the North-South Korean border, trapped inside a tunnel? An enemy tunnel, like the ones the lieutenant told them about: built by the Chinese, branching out like an old oak, where the enemy can crawl out—right behind them. Just a few months ago, he was with his mother and sister—working, delivering water in Busan, waiting for Ahpa to come. Now . . . his hands, they're shaking so hard, Myung-gi can't even recognize them.

The barrage outside echoes against the rock walls. He wonders how the Chinese could dig such an intricate underground passageway without large machinery, using only hand tools. Myung-gi tries to stand but can't. The shaft is only four feet wide and five feet tall.

He takes a deep breath. The air is stale. There are strange smells like burning pine and petroleum and deep earth. And something putrid, close enough to get in the back of his throat where he can taste it. He spits on the ground, but it's still in there—up his nostrils, in his mouth, filling his sinuses.

At least he's sheltered from the pinging bullets. That's what he keeps telling himself, anyway, and slowly his shaky breath begins to steady.

But not for long.

Because he hears them, somewhere deep in the tunnel. Voices shouting. Pistols firing. And screaming—grown men screaming. His fellow South Korean soldiers must have found another entrance, slipped inside, and are now fighting the enemy—hand-to-hand, in the dark. Myung-gi shudders so hard, he has to lean away from the sharp, stony walls.

He gropes around like a blind person. There are sharp objects on the rocky ground. Garbage, too, maybe. He tosses a crumpled paper to the side. Then he feels his belt, feels the sheath, and pulls out the only weapon he has left. Myung-gi thumbs the edge of the sharp blade, then puts it back inside its case. *God, please don't make me use it.*

Above, artillery pieces shell the hill.

And the earth breaks.

Myung-gi's head snaps back, hits the rock wall, jolts back into place. As if the giant hand of God just shook the boy out of him.

Myung-gi-ya, sixteen is still a boy, too young to fight, Uhma had argued.

But not for this war, he had shot back. *Any age will do, especially if you lie about it—even if they* know *you're lying about it. I'm living proof of that.*

But now . . .

Sorry, Uhma. I haven't been a good son. You told me not to enlist, told me this was not a good way to find Ahpa, told me this was not who I was. But now this is who I am, a recruit in the South Korean army, buried inside an enemy tunnel, about to die. And I don't know how my plans went so wrong.

CHAPTER 2

August 15, 1945: Myung-gi, Age 9

Something was wrong. Ichiro looked up from his book and listened to the strange ruckus outside—crying, shouting, pans banging. What was going on? Had the villagers gone mad? Before closing his book of folktales, he made a mental note of the page where he'd left off reading, not wanting to fold the corner and ruin the crisp sheet.

Peering through the rice paper of his wooden lattice door, Ichiro didn't see anyone in the main room—not even Uhma, who usually sat at the low dining table snapping off the root ends of soybean sprouts in preparation for a week's worth of side dishes.

He slid open the door. The sounds outside grew louder, almost as if they were right there, inside the house. Ichiro looked across the courtyard. The main gate was propped open. A stream of people were walking past, yelling and crying.

Along the street's edge was his mother's long skirt blowing in the hot breeze, his father's back beside her, his seven-year-old sister's feet jumping up and down in front of them. What were they looking at? Were they going somewhere—just the three of them? Why hadn't they told him? It seemed he never knew what was going on outside the worlds of his books.

Ichiro shuffled toward them. His feet suddenly turned as heavy as the rocks he and his fourth-grade class had to carry to build dams—children doing the job of men who were off fighting the war in the Pacific. When carrying, Ichiro would always pass the freshly painted Japanese schoolhouse where only Japanese children were allowed to attend. He often saw them watching from their windows—some wide-eyed and solemn, others laughing and pointing. The Japanese children did not have to haul any rocks.

What if all this noise outside had something to do with the Japanese? What if those pans banging was the sound of metal against the side of someone's head—someone who wasn't doing their share in serving Emperor Hirohito, Japan's living god? Ichiro was not good at carrying all those rocks—the worst one, actually. Sweat glazed his forehead, and his glasses slid to the tip of his nose.

Just then, his father strode back to the house, followed by

Ichiro's mother and sister. A small Korean flag—one that they'd always kept hidden in the back of a drawer—now swung from a stick in his little sister's hand.

Ichiro couldn't stop staring at it. "Uh . . . Ahpa, shouldn't you put that away? What if someone sees it?" No Korean flags were allowed to fly under Japanese rule. They weren't even allowed to speak the Korean language in public (though he and his sister used certain Korean words—like Ahpa and Uhma—in private). Koreans were a lower class whose culture had to be erased. Even Ichiro knew that.

"Son, we can fly our Korean flag proudly now," his father said, grinning. "The Japanese have lost the war in the Pacific. They've been ousted out of Korea. They're all leaving, even as we speak. We are free, son! Free!"

Ahpa hoisted Ichiro in the air, his arms as sturdy as a bull's horns. Uhma laughed, while Ichiro's little sister whined to be picked up too. But Ichiro just held on tight, still wondering what this all meant.

Setting Ichiro down, his father looked him in the eye. "Your name is no longer Ichiro. That was *their* name, the one the Japanese made us use in place of your Korean one. Son, your Korean name, your *real* name," he said, his lips a trembling line, "is Myung-gi. Kim Myung-gi. We will never use the Japanese name Ichiro again. Do you understand?" The line of Ahpa's mouth returned to normal—straight and steady.

"Yes, Ahpa," Ichiro said, then whispered to himself: "Myung-gi.

Kim Myung-gi." How strange it felt in his mouth and then in his ears. All his life, he had been Ichiro, and now he was Myung-gi. But who was Myung-gi? He looked to his father, who always had the answers.

But Ahpa only picked up Myung-gi's little sister and said, "Hideko is no longer Hideko. You, my pretty girl, are now Yoomee, meaning 'having beauty.'"

It was as if their father had just anointed her Queen, the way she stood there for a second, unmoving, her mouth slightly agape. "Yoomee," she whispered, her eyes gleaming. "My name means beauty." And she dropped to her knees, grabbed some paper, then started drawing flowers and stars and rainbows, her feverish hands finally claiming all those beautiful things.

"And my name, Ahpa?" Myung-gi asked, peering above the rim of his glasses. "What does my name mean?"

That was when Uhma stepped in and straightened her son's frames, her smile full of so much pride, it was bursting through the balls of her cheeks. "Your name means 'having cleverness and strength,' a name picked specially by your father," she said. "Because you are just like him."

Somewhere in the periphery of the room, Myung-gi could hear his sister nagging for everyone to look at her drawing, but he only sat and stared straight ahead, turning his new name around in his head. He knew he had some book smarts, always getting good grades at school. But cleverness? Strength? He wasn't so sure about those things. He looked up at Ahpa standing there in the middle of the room, his shoulders broad, his smile wide. Everyone in the village respected and liked his father. Men went to him for business advice. And he was once part of an army—just like Myung-gi's grandfather—and had carried two injured soldiers across a battlefield during the early clashes against the Japanese, one on each shoulder. Maybe Uhma and Ahpa had given him the wrong name.

"I'm in the mood to make a feast," Uhma said, her eyes sparkling like the jeweled brooch on the lapel of her silk hanbok. "I'll make galbi-jim so soft and tender, it will fall off the bone. Oh, and some radish soup, kimchi pancakes, and marinated cucumbers. And if I have any pots left, I will make some sweet rice with chestnuts and dates!"

Myung-gi could practically taste it—meat stewed so rich and dark, fried pancakes sizzling on his tongue, crisp cucumber sliced paper thin. He leapt onto a floor cushion, surprising everyone. Aside from a good book, few other things could make him feel this way.

"Why didn't you tell me you were short on pots?" Ahpa said, tuning the radio to a lively trot song. "I will buy you pots tomorrow—the best pots I can find!" Sweeping Uhma into his arms, he danced her around the room, making her squeal with laughter, and Myung-gi looked away, his cheeks growing warm.

"Do you like this picture, Oppah?" Yoomee asked, smiling shyly at her older brother. She pulled out a piece of paper from behind her back and shoved it in front of Myung-gi's face.

It was too close for his eyes to focus, but he told her he liked it any-way, until she pulled it back, and he could see the drawing of a monkey sniffing its own armpit, the words "Myung-gi means monkey" scrib-bled at the top. Maniacal laughter—as loud as any man out drinking with his buddies—burst out of her small, seven-year-old body.

Oh, how Myung-gi regretted Ahpa teaching her some English words.

"Give that to me," Myung-gi said, trying to grab the drawing. He didn't need that picture making its way to school—something Yoomee would be sure to do.

But Yoomee darted away, knocking over a pile of books on the floor.

"Yah! What's going on here?" Ahpa said, giving them both stern glances.

Uhma shook her head at her two children, but a smile lingered in her eyes as she headed into the kitchen.

"Sorry, Ahpa," Myung-gi said, his gaze faltering. He kept looking at his sister, waiting for her apology too, but she only stared down at her picture, her face a tight fist.

"There will be no fighting. Especially not on this glorious day," Ahpa said, his hands on both their shoulders.

In the silence that followed, Myung-gi could still hear clanging pots and shouts of joy outside. Ahpa was right; this was a special day, a glorious day. Today was the day they were finally free from years of Japanese rule.

Which he guessed would mean no more segregated schools, no more carrying rocks to build dams and bridges, no more hiding their Korean language and Korean names. He was truly no longer Ichiro. From now on, he would be Myung-gi—whoever that was.

"Now . . ." Ahpa said, his tone pretending to be low and serious. "Should we play some jegi chagi?"

Before anyone could answer, Yoomee was already up and running to get the jegi, a silk-wrapped coin, from the drawer. For the rest of the afternoon, the three of them stood in the courtyard, kicking the jegi with the sides of their feet, trying to keep it up in the air, the savory aroma of roasting spareribs threatening to break their concentration. But they kept going, laughing and tossing the jegi back and forth. And though Myung-gi couldn't keep his balance, couldn't kick the jegi more than twice, he had to admit that Yoomee was pretty good, sometimes keeping the sack up in the air eight kicks in a row. In the end, it was Ahpa who had won.

By the time Uhma called them for dinner, an ache was running down Myung-gi's leg, Yoomee was complaining that something wasn't fair, and Ahpa was patting Myung-gi on the back, saying, "Maybe you'll do better next time, son." But none of that mattered. Because today he had a new name, picked to be just like his father. And Ahpa was theirs and they were his, and sometimes, even if you weren't a winner, it was good enough just to stand close to one.

CHAPTER 3

August–September 1945: Myung-gi, Age 9

For some, it lasted only a few hours. For others, it lasted a few days. For Myung-gi and everyone in his village, the celebration of freedom lasted only one night.

The next morning, as quickly as the Japanese authorities had moved out, the Soviet soldiers moved in, marching into the village from the train station. Myung-gi had never seen a white person up close before. They were giants, carrying large rifles. Their cheeks were chiseled and sharp, their blue sapphire eyes mined out of the hard rock of their faces. Even in summer, they wore long coats that whished as they walked, blowing the stench of hot and humid sweat across everyone's faces. One of them spat the shells of sunflower seeds right into an old couple's courtyard.

Weeks after they swooped in, it was announced that Korea had been divided in half at the 38th parallel, a line of latitude on a map— the Soviets occupying the North and the United States occupying the South. The Russians said they were there to free the people of northern Korea from Japanese occupation.

Then they shut down all the newspapers.

No one seemed to know what to make of these new foreigners, all the villagers only blinking at one another in silence. Were the Russians just passing through? Would they stay for good? Or would the Americans eventually come? Just you wait and see, a few argued, the Americans will be here soon—but they never came.

Mrs. Song, Myung-gi's next-door neighbor, said that the Soviets were their liberators, that everyone should be grateful to them, that no one could be worse than the Japanese imperialists.

"Was that true, Ahpa?" Myung-gi had asked before they all headed to a village funeral. "Are the Soviets our liberators? Are they good?"

But Ahpa only rubbed the back of his neck, that wide smile from Liberation Day now pursed and shriveled like a prune.

It was the third funeral they had attended since the war in the Pacific had come to an end—the young Korean men who had served in the military now returning home injured or in body bags. The lost son of one villager was like a lost son to all—nearly everyone showed up to pay their respects.

Myung-gi and Yoomee stood close beside their parents. Though Myung-gi did not know any of these fallen young soldiers, he recognized their faces from the older boys' schoolyard. He couldn't believe they were now gone, disappeared from the face of the Earth. A chilly wind blew hard against his back, and Myung-gi dug his feet into the dirt.

One of the weeping mothers stood beside him, the white hemp of her dress as colorless as her pale face. With nothing but a photograph of her son—not even a body to lower into the ground—the woman started wailing and moaning, deep and raspy, like a rusted ship being dredged.

Myung-gi bit his lip, dug his nails into his palms, but he could still feel a well of sadness rising in his throat. So he pinched himself hard—anything to stop the tears that were already starting to dribble down his cheeks. Wondering whether Ahpa felt it too, Myung-gi glanced up at him, but his father's jaw was set tight. Ahpa never cried.

After the funeral, everyone headed home. Myung-gi ran ahead, hoping the wind would dry his face. He gulped mouthfuls of air. Made sure to stay in front so no one could see his watery eyes and trembling lips.

But he could feel someone getting closer—quickening feet, panting breaths. Before Myung-gi got the chance to wipe his eyes and straighten his face, Yoomee caught up and started trotting alongside him.

"You crying, Oppah?" she asked suspiciously.

"What? No," Myung-gi said, staring straight ahead.

Yoomee examined him closely. "Yes, yes, you are! Oppah's crying!" she shouted, as if she'd just discovered some rare artifact that everyone had to come and see.

"Cut it out," Myung-gi said, picking up his pace.

"You're crying."

"Go away."

"But you're too big to cry."

Myung-gi kept walking but closed his eyes and covered his ears. Ignoring her was the best way to get her to shut up. He knew this from experience.

But maybe closing his eyes and covering his ears was not the best way to walk.

Myung-gi collided with a Soviet soldier, who did not even acknowledge him. Mrs. Song strode beside the man, a stack of pamphlets in her arms. She looked at Myung-gi, then at the soldier, who nodded. She began handing out the papers to everyone on the road, forcing one into Myung-gi's hands. The words LEARN FROM THE SOVIET UNION were printed across the top. When the man spoke to her in Russian, she turned to the crowd that was now forming.

"The Soviets are our liberators from Japanese oppression. We will be allowed to fly our Korean flag and preserve our Korean culture. They will ensure equality for all under communist rule. They will protect us from the imperialist Americans. They are here to save us," the woman said.

To which the crowd cheered. Myung-gi looked around at all the villagers, their tear-stained faces still damp from burying their sons who had been forced to enlist in the Japanese army under Japanese names. Certainly, anyone who was against the Japanese had to be good, right? But Myung-gi noticed that Ahpa wasn't cheering.

The Soviet soldier smiled at the crowd, then folded his arms across his chest, three watches on each wrist showing past his sleeves.

CHAPTER 4

September 1945: Myung-gi, Age 9

"They're looting people's homes," Ahpa said the next morning at breakfast. "Those watches on that soldier's wrists—they were all stolen from villagers."

Uhma reached over and ladled bean-sprout soup into everyone's bowls, her hand shaking. Looking up at his mother, Myung-gi took the ladle from her and finished serving.

"We should get rid of our valuables," Ahpa said, his eyes moving from the blue and white tea set on the table to the painted scrolls on the walls. A beam of morning sun streamed into the room, turning the golden scrolls even more brilliant, the stark black of the Chinese and Korean calligraphy even darker.

Uhma spilled hot soup on her finger. "Everything? Do you mean we should just throw out everything?"

"Some of it, yes. But a few things we can hide. I don't want to bring attention to our house. We must be careful and vigilant. We must keep our eyes wide open." That was when Ahpa set his spoon down and rubbed his forehead, hard. "I hear they're hurting women," he added, his lips drawing up as if he were getting ready to spit.

At that, Myung-gi stopped chewing. Hurting women? Why would they do that? These soldiers were nothing but big bullies, picking on those smaller than them.

"Will they hurt little girls too, Ahpa?" Yoomee asked, tugging on his sleeve.

It seemed that tug managed to pull Ahpa back to this world, instead of the far-off place his mind had been wandering lately. He cupped Yoomee's face in his hands and looked straight at her. "No, my beautiful girl. No one will hurt you. I will never let that happen."

Yoomee sniffled and nodded, and Myung-gi exhaled in relief.

"So wipe off all your makeup and take off all your jewels," Ahpa said to Uhma. "Wear only your plainest clothes. Don't bring any attention to yourself. Do you understand?"

Uhma nodded, barely. She clasped her hands together on her lap, as if to stop them shaking. The jeweled brooch on her hanbok sparkled, picking up the red in her painted lips and the peach in her powdered cheeks. She always took care in fixing her hair, preparing her face, adorning herself in fine silk. Everyone in the village always said she was kind and beautiful—the most fashionable woman, with sophisticated tastes. Uhma touched the edge of her brooch, then stuffed a spoonful of rice into her mouth.

"I want you to do it now," Ahpa said, low and steady.

"Now?" Uhma answered.

"Now!" Ahpa said, his voice cracking.

Myung-gi jumped in his seat. He had never heard his father raise his voice.

Myung-gi watched his mother scramble for the dishrag at the edge of the table and wipe the red from her lips and the peach from her cheeks, a muffled cry bleeding into the rag and then into his ears.

Myung-gi wanted to go and wrap his arms around his mother and tell her that she still looked beautiful, but he just sat there, afraid of embarrassing her and himself.

Finally, Ahpa reached across the table and put his hand over Uhma's. "I'm sorry, dear," he said. He got up to leave, but first he took down the painted scrolls that had been in his family for generations, only to end up now under a floorboard or thrown away.

The empty walls stared blankly.

Uhma unpinned her brooch and put it in a lacquered drawer, then finished wiping the last bit of makeup from her face. Myung-gi reached for his book of folktales and held it close, his eyes fixed on a bowl of pale winter melons, and wondered whether this was how everything was going to be from now on.

CHAPTER 5

October 1952: Myung-gi, Age 16

> You, mountain, here since mountains began,
> slopes where nothing is built,
> peaks that no one has named…
> Do I move inside you now?
> Am I within the rock
> like a metal that hasn't been mined?
> Your hardness encloses me everywhere.
> —Rainer Maria Rilke, *The Book of Hours*

Myung-gi starts crawling. Because this cannot be the way everything is going to be from now on. He must get out before another shell lands on top of the tunnel, before it fully collapses, before an enemy soldier finds him.

He must get out to find his father.

But when he moves forward, his head hits a rock wall so rigid and sharp that it opens yet another wound on his body. He's full of holes and gashes and broken parts that might never heal right.

Gravel grinding against skin, he turns on his knees in that tight and narrow space to head in a different direction, only to face another wall and another and another. Heat starts rising on the back of his neck. Where is a way out? Feeling around in the dark, his hands frantically skim the rocks beside him, above him, behind him. But he's surrounded by jagged walls.

For some reason, Yoomee pops into his head. He pictures his little sister standing here, arms crossed, foot tapping.

What made you think you could find Ahpa by joining the army?

Because, he answers, *the army has intelligence; it has weapons; it has thousands of men. With all those things I thought I could find him.*

For someone so smart, you sure can be dumb sometimes!

Why didn't he ever listen to her? Sure, she was two years younger than him and liked to show off to her friends. But she was smart, so smart. His little sister.

Outside, there are booms and shots. But they're muffled, as if he's gone partially deaf. He digs his finger into his ear. Maybe those blasts damaged his hearing. Maybe the earth is now so thick around him that sound can barely get through.

And now he's trapped. Truly trapped. His insides about to implode.

This was supposed to be his chance—so close to the North!—where he could slip away and search for Ahpa. Instead, he is stuck inside this *mountain, here since mountains began, slopes where nothing is built, peaks that no one has named . . .* No, no, no—not those words, not that poem. Myung-gi squeezes his eyes closed, hoping to shut them out. But he can't stop them from floating toward him. *Do I move inside you now? Am I within the rock like a metal that hasn't been mined?*

Enough, that's enough of those stupid words. All those useless books he's ever read from all over the godforsaken world—books that aren't going to help him!

His legs pedal into the ground, pushing his back up against the jagged sides of the tunnel. Because this is the part he doesn't want to hear, the part that fills him with terror: *Your hardness encloses me everywhere.*

He clasps his ears, as if that can do anything to keep out the words that are already inside him. "Stop, just stop!" he mutters to himself.

But all the words he's ever read will keep coming, in this dark and lonely place, where there is nothing to do but sit and think and wait.

CHAPTER 6
January 1947: Myung-gi, Age 10

More than a year had passed since the Soviets took over northern Korea. It turned out they were just as cruel as the Japanese—no, they were worse. Soldiers roamed the village, getting drunk, firing guns in the air, barging into people's houses, tracking snow and dirt onto their glazed paper floors, and taking whatever they wanted. Soon, Russian-style homes began appearing not too far from Myung-gi's tile-roofed house. He could spot them easily with their bright blue and red roofs.

Everything seemed on the brink of collapse. Under a new law, the Red Army took almost all the farmers' harvest—not unlike the Japanese—and in return they strangled and mismanaged production.

Farms faced a fertilizer shortage; factories stopped running; and people were starving.

Even Ahpa's large fabric business closed its doors because no one could afford new clothing or scarves or blankets. Still, he vowed that his family would never go hungry. Myung-gi marveled at his father's ability to keep that promise, listening to other kids' stomachs growl at school while his and Yoomee's always stayed full of rice. As a growing ten-year-old boy—his face buried so deep in his bowl—Myung-gi couldn't have noticed when Ahpa often claimed to be too tired to eat, giving his portion to Myung-gi and Yoomee instead.

"I got the job," Ahpa announced one afternoon.

Uhma looked up from the round iron fire pot where she was roasting chestnuts. A slow smile started forming. "You got it? The principal job at the boys' school?"

Ahpa nodded, grinning.

Yoomee squealed and jumped up to hug him.

"How on earth? How did you . . . ? How did they . . . ?" Uhma said, untying her apron and getting ready to listen.

"I just told them how managing a large business is not unlike managing a school."

"Ahpa, are you going to be the principal of my school?" Myung-gi asked, looking up from his book.

"Yes, son."

Uhma laughed. "Your father's cleverness never ceases to amaze me. No one is more capable than your father."

Myung-gi nodded. This was true. No one was like Ahpa. Not even close.

"Myung-gi-ya, do you want to go to the city with me today? They're sending me to order some books for the school," Ahpa said enthusiastically. "I bought one extra bus ticket. What do you think?"

"Yes! Yes, I want to go." Myung-gi jumped up to put on his shoes. The warm, sweet aroma of roasted chestnuts wrapped around him.

"What about me? I want to go!" Yoomee pouted.

"Yoomee-ya," Ahpa said, gently, "Ahpa doesn't have another bus ticket. And since Myung-gi is older, I think he should go. Next time, when you're a little older, you can come with me. Okay?"

"But I'm eight. Isn't that old enough?"

"Next time, okay?" Ahpa said, firmly. "This way, you and Uhma can have the chestnuts to yourselves!"

But she only crossed her arms and glared, all that prickly heat boring into her older brother. Then she picked up her sketchpad and stomped off to her room.

❦

Myung-gi could hardly remember the last time he had ridden a bus. The shuttle sputtered and wheezed up a narrow road. In the back was a large cast-iron boiler for burning wood and producing steam to get the bus moving. *Gasoline shortage*, Ahpa had said, pointing to the strange contraption.

Sitting by the window, Myung-gi watched bare trees and barren farmlands crawl past under leaden skies, the smell of burning fuel filling the cabin. He pressed his forehead against the cold glass and watched his breath fog the world away. When he sat up straight again and the condensation started clearing—the outside edges working their way inward—he could see, as if waking from a dream, Soviet and North Korean soldiers standing side by side at the edges of the farms, watching back-bent farmers leading their skinny cows.

Myung-gi turned away from the window. "Ahpa, would you rather be hungry or thirsty?"

Ahpa sat back in his seat and chuckled. "Oh, are we playing this game again? Okay, let me think. Hmm . . . I would rather be hungry because hunger pains can go away, but your thirst never leaves you."

Myung-gi nodded.

"Okay, my turn," Ahpa said. "Would you rather be a professor or a principal when you grow up?"

Now it was Myung-gi's turn to chuckle. Those weren't interesting choices. Ahpa didn't know how to play. "I wouldn't want to be either of those things."

"Oh, really?" Ahpa turned to look at his son, as if seeing him for the first time. "Then what do you want to be when you grow up?"

"A writer," Myung-gi said, staring up at his father from behind thick lenses. How could Ahpa not know? He was the one who encouraged him to read, who found books for him—even foreign ones, like *The Call of the Wild* and *Treasure Island* and *The Red Badge of Courage*. Myung-gi loved all kinds of books—history books, fantasy books, even the nonfiction ones that made his eyes grow wide in

27

wonder. He loved the way a certain word could be *just* the right one, stirring something deep inside him. It was magical, really.

"Not a principal or professor? Or even a businessman?" Ahpa pressed, gathering their things as the bus came to a stop.

Maybe a writer wasn't big enough, important enough. Myung-gi shook his head slowly, but he was no longer sure what he wanted.

"Ah, look, we're here!" Ahpa said, leaning over Myung-gi and looking out the frosted window.

Snapping to attention, Myung-gi stared out. There were wooden storefronts lining a hard-packed road with signs for a dentist, a tea house, a movie theater, and more. Electric poles ran along the street. People milled about, buying and selling fruits and vegetables, surrounded by patrolling soldiers. An ox clip-clopped beside the bus.

"Where's the bookstore?" Myung-gi asked.

"Right there," Ahpa said, pointing. "That little storefront with the wooden awning."

They scrambled off the bus and headed toward the shop.

Myung-gi stepped inside, and when the door closed behind him, all the sounds of a dirt-kicking, clip-clopping, engine-roaring city ceased.

It was quiet. And small.

But books covered every wall from floor to ceiling. They were piled up high on long tables, too—stacks three feet tall balanced precariously, and Myung-gi held his breath, afraid that it might all come tumbling down: the words, the stories, all those colorful spines.

Tiptoeing around the tables, he went deeper into the store, until he stood surrounded by books of every shape and size. The smell of wood pulp hung thick in the air. Mesmerized, Myung-gi picked a paperback off a shelf, and when he flipped the pages, that earthy book scent fanned against his face, battering his senses. He closed his eyes and breathed it in.

"What do you mean, 'they've gotten rid of the books'?" Ahpa asked the store owner, a little old man dwarfed by all the stacks.

"The authorities came and told me that I couldn't sell them anymore. No American books. No European books. No Japanese books. Not even any Korean books if they go against communist ideology," the old man said, the lines on his face crinkling in apology. "I'm sorry. I'm just the distributor; I don't make the rules."

"Surely you must still have something, anything—a few of the old books left somewhere," Ahpa said, pressing harder.

"Well . . . let me see . . . who did you say you were? Who was your father? What province?" the old man asked, but Myung-gi stopped listening and stepped closer to the books instead.

Examining them, he noticed a pile of red ones with a hammer and sickle on the front covers—the symbol on the Soviet flag. Many others were written by people with Russian names, but where were the other authors, the other books? Were they really all gone?

"Come, let's go, son." Ahpa said, turning to leave. "And thank you very much, sir. I truly appreciate your help."

The store owner nodded slowly, as if the weight of the heavy world were on top of his head.

Myung-gi shuffled toward the door, shoulders drooping. Why was Ahpa thanking the store owner? They hadn't even bought a single book.

Outside, a bitter wind slapped the side of Myung-gi's face, and he huddled deeper into his coat. He walked alongside his father as they headed toward the bus stop, passing stores and cigarette-smoking men on the way. Down an alley, a ghetto full of crumbling houses and garbage-strewn streets was loud and filthy. "Ahpa, who lives down there?" Myung-gi asked, unable to tear his gaze away.

"The Japanese who never left Korea after Liberation Day."

A gang of Korean boys ran past, laughing and throwing rocks into the littered street. "Serves you right! Here are some rocks for you to haul!" they shouted.

Ahpa shook his head sadly. "When will we ever learn that it's not the people who are to blame? It's the handful of evil madmen in charge."

Myung-gi stared at the Korean boys, at the Japanese kids, at the rocks chucked into the alley, and began to feel queasy, as if the world were tilting on its side, his stomach turning upside down.

CHAPTER 7

August 1948: Myung-gi, Age 12

Over the next year and a half, as North Korea became a communist state, Myung-gi hardly saw his father. At school, Ahpa was always stern-faced, sitting in his principal's office. Outside of school, he was working and meeting with people, disappearing for hours at a time. Now that Myung-gi and Yoomee were older, maybe Ahpa didn't feel the need to be around as much.

Myung-gi lay on the table in the courtyard, looking up at the summer sky as it darkened, daylight still lingering in the distance. A few boys at school had asked if he wanted to join in a game of chuk-guk, but he wasn't very good at kicking the ball or earning points for the team. In fact, he didn't even know all the rules of the game—his mind wandered whenever someone had tried explaining. *No thanks*, he'd told them.

Red and purple clouds swirled above, and Myung-gi imagined how much brighter it must be up where they were. He grabbed two books and headed out the front gate, following the glowing sunset to where Sora lived.

Hers was a thatched-roof house, small and tidy, so different from Myung-gi's large tile-roofed home. But he liked the cozy feel of this place, nestled in the foothills not too far from the shimmering river. Sora's mother stood in the courtyard, broom in hand, trying to stamp out the field mice running along the fence. Though their families were close, and Uhma had always said he should consider Mrs. Pak an auntie, his palms turned slick with sweat watching her beat those "disease-carrying vermin" away.

"Hello, Mrs. Pak," he said, bowing by the open gate. "Is Sora home?"

Before she could answer, Sora came rushing through the sliding paper door and across the courtyard, her words tumbling out in one breath: *Bye, Omahni, bebacksoon. Myung-gi Oppah, let's go!*

"Yah, Sora-ya!" her mother shouted, that broom now pumping the air. "You have chores to do!"

But Sora was already out the gate, running past Myung-gi down the gravel road and heading for the willow tree by the school, her long, wavy hair rippling like a kite. "Race you!" she shouted, her voice whipping past and fading.

Myung-gi started running, his stride long and steady, but no match for Sora's lightning-quick feet. She was more than a year younger, and shorter too. But he always ended up chasing after her.

"Slow down!" he yelled, a book in each hand, like oversized mitts dragging against the wind.

"Why?" She sprinted toward the horizon as if it were some fiery finish line, her hair ablaze in the setting sun's light.

By the time he caught up with her, she was already sitting under the willow tree, grinning. "What books did you bring today, Oppah?" she asked, affectionately calling him "big brother."

Myung-gi dropped them by her feet. Sometimes he wondered whether she liked spending time with him or just his books. But no matter—he knew Sora's family couldn't afford such luxuries, and he was happy to share his wealth of words.

Myung-gi bent over to catch his breath. "How do you do that? Run so fast?"

"I just pretend I'm being chased."

"You didn't have to pretend. I was chasing you."

"No, I mean being chased by something scary."

"Did you hear your mother yell when you ran out of the house? Something about chores?"

At that, Sora frowned. "No, I didn't hear that."

"Well, no matter," Myung-gi said, wishing he hadn't brought it up. "I'm sure it wasn't too important."

But Sora sat still, thinking, her gaze stuck on the barb of a rose bush.

Myung-gi didn't want her to worry. "I brought that folktale book you like and a book of Kim Sowol's poems."

Just as he hoped, this stirred her from her stupor. She grabbed the book of folktales.

Like the tigers in all the fairy tales, she brought it close to her face and sniffed deeply, as if the musty paper were fresh meat. She leaned against the tree trunk and opened the book, her eyes prowling back and forth across the page hungrily.

Settling beside her, Myung-gi looked up at the sky turning deep purple and wished he'd come sooner. In the daytime, the canopy of draping branches cupped them, a giant hand made of bright green leaves. But under the darkening sky, the thin boughs started turning into black veins, the leaves into liver spots. Unsettled, he looked over Sora's shoulder to read the story of a boy and girl who had turned into the sun and moon.

Footsteps crunched on the gravel road. Myung-gi glanced away from the book, then stood and poked his head through the shivering curtain of willow branches.

He stopped breathing.

"Hey look, it's Myung-gi!" a boy shouted. "I thought you couldn't play chukguk because you had homework."

Snickering followed.

Another one said, "Let's go see what he's up to."

Feet trudged up the hill.

Myung-gi pulled his head back inside and stared at the tree roots, his hands on his knees. Maybe he shouldn't have come here. Not with Sora. Turning to her, he said, "Listen, when I tell you to run, I want you to go around the back and head home. Okay?"

"Huh? What are you talking about?" Sora asked, putting down the book.

That was when the curtain of branches parted. Five boys stood in the opening. "Look here," a tall, skinny one said, stepping inside as if he'd been invited. "It's like a secret hideout. Oh, for just the two of you. How adorable."

That set the others howling.

"So . . . is she your girlfriend? Do you kiss and stuff in here? Is that why you wouldn't hang out with us?"

Myung-gi glowered behind his glasses.

"I think you're a Jap lover, or one of those bourgeois fools waiting for the American imperialist pigs to save you from the common people! Isn't that why you don't wear the red band on your arm like the rest of us? Because your pig father used to own a factory? Because you're so stupid that you don't know what's good for you?"

"Actually, he gets good grades in school," mumbled an overgrown boy, his back slightly hunched. Myung-gi recognized him from history class—Byongho. Yes, he was pretty sure the name was Byongho. A boy Myung-gi had once helped with his reading assignment after the teacher told him he was failing.

"Shut up! Who asked you?" the tall skinny one demanded. "Why do you think he gets good grades? It's because his daddy is the principal!"

"I get good grades because I like to read. You should try it sometime," Myung-gi said, still staring at the ground.

It was the swift fist to his ribs that sent him reeling, breath catching, vision dimming. But Myung-gi still managed to tell Sora to run: "Go!"

In an instant, they were on top of him—punching, kicking, pinning. Nothing but shadows wrestling in the dark. Myung-gi winced, curled up, covered his head, but his glasses broke anyway—flung off his face, ground into pieces. When he tried to stand, the boys only kicked harder. Sharp pains pierced his sides.

Myung-gi started leaving his body. He hovered over himself and the pack of boys, all of them swarming like so many maggots over an open wound.

CHAPTER 8

August 1948: Myung-gi, Age 12

"Oh God! What happened to you?" Uhma cried the next morning.

Myung-gi walked into the main sitting room, his hair brushed down over one eye. Though his ribs ached, he made sure to walk without a hitch in his stride. "It's nothing, Uhma. I just tripped and fell down the hillside."

"What? There are big rocks jutting out of the mountains. You could have gotten a concussion. Aigoo, you have to be more careful!" Uhma said, wetting a cloth in the clay water jug just inside the kitchen door. "Here, put this over that bruise on your cheek."

Ahpa sat up straight at the table, tossing his newspaper aside in a crumpled heap. "Can you walk just fine? Does it hurt anywhere? Do you think you broke anything?"

"No, I'm fine. Really. The bruises are a little sore, but nothing's broken."

"You look like you got in a fight, Oppah," Yoomee announced, slurping her oxtail soup before wiping her mouth with the back of her hand.

Glaring at her, he reached for his spoon—but winced at the sharp pain in his side.

Ahpa leaned in closer, his fingers tracing the cuts and scrapes on his son's face. And Myung-gi held his breath, hoping he wouldn't connect the lines enough to map out the whole story. "Hmm . . ." was all Ahpa said.

"Oppah, you should learn judo or that new martial art called taekwondo. Right, Ahpa? Didn't you know judo when you were younger? And Grandfather, too? Wasn't he like a judo master or something before he died?" Yoomee asked, sucking the marrow out of an oxtail bone. Then, as if a switch had flicked inside her, she stopped and looked straight at her big brother. "Actually, never mind. I can't see you doing those things. You're always just reading in your room."

"I wasn't in a fight," Myung-gi said, an edge in his tone.

"But you look like you got beat up."

"It's just a small contusion."

"A what?"

"A contusion. It's what happens when a blood vessel gets

damaged and starts bleeding under the skin. You know, like when you bump into something hard?"

"Uhma, he's using big words and trying to make me feel stupid," Yoomee whined.

"Enough, you two," Uhma said, still fussing over Myung-gi's bruise. "What about your communist youth meeting this morning? Will you be able to go?"

"I'll tell them he's not feeling well," Ahpa said.

"Are you sure that will be good enough for them?" Uhma asked anxiously.

"What do you mean? I'm the principal. I'm the one to decide."

That made Uhma quiet. But they all knew it *wasn't* up to Ahpa. The Party leaders were always watching.

But Myung-gi had never missed a meeting before. Maybe missing this one time would be fine. The ache in his ribs sharpened, and he lowered himself to sit on the floor, slowly.

"If someone ever tried to fight me, I would pummel them into the ground," Yoomee said, slamming her fist on the table.

"Yah, Yoomee-ya! You're spilling soup everywhere," Uhma scolded.

"And poke their eyes out!"

"Aigoo . . ." Uhma shook her head.

"And scream in their ear!"

Myung-gi closed his eyes. Maybe she would shut up. Maybe she would disappear. Ignoring her was his best defense.

"Where are your glasses, son?" Ahpa asked.

Myung-gi's eyes snapped open. "Oh. I lost them." His cheeks started burning under the strain of all these lies and humiliations. Ahpa would've never lost a fight, not with his judo and street smarts and muscles. From the sound of it, not even Yoomee would've gotten beaten up like this.

Ahpa sighed. "I see. . . ."

That was when his father's gaze met with Myung-gi's and darted away, as if it were too embarrassing to look at him.

CHAPTER 9

October 1952: Myung-gi, Age 16

I hunger after this brightness.

I have been in my room, door shut, breathing at the walls.

—Kim Yeong-nang, *Brightness*

Flickering light streams in through the tunnel's cracks and crevices. Myung-gi raises his hand, closes his fingers around it, tries to grip it like a rope. But he stops, thinking himself strange and embarrassing, even alone in the dark.

Myung-gi sits, knees up, ears covered, and stares at the light. It couldn't be the dawn—it's too white, too flashing. And no sunrise is ever accompanied by the sounds of explosions.

Everywhere, the walls shudder.

Though Myung-gi begins to understand what the white light is—the burst of grenades and bombs, the last thing a soldier sees before he is blown up—he still *hungers after this brightness*, as if he were home, rubbing his eyes, walking out of his room into the daylight after a marathon of reading. God, how he misses those days! But he is not in a stupid poem, and this light is not the kind he should hunger after—not when every flash means a man is dying.

Myung-gi doubles over, clutches his stomach. Terrified, he can't stop watching for the light, waiting for it, hoping for it—especially when the moments in between are so pitch black that even the air turns thick and tarry. It is *then* that he can't breathe, darkness heavy as stone on his chest, his lungs hardly able to push out as the air begins crushing him.

Until, finally, another flash flickers through the cracks and crevices, and he can breathe again.

Guilt washes over him.

He hopes he can be forgiven.

CHAPTER 10

September 1949: Myung-gi, Age 13

A year later, all the cuts, scrapes, and bruises of the fight under the willow tree had healed. But something had started to fester deep inside Myung-gi—the gnawing certainty that he would never live up to his name. It permeated the classroom, where he kept to himself. It took a seat at dinner, where he sat quiet. It even followed him to bed, where he would lie on his back, staring straight up, replaying all the events of the day—reading outside during break time, a ball hitting him on the head, everyone laughing.

He wasn't strong. Not like Ahpa.

That was what Myung-gi was thinking while heading home from school one day.

He was walking on the gravel road when it happened: Yongshik—an older boy in the village who had started organizing a protest against the government—was strolling a hundred yards ahead of him. Like all the boys in Myung-gi's school, Yongshik was good at chukguk, even serving as team captain—but unlike them, Yong-shik was kind, often helping younger boys, like Myung-gi, practice kicking the ball.

Myung-gi studied the way he moved, one hand in his pocket, the other on his shoulder bag, a slight swagger in his step. Though he'd never seen a photo of his father as a teenager, he imagined he might've looked something like Yongshik.

Carrying a bag full of communist-approved books, Myung-gi followed at a distance, the autumn leaves drifting in the wind. Later, he would wonder whether those leaves—swirling in the air like an exploded bag of feathers, enticing him to watch their flurry of light and color—had distracted him from seeing what really transpired.

Because one moment Yongshik was there, and the next he was gone—vanished, never to be seen again.

A military truck rumbled away. Myung-gi looked left and right, but there were only open fields on either side, mountains rising in the distance. Had the soldiers taken him . . . ?

Only after Myung-gi got home and ate dinner and finished his homework did he tell his father. Ahpa just shook his head, his lips in a grim line. *This is what they're doing now—kidnapping anyone who speaks up against them*, he said. The floor dropped out from under Myung-gi's feet.

❧

Later that evening, Ahpa came into Myung-gi's room. "Son, I have a surprise for you." He pulled out two books from behind his back: *Twenty Thousand Leagues Under the Sea*, by a French writer named Jules Verne, and *Ivanhoe*, by a Scottish writer named Sir Walter Scott—both written in English, which was not a problem; Ahpa had taught him several foreign languages.

But Myung-gi only stared, those book covers pulsing before his eyes. "Ahpa, aren't all Western books banned? Isn't—isn't that what the bookstore owner said? How did you get them? What if we get caught?"

"You don't need to know how I got them," Ahpa said, closing the door behind him and then pushing Myung-gi's wardrobe to the side. "And we just have to be careful, that's all."

"What are you doing? Do you need help?"

"No, no, I got it, son."

Myung-gi watched as his father took out a pocketknife and started cutting out a square hole in the wall.

"Ahpa, what are you doing?"

"This is where we'll hide your books. Because there will be more coming your way and you'll need a place to keep them."

"More *banned* books?" Myung-gi didn't know whether to laugh or cry. More books meant more stories. He could already feel his heart opening and unfurling—like a flock of birds beating their wings, flying high into the sky. But this also meant more to worry about. What if someone found out? Would he get abducted like Yongshik?

"Why? Don't you want them?" Ahpa asked, still working on the wall.

Staring hard at the books on the floor, Myung-gi thought about that bookstore and all those volumes piled high. Those days of reading under the pines out back, or in his room, or under the willow tree with Sora. Hours spent in far-off worlds, laughing or gripping the spine or weeping in private, then taking a deep breath and closing the book, satisfied.

If he was very careful, he might not get abducted on his way home from school.

Nodding, he said, "Yes, Ahpa. Yes, I want the books."

CHAPTER 11

February 1950: Myung-gi, Age 13

Autumn colors soon gave way to snow and ice. A white sheet draped over the jagged mountains. Myung-gi was on his way to Sora's house to deliver the sweet rice cakes that Uhma had made, Yoomee tagging along beside him.

He didn't want to go. Ever since that day under the willow tree when those boys had barged into their secret space, he hadn't wanted to see her. Sora never mentioned that day or those boys or what happened afterward, which he appreciated. But still, it made him wonder whether she had seen everything and was embarrassed for him. And now he couldn't quite look her in the eye. Besides, he was thirteen and Sora was almost twelve, so maybe they were getting too old to read under trees together anyway.

"Oppah, you're not friends with Sora anymore, are you?" Yoomee asked, examining the ends of her hair.

"Why do you ask?"

"Because you never spend time with her. It seems like you don't like her—and I get it, trust me, she's not the nicest person, you know."

Myung-gi sighed and glanced at his sister sideways. "Why would you say that? She's plenty nice. Nicer than you."

At that, Yoomee huffed and ran ahead to a group of girls washing laundry along the river. Myung-gi watched the girls roll their eyes as Yoomee came bounding toward them. They were older, around Myung-gi's age, and when they caught him watching, they softened their gazes, one of them turning pink and waving shyly.

After waiting a few minutes, he shouted, "Yoomee, let's go!" He knew how his sister acted around other kids—always showing off—but something still ached inside his chest when she turned and ran back, the girls snickering once she wasn't looking.

"What did you say to them?" Myung-gi asked.

"Nothing. I just told them about the pretty hairpins Uhma gave me and how the jewels in them were real."

"Were they nice to you?"

"Yeah," Yoomee said, staring at the ground.

Sora's little brothers, Youngsoo and baby Jisoo, sat in the front courtyard, building a tower of sticks. When they saw Myung-gi and Yoomee, they scrambled toward them, their small hands reaching for the sweet rice cakes wrapped in a colorful cloth.

"He's so cute," Yoomee said, picking up Jisoo and squeezing his chubby cheek.

Myung-gi extended a hand toward him—as if reaching for a wild animal—and Jisoo latched onto his finger and stuffed it in his mouth. "Help, what do I do?" Myung-gi asked, his eyes growing big.

Hysterical laughter.

It was Youngsoo, rolling on his back. "Let him eat you!"

Yoomee smirked, but Myung-gi started pulling his finger away from Jisoo's grip, which was tightening. Who knew a baby could be so strong?

"Jisoo, no!" a voice cried.

When Myung-gi looked up, Sora was standing in front of the sliding rice-paper door, a bit of sticky rice flour dough stuck in her hair.

"Sorry," she said, shooting forward and taking Jisoo from Yoomee. "They're a little hard to handle sometimes."

She'd grown taller since he last saw her. Even prettier, too. It took Myung-gi by surprise and turned his face bright red.

"Did you come to see me?" she asked, looking right at him.

"Uh, I have something for you. Here," he said, holding out the rice cakes, wrapped and knotted at the top. "Our mother made this for your family. She wanted me to drop them off."

"Oh. Thanks." Sora took them and went inside, probably having more important things to do.

Myung-gi turned to leave, Yoomee scrambling to catch up with him.

"You like her, don't you?" Yoomee demanded, grinning and bobbing alongside him.

"No. I don't."

"Then why did your face turn red?"

"It didn't." But denying it only made his cheeks burn brighter.

At that, Yoomee started cackling. And Myung-gi covered his ears.

CHAPTER 12

June 1950: Myung-gi, Age 14

Over the next few months, Myung-gi kept to himself, doing nothing but eating, sleeping, and reading. When he turned fourteen in the middle of June, he told no one at school. All that mattered to him now was the steady stream of books—everything from Kim Yeong-nang's poems to *Frankenstein*—that kept him company. And he worried about running out of reading material. When he had asked his father why the schools couldn't just *add* books about communism rather than take away everything else, Ahpa had told him that the Reds didn't want them to know more; they wanted them to know less.

It was a Saturday afternoon when Myung-gi tiptoed toward his father's room and slid open the door.

"Ahpa, I'm running out of hiding space," he whispered.

Getting up from the floor cushion, Ahpa said, "Show me, quickly."

Myung-gi led him into his room and shut the door behind him. The lacquered chest stood off to the side where Myung-gi had dragged it away to expose the hole in the wall.

Folding his arms, Ahpa stared at the opening and frowned. "You should never leave this hole uncovered and unattended, even for a few seconds, son."

"Sorry," Myung-gi said. Ai, how could he have forgotten? He adjusted his glasses.

Ahpa stepped forward and examined the shallow cutout filled with books. "You read every single one?" he asked, putting his face up to the hole.

Myung-gi smiled. Of course he'd read all of them. He wasn't sure how Ahpa got these smuggled books, but he guessed his father, as principal of the boys' school, had his ways.

"Maybe we should get rid of a few so it's not so crowded in here. You wouldn't want a book to spill out from behind the dresser," Ahpa said.

"Oh. Do we have to?" Myung-gi said.

Ahpa didn't answer. He pulled one out—a shiny paperback. Myung-gi could smell its wood-pulp scent even from where he stood.

"Ah, this one was interesting. . . ." Ahpa muttered to himself. "Did you like it?" he asked, flashing the cover to his son.

Myung-gi jumped back—*Nineteen Eighty-Four* by George Orwell, out in the open, under the brightness of his lamp. It was, by far, the most dangerous book. Getting caught with that one by the secret police meant death, Ahpa had told him. But even so . . . he didn't want to let it go.

Myung-gi took it from Ahpa and held it tightly against his chest, which was pounding.

"Yes, I liked it," he whispered, even though the story's futuristic world filled with Thought Police and Big Brother gave him nightmares. He wondered, sometimes, whether that future was already here in North Korea.

Ahpa ran his hand over the wall. "I'll see if I can make another cutout for you."

Myung-gi exhaled in relief. Ahpa had always said that books were their window to the world. But for Myung-gi they were more than that—they *were* his world. They let him live in other times. They let him see other places—places beyond his country's borders, where armed soldiers now stood guard to make sure no one left. These books . . . they let him *feel* things. He even loved the hefty weight of the thickest ones, as satisfying as a sack of rice. He knew his father understood. "Thank you, Ahpa."

"But I'm afraid I will not be able to bring you more banned books. It's getting too dangerous these days, son," Ahpa told him.

"Yes," Myung-gi replied, trying hard to hide his sudden disappointment.

Of course it was too dangerous; it always had been. He was lucky to even have the books that he had. Ahpa had been risking his life to get these books. What kind of son would he be if he wanted *more* books?

All at once, he could see how childish and selfish he had been, expecting an endless delivery of banned reading, and the realization spread across his cheeks.

Uhma called them from the main sitting room. "Time for dinner!"

"Quick, help me move this back," Ahpa said, grabbing one end of the lacquered chest. "If your mother knew about these books, she would never stop worrying. We would have to burn them right in front of her so she could sleep at night."

Myung-gi nodded and pushed from the other end. But he knew Yoomee was the one he really had to watch. She would notice if the chest was off by just a few inches. Which would lead her to snoop. Which would lead her to discover the hole in the wall. Which would turn this thing between Ahpa and him into some banned-book club where she was president. And even if he *told* her that it was a secret, she wouldn't be able to resist telling those mean girls in her middle school who always excluded her anyway. And those girls would tell their new teacher, Comrade Lee, whose ears would prick at the news. And then . . .

It wasn't that he didn't love his little sister, but sometimes he had to keep things from her.

Pushing his glasses up higher, Myung-gi stepped back and

looked at the chest, its metal hardware holding the double doors closed. Would it keep his secret? But when he stared hard enough, the swirling wood pattern seemed to pulse—almost as if it wanted to open up and speak.

Myung-gi followed Ahpa into the main room, where the walls were bare and Uhma, without makeup, sat at the table with a simple meal of kimchi, rice, and broth waiting.

"You two . . . like a dragon and its tail," Uhma said, shaking her head. She put on a smile that couldn't quite reach her eyes.

Yoomee plopped on the floor beside Uhma, who sat at Ahpa's right side. Hot steam turned their faces rosy and shiny—even Ahpa's—as they sat together as a family, their house still not ransacked, everyone unharmed. Myung-gi sat beside his father, the faint sounds of summer wafting through the open window: dogs barking, children squealing, and a radio playing a song about the Soviet-appointed Great Leader that he'd heard enough times to no longer notice:

So dear to all our hearts is our General's glorious name!
Our own beloved Kim Il-sung of undying fame!

The setting sun shifted across the room, lighting everything in its path—the low dining table, Myung-gi's open rice-paper door, his lacquered chest. And in the orange glow the four of them sat and ate, that tune floating on a breeze.

CHAPTER 13

June 1950: Myung-gi, Age 14

Sunday morning, Myung-gi checked the positioning of the chest before heading to school for his weekly communist youth meeting. Attendance was mandatory; nowadays, no-shows ended up in jail or missing. Everyone knew that.

He walked alongside Ahpa, whose principal's jacket flapped in the breeze of their brisk and synchronized pace. Spiked mountains towered in the distance. A light drizzle hit the ground. Myung-gi tugged on the red scarf of his uniform, which was now damp and scratchy. He would never get used to wearing that thing.

"Have a good day, son," Ahpa said before heading to his office. "Oh, wait, Myung-gi-ya!"

Myung-gi spun around.

"Neither," Ahpa said.

"What? You can't say that. You have to choose. That's the rule of the game," Myung-gi argued. "Would you rather live in the past or in the future?"

Ahpa grinned and walked away, his arms spread wide. "The present," he said. "I would rather live in the present, because it is all part of the good Lord's plan."

Myung-gi shook his head and laughed—Ahpa was never good at this game. He watched his father go, then headed toward his classroom, hoping no one had heard Ahpa mention God. God Himself was banned now; the churches sat empty, the pastors taken away.

Students thundered past—boys to one building, girls to the other. But Myung-gi walked slowly, dreading the boring meeting and the droning student body leaders—sons of farmers and laborers who had just returned from their trip to the Soviet Union, freshly indoctrinated and glazed over and ready to lecture about the exemplary model of Soviet society.

Inside the school, however, he found a commotion buzzing through the corridors.

"There's a special meeting in the large hall for everyone! A big announcement," someone shouted into the crowd.

Special meeting?

Myung-gi headed toward the assembly room, wondering why

Ahpa hadn't mentioned anything about a special program. Maybe the student body president had something to say.

Myung-gi sat on a wooden bench in the back, a group of girls sliding in beside him. One of them kept glancing his way and giggling, but he took out his science textbook and started reading about the moon and the stars and the sun—at least those things had not changed under the new curriculum. Around him there were wide eyes, uneasy laughs, a few shouts across the room.

Comrade Lee stepped up to the podium, her chin angled up as if trying to show off the crisp red necktie knotted neatly around her neck. She cleared her throat.

"Settle down, boys and girls. I have an important announcement to make." A sudden smile appeared on her face. "Today, South Korean forces invaded the North. But fear not, because our valiant North Korean army decimated the South Korean puppet regime of the imperialist Americans! War has been declared! We will soon be a unified nation again under communist rule!"

The hall roared with cheers, but Myung-gi stayed quiet.

After a few minutes, Comrade Lee lowered her arms to silence the crowd. "Today, I am also happy to announce that we will have a new principal to head the boys' school—Comrade Ahn, a mine worker who has never hobnobbed with the elites who seek to undermine the collective. He is a true proletarian, a representative of the masses!"

Another burst of applause.

Was this about those banned books? He should've burned them, never should've read them. He searched the room, his eyes darting left, then right. Where was he? Ahpa.

"Before I dismiss you early for the day, you must all help in the war effort by collecting metal scraps for weapons and bullets to aid our noble North Korean soldiers. And please do your part in strengthening our nation by reporting any anti-communist behavior to authorities—even if it's your parents who are the ones straying from the teachings of our benevolent Soviet leaders. Now let's go out there and do our part to fight those evil American dogs!"

More cheers burst through the hall.

But the sounds were like a rotten egg cracked open on top of Myung-gi's head, dripping into his ears, over his shoulders, down to his feet. Everyone stared curiously into his face as they passed him. And he nodded, tried to act sociable—normal—but he was never good at that sort of thing.

"Let's see if he can still be a straight-A student now," someone in the crowd said.

Myung-gi whipped around, but the voice had already drifted down the hall, and like a noxious odor, lingered over all those who had heard. He darted out of the assembly hall and toward the principal's office, pushing open the door.

Ahpa's chair sat empty. His desk had been swept clean. No books, no pens, no framed degrees, no silver clock.

Wading back through the crowds, he asked anyone who would

listen: *Have you seen my father?* But they all shook their heads. He sprinted past the Soviet painting—Stalin's hairy face and giant nose so different from theirs—and hurried out of the building. Maybe Ahpa had already gone home?

His legs scissored through the woods in long strides. Past a stream, over a hill, down the gravel road to their house. He remembered Yongshik, on this very road, nearly a year ago, abducted on his way home from school. Never to be seen again.

Myung-gi looked over his shoulder. His hard schoolbag knocked against the bones of his back, full of all those books he always carried. The hot sun burned on the back of his neck. Sweat tingled on his scalp. He ran and ran, until finally he burst through the door of his house.

CHAPTER 14

October 1952: Myung-gi, Age 16

I'm just pain covered with skin.

—John Steinbeck, *The Grapes of Wrath*

The flashing lights have dimmed. The rock walls are no longer trembling. The battle sounds farther away.

Myung-gi blinks in the dark and starts touching his head, patting his chest, feeling around for any gashes, aware again of his own body. Grit and dirt sting his cut-up knees and elbows. Sticky blood oozes from the back of his head. He touches his face, and it's wet there too. More blood, he thinks, because it couldn't be tears; he's not crying. He rips the sleeve off his shirt and ties it tight around his head to stop the bleeding. And he wonders if he looks savage now.

The bandage may help his head, but his ankle is swollen and numb. When he tries to crouch, something snaps, and sharp pain shoots straight to the top of his skull, burning behind his watering eyes and his contorted mouth where a scream is piercing. It knocks him down. That pain, it knocks him down.

Everything throbs. He is *just pain covered with skin*, like he once read. This time, he decides not to curse the book for lingering inside his head.

But he realizes that he's trapped not only by the tunnel, but by his own broken self. Slumping against the wall, shoulders low, Myung-gi tries to think.

His hands. He still has his hands.

He claws at the rocks. The small ones come loose. Gravel and dirt slide away. He's making progress! His fingernails feel full underneath—soil and clay and grit packing them tight. But he doesn't stop to scrape them out. Just keeps digging until his fingertips turn numb. Because he needs to get back out there so he can defeat the enemy, so this stupid war will end, so he can go find Ahpa. *Wah, did you make this at kindergarten today? Yes, Ahpa. A picture just for me? Yes, Ahpa. What a good boy.*

Ahpa.

Myung-gi's chest burns. He can barely keep it together, pain now seeping into parts he cannot reach or bandage. But he bites his lip, pushes Ahpa out of his mind, keeps digging.

For hours.

Now Myung-gi can't even feel them—his fingertips. He stops for a second. There are no blasts in the distance, no guns firing.

Everything has turned quiet. Did the battle end? Which side won? Has his platoon left him? He brushes his fingertips against his face just to know that they're still there, that they haven't fallen off.

Reaching up, he continues clawing—because what is a little more pain on top of all the pain he's already carrying?

Myung-gi digs until the dark starts forming shapes, until a rhythm takes over his body, until his fingertips are scraped raw. And then he feels it. Against his palms, where there is still sensation.

Something smooth and thick and unyielding.

A boulder.

No, no, no. He can't dig through a boulder. Myung-gi sweeps his arms and hands around it. It's solid and massive, like the side of a whale. And though it's too dark to see, he presses his forehead against it, his breaths coming fast and hard.

"Let me out! *Let me out!*"

He pounds the boulder. Hard. His hands ache; his foot is still dangling strangely. Myung-gi stops.

Now what?

CHAPTER 15

June 1950: Myung-gi, Age 14

Closer to the house, Myung-gi could hear crying. So he quickened his pace and burst through the door.

It was Yoomee sitting on a satin floor cushion in front of Uhma's mirrored chest.

"It's too short!" she cried, tugging on her bangs. "I look like I'm ten years old!"

"Don't be so melodramatic," Uhma said, putting the scissors back into the velvet drawstring bag Ahpa had bought for her. Myung-gi could smell the honeysuckle scent of his mother's perfume. "You look like the beautiful twelve-year-old girl that you are, sweet and innocent." She leaned to hug Yoomee.

"Where is Ahpa?" Myung-gi cried, kicking off his shoes and tossing his bag onto the floor.

That was when his father slid open the bedroom door and stepped into the main room.

"Ahpa, what happened? They said there's a new principal, and that the South invaded the North! What's going on?"

At that, Uhma dropped her velvet drawstring bag.

"I hope you don't believe that for a second—the South invading the North. The rest of the world is saying it was the other way around," Ahpa said, holding up his black-market foreign radio.

"But this—this is just another border skirmish, right? Not an actual war?" Myung-gi asked, the room growing warmer.

Ahpa didn't answer.

"What about your job? Did they reassign you?" Uhma asked. Her shoulders started curling, as if worry were gripping her by the back of the neck.

"No reassignment. They just let me go. Which is not a good sign. The Party might know things."

"What things?" Uhma gasped. Her face turned white.

That was when Ahpa sighed and told them. "I was involved in organizing those student protests a few years ago. And I've been getting banned books from the bookstore—circulating forbidden ideas. They might have caught on to me."

A bead of sweat dripped down Myung-gi's forehead, but he didn't wipe it.

Was that why his father had always been so busy with work—coming and going, meeting with people? He was organizing protests? Going to the bookstore in the city? Was that where he got those smuggled books?

"Some of those involved in the protests were my former students—some even around your age, Myung-gi. I couldn't just stand back and watch. They were getting shot and killed just for voicing their opinions. Shot and killed."

Shot and killed? *Shot and killed?* An ant crawled onto Myung-gi's foot, so he went to the door, dazed, and gently pushed it off.

"Oh God, what if they hurt you?" Uhma said, her hand trembling against her lip. "What if they take you away? What about the children? How are they going to live? We'll have no source of income."

"It won't happen, because I have a plan," Ahpa said, grabbing a pen and paper from his writing desk, his movements quick and assured. He motioned for them to gather around on the floor. "You know that I've been planning our escape for years now, but there was never a good time. It was always too dangerous with guards checking all the borders. But now things are different. Now there is a war, a distraction. I think this is finally our time to go."

Myung-gi sat there, stunned. The last time Ahpa had gotten close to carrying out their escape, they had aborted after his colleague Professor Song was shot trying to cross the border. He looked at Uhma; sweat glistened on her nose. She and Yoomee huddled together.

"We're going to head south to the mouth of the Yesong River where it empties into the Yellow Sea. It's about a hundred miles from here, right at the border of North and South Korea," Ahpa said, his hand flying across the paper. He made a rough sketch of both countries, then drew a line from their village to the Yesong River.

"I heard from one of my former students living there that there are boats smuggling people south," he continued, drawing an arrow through the Yellow Sea to the west coast of South Korea. "From there, it is a short boat ride to the seaport city of Inchon. Then we will walk to Busan on the southern coast—as far from the North as we can possibly go."

Myung-gi remembered reading about the Yellow Sea. It had some of the most extreme tides in the world. He imagined getting swept out to sea—arms flailing, head bobbing, water shooting up his nose—and a shudder ran through him.

"When do we leave?" he asked.

"In a few days. I have to prepare for our journey, confirm word about the boats, talk to the Paks about our plans."

The Paks, their closest friends. Was Sora still Myung-gi's friend? Myung-gi worried his hand through his hair, over and over.

At the mention of Sora, Yoomee couldn't help but chime in. "I saw Sora hiding under the willow tree outside my classroom window the other day," she said. "It was like she was sneaking around or something. Definitely not to be trusted."

"Her mother pulled her out of school to look after her little brothers. She was probably just trying to listen in on the lessons," Uhma said, staring at Ahpa's map, her mind far away, maybe already sailing across the Yellow Sea.

Myung-gi looked at his sister. This was why those girls by the river had rolled their eyes at Yoomee. When would she learn? "You shouldn't make snap judgements about people," he said.

"She's not the smartest person in my grade, you know," Yoomee blurted.

"What? What does that have to do with anything?"

"I'm just saying. I don't think she's nice."

"That's ludicrous."

"Uhma!" Yoomee cried. "He's using big words again!"

"Enough," Ahpa said, holding up his hand.

They stopped arguing.

"They've invited us for dinner. I'll tell them tonight."

"Do you think that's wise?" Uhma said, her forehead creased with worry. "I know they are our closest friends, but still . . ."

Ahpa took her hand. "I have to give them the chance to come with us."

Myung-gi knew that Ahpa and Sora's father were like brothers, though you'd never guess it by looking at them. In grade school, Ahpa was the popular one—winning competitions and good at everything—while Sora's father was quiet and always content to be last, according to Uhma. The only thing they shared was their sense of justice—both standing up to the Japanese teacher who had wrongfully accused someone of speaking Korean. But would this long friendship really be enough to keep them together through an escape? Across armed borders? Where getting caught meant getting killed?

"The Paks were prominent members of the church once; I'm afraid the Reds might come after them too," Ahpa continued. "It would be good if they came."

"Why do they always have to come with us?" Yoomee mumbled.

Ahpa stared at her long and hard. "Because the Reds are arresting and killing Christians. The Paks don't have to come with us, but I certainly hope they do."

Yoomee lowered her head.

"What about school?" Myung-gi asked.

That was when Ahpa looked him level in the eye. "You should continue going, son, up until the day we leave. If you don't show up, they might get suspicious and figure out our plans to escape. So be careful of what you say, and watch for anyone following you home. If you notice anything strange, run and find me. You can't have your head in the clouds. You must be vigilant, always."

"Yes, Ahpa," Myung-gi said, nodding too vigorously.

"When we do leave, we will escape at night. Hopefully no one will know we're missing until we're long gone," Ahpa said.

Uhma closed her eyes and started whispering a prayer.

"And if something happens to me, I want all of you to follow the escape route," he continued, holding up the map he had drawn. "Don't wait even one hour, just go."

"What? No!" Yoomee shouted, throwing her arms around Ahpa.

Pulling her slowly away, Ahpa told her—told all of them—that even if the secret police were to take him away, he would make his way to Busan. "I will find a way to you. Busan will be our meeting place," he said.

"But, Ahpa, I . . . I don't know if I would be able to leave you," Myung-gi said, his voice getting stuck in his throat.

"Listen, they could even come for you next, Myung-gi," Ahpa said, his eyes boring into his son. "Remember, go a hundred miles south to the mouth of the Yesong River. My former student will be there—Ko Jusung. Say it: 'Ko Jusung.'"

"Ko Jusung," Myung-gi said. But it sounded timid and unsteady, like words stepping out on a plank.

Ahpa nodded. "Don't be afraid to go on without me, son. Do you understand?"

Myung-gi gripped the edge of the table. "Yes, Ahpa," he said again, his face as solemn as an oath.

CHAPTER 16

June 1950: Myung-gi, Age 14

It was evening, and Myung-gi was inside the Paks' thatched-roof house, sitting cross-legged on the floor at the low dining table. Sora sat beside him, her knee touching his. But he hardly noticed.

Because they weren't coming—Ahpa had asked the Paks to escape with them, and they said no.

Uhma tried to make amends with Sora's mother, who was still upset over Ahpa's dangerous proposition of escape. Mr. Pak tried to soften the moment by offering Ahpa the name of his brother-in-law in Busan as someone who could help. And Sora, Yoomee, Youngsoo, and baby Jisoo were doing what kids did when their parents argued: pretend to be engrossed in something else.

If the Paks had agreed to come, it wouldn't feel so much like a treacherous escape as an ordinary trip—the fathers walking together, the mothers chatting alongside them, the kids clustering behind. With Sora by Myung-gi's side, wrangling the little ones wouldn't be hard. And Mr. Pak could help protect Ahpa, so that Myung-gi wouldn't ever have to go on without him.

Don't be afraid to go on without me. What did that even mean? Was something terrible going to happen to Ahpa? Did his father know more than he was telling? Myung-gi couldn't get those words to stop repeating inside his head—and now they were throbbing behind his eyes.

"Myung-gi-ya, stop tapping your finger," Uhma snapped.

He stopped, then looked over at Sora, whose eyes were dark and somber. Like the bark of the willow tree after a long, hard rain. When was the last time they had sat together under its branches reading books? A year ago? He knew she still went, but he was too old for that sort of thing. And wouldn't it be unseemly if he kept meeting her there at their age?

Sora glanced toward him, and he darted his gaze in the other direction. He didn't mind admiring her from a distance—the warm glow of her skin, the way she could recite long poems. But now he would have to regard her from even farther: from across a border, hundreds of miles away, like a character in one of his books.

Maybe he would never see her again.

A teapot sat on the table, a crack running up its side—maybe from when Sora's mother set it down harder than anyone was expecting. *You shouldn't have said any of this out loud. It puts us all in a dangerous position! Who do you think the police will interrogate? My husband and me!* she'd cried. Maybe it *was* selfish of Ahpa to ask them to come, and selfish of Myung-gi to hope that they would—especially when one of Sora's relatives had been executed for going against the state. Their family was already under suspicion for that.

Staring at the tiny bubble of hot water forming along the fissure, Myung-gi wiped it away with his thumb, only to watch another one squeeze out, this time a little bigger. The crack was widening, and a tiny puddle was pooling, and soon there would be a mess of hot tea on the table and an empty pot.

No one seemed to notice except Sora's little brother Young-soo, who was carefully watching Myung-gi—the only older boy he knew—and then copying the way he sat slumped on his floor cushion, one hand holding up his head, the other one resting on his knee at an angle. Myung-gi nodded once, and Youngsoo nodded back.

After a while, no one knew what else to say. Myung-gi sat still, the silence growing so taut that he could pluck it with his fingers, hear it reverberate inside his head.

He got up and left.

CHAPTER 17

October 1952: Myung-gi, Age 16

I love to be alone. I never found the companion that was so companionable as solitude.

—Henry David Thoreau, *Walden*

Myung-gi wants to get up and leave. Now. Because strange sounds are reverberating inside the tunnel.

Breathe in and out. Nice and even. If he can't get out past the rock walls, then maybe the enemy can't get in past them either. No one can get to him. He's safe here, for now.

But if he thinks too hard about it—being trapped underground, in a four-by-five space, the air dank and thick . . . if he lets his lungs draw in too quickly, too deeply, only to suck in too little air in return . . . if he dwells for even a second longer on the idea of being stuck deep in the earth, like a corpse . . . he might let that cork of composure pop and start ramming his back into the rock wall—shoulders jabbing, bones breaking, head smashing. A wild animal throwing itself against its cage. Again and again, to no avail.

But something has to give.

Myung-gi screams. Long and hard. But the shelling has begun again. And his voice is drowned out by all those blasts above, where everyone is busy dying.

No one knows he's here. Oh God, no one knows he's here. And this is the idea he can't shake: of being alone, in the dark, forever.

That scream has scraped his throat raw; when he swallows, it doesn't feel right. So he quiets himself, does his best to bottle everything up, put that cork back into place—like Ahpa, like Uhma. And he sits there, knees up, head down. Shivering.

It is in that dark and lonely place that words from a book pop into his head, as if they are his own: *I love to be alone. I love to be alone.* All those hours spent in his room, away from everyone, always reading. Wasn't he happy then? Wasn't he alone? This is no different, except he doesn't have books to keep him company, doesn't have anyone to talk to about them.

Enough—that's enough.

He will keep himself together until morning.

CHAPTER 18

June 1950: Myung-gi, Age 14

Next morning, Myung-gi got ready for school.

"Don't talk to the other students," Uhma said, ironing Myung-gi's red scarf. It was the first time she'd told him to keep to himself; she was always encouraging him to make friends instead. *He never lets me hug him anymore, never tells me anything*, Myung-gi had once heard her complain to Mrs. Pak. *That's just the way boys are. He's growing up*, Sora's mother had replied. Uhma had sighed longingly, and a pang had shot through him.

"Just focus on your studies," she continued.

"Yes, Uhma."

"If anyone asks about your father, say you don't know. We're counting on you to buy us time."

"Yes, Uhma." Myung-gi took the hot scarf from his mother and tied it around his neck, the heat from the iron burning into his skin.

A tremor rattled his hands, but he gathered his books—including an extra one he planned to leave under the willow tree for Sora, just to let her know they hadn't left yet. He'd never left her books before, but he was sure she would find it, and she would know it was from him.

"What are you doing with *that* book?" asked Yoomee, still in her pajamas. Classes for the younger grades had been canceled because of the war.

"What? Oh, it's for school," Myung-gi said, putting on his shoes. How did she always notice everything?

"But you already read it last year for school. I remember the funny title: *How the Steel Was Tempered*. You said it wasn't good!"

He knew there was no fooling her; she remembered everything. Letting out a long, noisy breath, he said, "Fine, you're right. It's not good. But I'm going to leave it under the willow tree to let Sora know that we haven't left yet. Maybe she can still convince her family to come with us. It's not safe for them to stay here."

"Oh, so it's like a secret mission," Yoomee said, her eyes sparkling. "Can I come?"

"No."

"Please? I'll be good."

"Yoomee, this is serious. You saw how scared Mrs. Pak got last night when Ahpa shared our escape plans," he said, trying to shut it out of his mind—Mrs. Pak's face as shiny and tight as thinly blown glass, a wild look in her eyes. He'd never seen their parents argue before.

"I won't tell anyone, promise," Yoomee insisted.

He looked at her—at the way she bobbed up and down like an overeager chick—and knew she was too young to be trusted. "Sorry," he said. "Maybe next time."

How the Steel Was Tempered was a novel. About the Bolsheviks, yes, but still a novel, and he knew how much Sora loved novels. It would catch her eye. And maybe, just maybe, after she had found it, she would know it was from him and could talk her family into coming with them.

For some reason, this thought was the only thing that calmed him.

The willow tree was on his way to school, so he dropped the book by the roots, tucked it under some leaves, and hoped for the best.

Then he set off again, keeping his head down, the back of his neck prickling as if he were under a magnifying glass, the hot sun blazing through from the other side. By the time he looked up, he'd reached the schoolyard.

Everyone was staring at him.

Just act normal, he told himself. But what was normal? He

straightened his shoulders, ran his hand through his hair, and then stepped inside the building.

First class. History. Comrade Hong sat at his desk waiting for all the students to enter. A low hum filled the room as boys greeted one another and talked about the homework. Myung-gi took his usual seat at the front. He pulled his notebook out of his bag and turned to his notes on modern history:

— 1910–1945, Japan rules Korea and oppresses the Korean people.

— 1945, Japan loses World War II and is ousted from Korea.

— 1945, the US and Soviet Union swoop in and divide Korea in half at the 38th parallel.

— Communist Soviet Union occupies the North. The democratic United States occupies the South.

And now here they were—the North and South fighting each other, as if they'd forgotten they were all Korean, forgotten they were all human. He looked at his notebook again and rewrote the last bullet point in case the teacher ever asked to see his notes:

— Communist Soviet Union occupies the North. The imperialist American dogs occupy the South.

There. He didn't want to get abducted on his way home from school. He slammed his notebook shut, and his desk rattled.

"Just look at him sitting there so smug. He thinks he's so smart, so good looking. I bet he thinks all the girls are in love with him," a boy said from behind. Snickers followed. Then the boy leaned in close and lowered his voice. "Once untouchable . . . but not anymore."

Myung-gi swatted his ear. He didn't turn around, didn't draw more attention to himself. But he clenched his jaw, could feel the length of his back tensing. He counted to ten. Someone's desk scraped the floor. He looked to his left.

It was Byongho, the overgrown boy who always went along with the crowd, whose name he almost couldn't remember. He was bigger and older than everyone else after taking two years off from school to work on the farm after his dad had passed away. Myung-gi had helped him with his homework once when his dad first got sick. Now he was laughing with the rest of them, until he caught Myung-gi looking.

Byongho stopped laughing.

Comrade Hong rose from his desk and told everyone to quiet down. "There will be no teasing or harassment here," he boomed, his voice a hammer coming down on the class. "Byongho, go to the principal's office."

"What? But I didn't do anything," Byongho said.

Comrade Hong was erasing the board. "Don't worry, you're not being punished. You've been picked for a great honor, actually," he said, turning around to face the boy. "You've been recruited to serve in our country's army and defend this great nation!"

"Recruited?" Byongho said softly, his mouth hanging open.

Murmurs rumbled across the room. Boys crossed and uncrossed and crossed their arms. No one dared look up at the teacher. Not even Myung-gi.

"Will I be able to go home and tell my mom?" Byongho asked.

"That's something you can ask once you get to the principal's office. Now go. They're waiting."

"But I have to say good-bye, or else she'll worry."

"That's enough talk now. You should go," Comrade Hong said, firmly, before turning his back to the class and writing on the board.

Everyone watched in silence as Byongho got up and gathered his things. A pencil rolled off his desk, and when Myung-gi picked it up to hand it to him, Byongho nodded politely before tucking it inside his bag.

Myung-gi had the urge to tell him that he was as strong as a bull—that he had horns that could gore, legs that could buck. He didn't have to go along with this! He could tell them he didn't want to go. But the thought petered out. . . .

Myung-gi knew there was no way out for him. Not really.

"Class, turn to chapter five of your textbook and take notes. Immediately," Comrade Hong said.

Papers rustled across the room. Everyone lowered their head and got to work. And Byongho shuffled out the door, one massive foot after the other. He was certainly big enough to be a soldier. But was he tough enough? Smart enough? Brave enough? He could get killed in battle—wiped off the face of the Earth, never to be seen again. This could be the last time Myung-gi ever laid eyes on him.

Even though Myung-gi never paid him much attention and didn't like the company he kept, he couldn't help but ache for this kid whose name he could hardly remember. Overcome, Myung-gi took out his textbook and started reading . . . when Comrade Hong crouched low beside his desk. Myung-gi looked up, startled.

"Myung-gi, how is your father doing? It must have been quite a shock for him yesterday," he said quietly.

There was concern in Comrade Hong's eyes. Maybe Myung-gi had misjudged him. Maybe some of the new teachers weren't so bad. "He's doing well," he answered cautiously.

Comrade Hong smiled. "Good, that's good." He got up to return to his desk, but then turned his head casually, asking, "Oh, but what will your father do now that he's out of work?"

Myung-gi paused.

They'd never discussed how to answer a question like that. People like his father were out of work for good.

He stared at Comrade Hong. The teacher stood there waiting, suspended between nonchalance and intensity. The morning sun streaming through the windows put a spotlight on him, exposing a flame in his eyes, wrinkle lines like splinters, a cigarette hiding inside his sleeve—and Myung-gi shifted in his seat.

"My father will join the proletarian masses and find a job working in the fields, of course, sir," he said, his voice unsteady.

A history book fell off a boy's desk—pages crumpled, front cover bent, spine twisted—but Comrade Hong did not turn.

Myung-gi lifted his gaze.

Comrade Hong looked back.

Myung-gi's face turned hot.

At that, his teacher flashed a smile, as if he'd just won a card game. "Of course. A job in the fields. What else would your father do?"

CHAPTER 19

June 1950: Myung-gi, Age 14

Every day was the same—go to school, try to stay invisible, race home, and hide.

It would be time to leave soon. For the past three days, Uhma had been packing rice, clothing, and money into bags, checking everything twice. Ahpa was going to secret meetings with people who could confirm their spots on those boats, and he had gotten word that Sora's aunt and uncle had found a place for them to stay in Busan.

Myung-gi was on his way home after dropping off another book under the willow tree to replace the one that was gone. They were disappearing, all the ones he had left, and he hoped it was Sora who was finding them.

The sky was blue. The air was warm. There was a button loose on his shirt. That was what Myung-gi was thinking on that 28th day of June in 1950, as he walked through his gate, across the courtyard, and through the sliding rice-paper door.

"Hand me those pots," Ahpa said, holding the jigeh back carrier with one hand and pointing with the other.

Myung-gi stepped down into the kitchen, stared at a shelf full of pots, then grabbed the three he knew his father wanted. "Is there anything else I can do to help?" he asked.

Ahpa was too busy strapping things into the A-frame back carrier to look up. "Hmm, let me think . . . not really. I've got to pack this jigeh myself so that it's balanced. Why don't you go outside and keep watch? Whistle if anything looks suspicious."

"Sure, Ahpa," Myung-gi said, running to his room and grabbing one of the books he kept on his open shelf. *The Structure of the Solar System*—always a good choice and safe to read outside. Now he wouldn't be completely bored while keeping watch.

He had a favorite spot—behind the house, on the other side of the stone wall, under the twin pines. No one ever bothered him there. Myung-gi went and scaled the back wall, then squinted at the summer sky, counting the hours before it would turn too dark to read.

Engrossed in the book—this one about the Earth's infinitesimal place in the universe—he didn't see men creeping along the side of the house, didn't hear the sticks broken underfoot, didn't keep watch or warn Ahpa like he was supposed to.

It was the grunting that jolted him alert. He jumped to his feet, the treetops sharp and clear against the blinding sun. Hurriedly he climbed the stone wall, slipped back into the courtyard, then peered slowly around the corner of the house.

The front door was wide open, the sound of a struggle coming from inside—headbutting, kicking, groaning, cursing. If sweat had a sound, it would be coming from that house too. What was going on?

Four men with rifles walked out laughing. They pushed Ahpa along in front of them.

Myung-gi flattened himself against the wall.

Ahpa's hands were tied behind his back, one eye swollen shut, a bright blue bruise on his cheekbone. He staggered, tripping on his own feet, looking like a drunkard beaten in a brawl—his gentleman father.

They were only a few feet away. What should he do? What should he *do*?

A shovel was leaning against the house—close enough for Myung-gi to grab. But he'd never hit anyone—never even stomped a bug. Could he do it? Could he strike those men with a shovel?

Myung-gi's shaking hand started reaching.

But Ahpa's gaze flitted in his direction. His one good eye lit on the shovel, then on Myung-gi, and he shook his head almost imperceptibly.

Myung-gi lowered his hand, then slid to the ground, his chest heaving.

He watched them take his father—the army men with their red and yellow badges, their rifles slung over their shoulders. They yelled at Ahpa to move faster, so he did. Then they pushed his battered head down and forced him into a car.

In an instant, they were gone.

Myung-gi sat on the ground, gutted.

Hot shame flooded him. He played everything over in his head: Reading behind the stone wall. Getting lost in the story. *Not keeping watch.*

His thoughts tumbled, one over the next. What now? What should he do? Run to the Paks for help? He imagined the panic on Mrs. Pak's face if he showed up at her door. His head pounded.

Then he remembered. Uhma and Yoomee. They would be coming home any minute now from washing laundry in the river.

He pictured their faces at hearing the news. The horror in Uhma's eyes, the rage on Yoomee's face. And Ahpa . . . he couldn't stop seeing Ahpa's eye, swollen shut and bulging like a tumor. . . .

Myung-gi clutched his stomach and doubled over.

How could this have happened? *How could he have not heard them?* It was as if his heart had turned into a hot slug and was sliding to the pit of his stomach.

He picked his book up off the ground, dusted its jacket, then hurled it as hard as he could.

Myung-gi could have warned him. He should have warned him. He should have been listening—not reading.

Dark clouds twisted across the sky, as if the heavens, too, were writhing with regret. Looking toward the setting sun, Myung-gi saw his family coming. Up the dusty road. Uhma and Yoomee, their faces still untroubled.

CHAPTER 20

October 1952: Myung-gi, Age 16

> The spirits of the dead, who stood
> In life before thee, are again
> In death around thee, and their will
> Shall overshadow thee; be still.
> —Edgar Allan Poe, *Spirits of the Dead*

In the darkness, Myung-gi can't stop tumbling through space. Faces spin upside down—Uhma's and Yoomee's—laughing and crying. Queasiness overtakes him, and he grabs onto the tunnel walls.

It's quiet outside. The fighting has stopped. But now there are other noises in the tunnel—chittering. Maybe it's just wind whistling through the corridors. Please let it just be the wind.

Though he's not sure, he thinks he's been sitting here for more than a day.

It's so black in here, Myung-gi doesn't know whether to close his eyes or keep them open; he decides to keep them open. Because he has this strange feeling that something is going to happen—his father's hand will emerge from the pitch blackness and tap him on the shoulder. He imagines Ahpa stepping into that father-shaped hole in the dark. And Ahpa will be grinning, as if this has all been a test to see how well Myung-gi could take care of things on his own, and now it's over.

Such a smart boy, he will say.

Except that's not true, Ahpa. Look at the mess I got myself into.

There's a matchbox in Myung-gi's pocket, but only one match left. He will use it now to assess his surroundings.

But his fingertips sting so much, he can hardly strike it. How is it possible to feel numbness and pain at the same time? Biting his lip, he winces, then figures out a better way: holding the match with his knuckles.

Strike.

Blinking, he looks around. There is a broken mirror on the ground; a tin cup; crumpled garbage. Behind him, where he first entered, the tunnel is blocked, as he suspected. In front, the shaft continues straight for a few feet, then hits another wall.

Myung-gi looks down. Black dirt and charcoal cover his arms. His fingertips—they're raw and bloody. He has to let his hands heal before he starts digging again.

The match is burning fast. If he lit some of that crumpled paper on the ground, he could see for longer. But then it would make too much smoke.

The match burns down to the end. He snuffs it out. It's dark.

Myung-gi hears something, something like the ocean inside a conch shell—the same resonating chambers, sound bouncing off hard surfaces, accentuating its natural frequency. He remembers when he was seven and the whole family went to the shore. Ahpa found a large conch shell, held it to everyone's ear, told them how it worked. *Wah!* Uhma said. *Let me see!* Yoomee said. *Listen!* Ahpa said.

And now, all their voices are howling inside Myung-gi's head. *Yes, the tunnel is like a conch shell, Ahpa. That's all it is—wind rushing through this tunnel like a conch shell.*

Myung-gi takes in a shuddering breath.

Enough of this. He needs to get out. He needs to find his platoon. And Ahpa—he needs to find Ahpa. Life can never be normal until he finds him.

Getting on his hands and knees, Myung-gi starts crawling forward, the stony ground jabbing his kneecaps. Maybe there's a different way out. Maybe he can dig again. Maybe he can still find his father.

If Uhma were here, she would tell him not to bump his head, not to make holes in his pants, not to hurt his knees. Then she would beg him to talk, share his feelings, let someone else in other than his father.

Myung-gi stops.

Someone is talking—not too far away, just on the other side of that wall at the end of the shaft. He listens.

It's quiet.

Shaking his head, Myung-gi starts breathing again. It was probably just his imagination—all those books he's read have spoiled his mind. Because isn't this how it always happens in a story: boy, alone in the dark, hears strange noises, and then something frightening happens? How many countless books like this did he read outside, in the shade, during recess? All those boys from his class snickering at him while playing games of war.

He keeps going, reaches the other rock wall, feels the edges for a fissure where he can dig. This boulder could be more yielding than the one behind him. With a little prodding, maybe he could tip it over and out of the way.

Myung-gi holds his breath. Because he hears it again. Closer than the thunder of distant shelling. On the other side of the rock wall. A human voice, quiet and low. It blows into his ears, dragging in something else uninvited: *The spirits of the dead* . . . No, not that one! . . . *who stood in life before thee* . . . He must cover his ears! . . . *are again in death around thee* . . . But the words of Poe don't need to travel through sound! . . . *and their will shall overshadow thee* . . . *be still.*

For a second, Myung-gi can't make out the mumbling. Until he does.

Chinese. Someone is speaking Chinese.

CHAPTER 21

June 1950: Myung-gi, Age 14

Myung-gi went inside the house before Uhma and Yoomee reached it. Chinese and Russian language books were scattered across the room, and he placed them back on the shelf. Their table was turned over, and he set it right side up. One end of the long chest was dragged away from the wall—as if someone had grabbed it in a desperate attempt to hold on—and he pushed that back too.

When they stepped inside, they brought in their usual chatter. He took it in like a warm breeze from past picnics, past trips to the beach, and held it for a few seconds, not wanting to let it go.

"Ahpa's gone. They took him," Myung-gi said, flatly.

The room fell silent. No one moved.

Then Yoomee burst into tears. Uhma let go an armful of clothespins, which clattered across the earthen floor as if her skeleton had come undone.

"When did it happen?" Uhma asked, the color draining from her face.

Myung-gi stood, back bent, hands on his knees. "About thirty minutes ago."

"Were you home?"

"Yes. No. I mean, I was outside."

"What were you doing outside?"

That was when he sat on the floor, the blood draining fast from his head. "I was reading," he said, not looking at her.

"*Reading?*" Uhma's eyes were wide. "Were you able to get a good look at them? What did they look like? What were they wearing?" she pressed, her tone ratcheting higher.

"They wore uniforms."

"Yes, obviously," Uhma said, closing her eyes and pressing her temple. "But were they secret police? Military? Local Party leaders?"

"I . . . I don't know."

"Where were you exactly? Can you show me?" She grabbed his hand and headed toward the door.

But he pulled his arm away—harder than he'd intended, the warmth of her hand threatening to dissolve the thin skin holding him together.

Uhma looked at him and at his reddening face, then sat on the floor.

"I'm sorry, I just don't know anything," Myung-gi said, not wanting to talk about it anymore. He stood there, the guilt growing like a weed inside him, already tangling with his thoughts, sprouting out through his mouth, winding around his neck.

✺

An owl hooted. Rain fell. Someone turned on a lamp, casting long shadows on the wall. The hours passed into night. Where was Ahpa now? At a labor camp? On the way to Siberia? Was he even still alive? Myung-gi couldn't feel his hands. What now?

"Let's go to the police headquarters or the Party leader and get him back," Yoomee demanded, already heading for the door.

"No," Uhma said, burying her face in her hands. "They'll never let him go. And they're recruiting every man into their army now. Going to them will only bring attention to the fact that we have one more male in our household." She looked up, her cheeks sagging. "They recruited a village boy just today—Byongho, I think was his name. He's only two years older than you, Myung-gi-ya. His mother was wailing on the road."

"I know," Myung-gi said, quietly.

"We can't let them recruit you. Do you hear me? We need to keep you safe."

Yoomee's head snapped toward her brother, panicked, as if he might get recruited right in that instant. She stepped away from the door.

Myung-gi couldn't look at them. Though he hated the idea of war and would never want to fight in one, Byongho was going to do the work of grown men. It was then that he remembered what Ahpa had told them to do if something were to happen to him. The thought made his insides twist, made him want to vomit, but he said it anyway.

"Uhma . . ." He could hardly get the words out. "Ahpa said if something were to happen to him, we should go . . . to the shore . . . and across the Yellow Sea. He said he would meet us in Busan. He even arranged a house for us there. Maybe . . . maybe we should go," Myung-gi finished, shakily trying on the words—like Ahpa's principal's jacket—worn only by the man of the house. But the words were too big.

"We can't leave!" Yoomee shouted, her face turning red.

Oh God, she was right. They couldn't leave. What was he saying? He put his head in his hands.

Uhma's gaze flitted from her son to her daughter and back again. She opened her mouth, but nothing came out. Which was when Myung-gi knew—even his mother didn't know what to do.

All night they sat, like idle pieces on a game board, no hand to direct them where to move. Eventually, Uhma got up and started washing barley in a pot. Yoomee took to old familiar ways, trying to glare at Myung-gi and spark a fight—*Who moved my sketchbook?* But without Ahpa to scold or pay her any attention, her whining hung in the air like an incomplete sentence.

"What are we going to do?" Yoomee asked eventually.

Myung-gi looked out the window. A faint orange glow tinged the sky. The sun would soon be up. And then what would happen? Would the authorities return? Would he have to go to school? How would they survive without Ahpa? How could they *leave* Ahpa?

"Maybe we should stay," Myung-gi ventured.

"Now, wait, let me think." Uhma's voice trembled. She wiped her hands on a rag, then smoothed the front of her dress and sat down. Though she'd stopped wearing red on her lips and peach on her cheeks, she still dusted her face with white powder, making her look pale as a ghost. "Your father told us to leave if anything were to happen to him, to meet him in Busan. That's what he said, isn't that right?" She looked at Myung-gi, and he could feel the weight of the world shifting from Ahpa's shoulders to his.

Uhma continued staring at her son, but he only sat mute. He knew what Ahpa had said—they all did. But what if Ahpa couldn't escape? If they left home, the distance between them would be so great, they might never see him again.

"I think we should leave. That is what your father instructed. It's not safe here for any of us. What if they came back, this time for Myung-gi?" Uhma said. Her sharp focus softened into a far-off gaze. "No, not my son. They will not take my son too."

Yoomee wiped her eyes and said in a small voice, "I don't want them to come back and take anyone else."

"Let's . . . let's make a list of leaving versus staying." Uhma grabbed a pencil—the one Ahpa had used to draw his map—but it slipped from her fingers, tumbled in the air, and fell to the floor. She closed her eyes and took in a shaky breath. "Well, no matter, we can just talk it out. If we *stayed* and your father escaped, he might miss us and head straight for Busan. And if he couldn't escape, we would all be stuck here without him—a family on the blacklist." Uhma nodded out the words, as if assessing each one carefully. "But if we *left* and your father escaped, he would head for Busan and try to find us, as he had planned. And if he couldn't escape . . ." She broke her far-off stare and looked straight at Myung-gi and Yoomee. "At least we would be safe in the South, where you two could both have a future." It was the most Uhma had ever spoken.

But Myung-gi couldn't imagine a future without his father. He needed Ahpa to tell him what to do, show him how to be. He needed to prove to him that he could be the kind of son to live up to his name—strong and clever, like his father. He needed to tell him how sorry he was for always having his head in the clouds and not keeping watch like he was supposed to. Myung-gi looked at the stack of books beside him and wanted to knock it over.

"Myung-gi-ya, I think this is what your father would want us to do. He told us not to be afraid to go on without him, didn't he?" Uhma said, that tremor still in her voice. "Let's not let him down, okay?"

At that, Myung-gi finally nodded. He'd already let his father down once. He couldn't let him down again. Yoomee sniffled and nodded too.

Uhma made radish soup and barley before they left, even though it was too late for dinner and too early for breakfast. The broth was thin and tasted like hot water. Barley clumped in Myung-gi's throat. Still, he forced down a few bites—they all did—knowing that they might not get another meal for days.

After eating, Uhma didn't wash their bowls and spoons. It didn't matter. But as Myung-gi walked toward the door, he couldn't help staring at all those dirty dishes scattered across the table.

It was humid out. The rain had stopped. An early morning fog hovered over the ground.

Myung-gi swung Ahpa's jigeh over his shoulders while Uhma and Yoomee clutched small bundles, all of them in a daze. He closed the door behind them. Uhma held Yoomee's arm. Then they stepped out into the murky white and disappeared.

CHAPTER 22

October 1952: Myung-gi, Age 16

No warmth could warm, no wintry weather chill him. No wind that blew was bitterer than he.

—Charles Dickens, *A Christmas Carol*

Myung-gi is disappearing—all that tunnel darkness erasing him from the head down. He pats his arm just to make sure it's still there, because no matter how close he holds it up to his face, he can't see it.

Maybe his mind is going, too. Because he thought he heard someone speaking Chinese on the other side of the rock wall. Unless the stress and dehydration and bump on his head are making him hear things.

"Who's there?" Myung-gi shouts, using the Chinese he learned from Ahpa.

Silence.

But he's *sure* he heard someone. A grown man's voice. Deep and low.

The darkness in the tunnel begins to seep inside Myung-gi. If China hadn't entered the war on the side of North Korea, then South Korea would've won. All Koreans would be free—free to travel, free to speak, free to worship, free to make their own fate. The war would be over by now. Myung-gi would've found Ahpa, and they would all be together.

He grinds his teeth, feeling the chill of half-forgotten words seep into him: *No wind that blew was bitterer than he.*

"Yah! I'm talking to you! *You've ruined my life!*" Myung-gi shouts so hard that his voice cracks.

At that, a few rocks crumble to the ground, as if someone is digging from the other side.

Myung-gi freezes. The vein on the side of his head pumps so hard it might burst. He can't stop thinking of the lieutenant's warning before this mission: *Inside these mountains, the Chinese are dug in—expect hand-to-hand combat in the dark.* Myung-gi had hoped he could fight this war from a distance, aiming through a scope—not so close that he could look into another man's face, not so close that the enemy would become human.

Myung-gi pulls the knife from its sheath and holds it straight out with both hands. The man might break through. But Myung-gi feels as ready as a boy playing pretend with a stick for a sword. *God, are you there? I already asked once: please don't make me use this.*

Sweat pours down the sides of his face. His hand trembles so hard, his knife hits the rock wall. "Ahpa," Myung-gi whispers, "help me."

"Why? Are you trapped?" asks the voice on the other side. It's speaking in a mix of Chinese and broken Korean.

Myung-gi stops breathing.

It's a trick. A plan for an ambush. Admitting he's trapped would make him vulnerable to attack.

"No," Myung-gi says. "I'm not trapped."

At that, laughter—deep and rolling—echoes through the tunnel. And Myung-gi clasps his hands over his ears.

CHAPTER 23

July 1950: Myung-gi, Age 14

Myung-gi shut the courtyard gate, the metal clang echoing in the predawn. At first no one spoke, the fog wrapping around their faces like a muffler. But gradually Uhma began trying to talk to Myung-gi as they walked, her terror hiding behind a tight smile. Myung-gi wanted to ease her mind, tell her everything she wanted to know. But every time she started asking another question, his heart would tumble down a long flight of stairs.

"So, tell me once more," she pushed. "How many men were there?"

"Four."

"And they didn't hurt him?"

"No," he lied, not wanting her to worry even more.

"Did they say anything? Did you hear anything?"

"No." *Except all that grunting.*

"Did they see you?"

"No."

"How did your father look? I mean, his expression. Was it a little defiant, you know what I mean, the way he looks when he has a plan?"

"I don't know."

After a pause, she said, "Ah, alright then," as if she didn't want to press her luck with a finicky cow that had already given her more milk than she'd expected.

Myung-gi quickened his pace and stayed two steps ahead, as if he were leading the way instead of avoiding more talk. Uhma patted him on the back, the way any good mother would, but his shoulders sagged.

Everything looked different in the gray murk. Mountains loomed closer. Pine trees lunged at their backs. Straw eaves on thatched-roof houses swayed like hair in the wind. The fog slowly started lifting, and when Yoomee turned to him—her eyes wide and glistening—even she looked different in the half light.

"Oppah, what if we get caught escaping? What if we can't get in a boat when we reach the sea?" she asked, her gaze fastened to him.

He wished she would yell at him about walking too slowly, or accuse him of using words that were too big—anything but ask questions. Because what was he supposed to do with a little sister who needed him to be strong? "Shh, we shouldn't talk. Someone might hear us," was all he could say, the sharp tang of pine slowly burning its way down to his stomach.

"And what about Ahpa? What if we never see him again?" she said.

Myung-gi tried to picture it but couldn't. Ahpa was the one who took care of them, provided for them, told them things about the world. When Myung-gi used to lie on his back in the courtyard and stare up at the night sky, Ahpa would stroll out and tell him about the moon, about the way it made the tides rise. He told him how people on opposite sides of the world could see the moon at the same time. And when Myung-gi didn't believe him, Ahpa sketched the moon and the Earth and the lines of horizons from different longitudes, until finally he could see it—the moon, a connecting dot in the sky. For a second, he closed his eyes, trying to hold on to this memory . . . but all he saw was the bright blue bruise on Ahpa's swollen cheekbone.

Myung-gi looked up just as rain clouds started moving in. Yoomee peered at him expectantly, but when he said nothing, she continued walking, quietly, by his side.

CHAPTER 24

July 1950: Myung-gi, Age 14

For weeks, monsoon rains soaked their clothes, froze their bodies, left them shivering. So they ran slightly hunched, protecting that soft spot in their middle, where they carried all their secrets and fears, hopes and dreams.

As much as possible, they stayed off roads, cutting through forests, pastures, and fields. Myung-gi led them south by the sun. Having to hide made their progress very slow.

One afternoon, as an earthy smell rose from the ground, the clouds ripped open wider than they ever had been. Droplets as big as bumblebees hit the ground and pelted Myung-gi's back. A loud thrumming filled his ears. The mountains blurred behind sheets of water.

He tilted his head and opened his mouth. Water hit his tongue, and he gulped whatever he could. When he turned toward Yoomee, she was doing the same.

"Do you know why I didn't say anything when you asked that question?" An answer had suddenly come to him, as if Ahpa had whispered it into his ear himself.

She stared at him. "What question?"

"A few days ago, you asked, 'What if we never see Ahpa again?'"

She stood there, waiting, her blurry body melting.

"I couldn't answer because you were asking the wrong question," he said, trying to wipe the water from his glasses. "It's not *if* we see him. It's *when* we see him. Because we *will* see Ahpa again. If we just stick to his plan, then he'll find us in Busan." For Myung-gi, there could be no other outcome: he had decided to believe Ahpa would find them.

The pitter-patter started to slow, and recognition bloomed across Yoomee's face, opening up like the *mugunghwa* flowers along the road. "You're right! Ahpa is the most capable person in the whole world. We can't forget that."

"That's right," Myung-gi said, taking off his soaked jacket and tying it around his waist. "Remember the time a part of our roof blew off, and he fixed it?"

"Oh, yeah!" Yoomee nodded and grinned.

The rain stopped. A hazy sun rose high. Hot steam rose from the ground.

Somehow they found themselves on a country road. Ahead of them, the towering trees and fields of tall corn they had traveled through now gave way to flat rice paddies—where there was nowhere to hide.

A hot breeze blew, but a cold shiver ran up his spine. A fly buzzed near his face, and he swatted it away.

The village was so quiet, all Myung-gi could hear was the high-pitched ringing in his ears, like a single note sawing back and forth on a string—louder and faster.

Uhma whipped around, as if she could feel it too.

On the far edge of the field, a farmer appeared, wheeling fertilizer over his crops. Behind him, a woman stepped outside their thatched-roof house to hang laundry. In the distance, a military truck rattled down a crossroad.

The farmer's face turned toward them.

"Keep walking, children," Uhma said, panting. "Myung-gi-ya, keep your head down, keep your shoulders hunched, don't let anyone think you're old enough to fight. And stay close, everyone."

So they did—Uhma and Yoomee, arms linked, Myung-gi trailing right behind.

Though he kept his gaze down, he could feel the villagers' curious stares burning on the back of his neck. Would they stop them? Notify the secret police? Demand to see a travel permit? Recruit him into the Red Army? Sweat dripped down his back.

"Hey! You, over there!" a man shouted from a distance.

Uhma and Yoomee paused for a second, then kept walking.

"Don't stop," Uhma said. "Pretend we didn't hear him."

Pretend? But Myung-gi was never good at pretending!

"Hey! Stop, I'm talking to you!" the man said, this time a little louder.

Myung-gi quickened his pace.

Footsteps pounded the ground behind him.

"Uhma, he's running toward us. What should we do?" Myung-gi said, the sweat now drenching the back of his white cotton shirt.

"Stop right now or I'll shoot!"

They froze. A soldier.

"Show me your travel permits!" The man pointed his rifle at Uhma but kept glancing at Myung-gi. "How old is he?" he asked, flicking his head toward the boy.

"Twelve," Uhma lied, not looking at the soldier.

"Hmm, he looks older than that," the man said, rubbing the stubble on his chin. "You aren't lying to avoid his conscription into the army, are you? That's a crime punishable by death."

Uhma shook her head vigorously. But Myung-gi just stood there, not able to look anyone in the eye—not even his mother.

"Well, show me your travel permit," the man said, holding his rifle higher. "And if you are lying about that too, the punishment will extend to both your children."

She opened her bundle slowly and began shuffling through

the small pack of rice and utensils and black beans. Furtively, she glanced up and met Myung-gi's gaze.

He knew his mother didn't have any travel permit.

Now this soldier was going to send them to prison—or worse. Ahpa would never know what happened to them.

Myung-gi shivered in his wet clothes. His mouth turned dry. He had to do something.

"I . . . I forgot to pack it, sir," he lied, his voice cracking.

Uhma's eyes flew wide open, and she shook her head slightly. Ahpa had looked at him the same way when he was arrested.

"I'm . . . I'm absent-minded, especially when I'm reading a good book," he continued, knowing this to be true. Everyone was staring at him—even the farmer far off in the field. "So I forgot to pack it."

Yoomee took a step forward, but Myung-gi pushed her back, giving her the sharpest look he could muster.

The soldier rubbed his face again, his eyes fixed on Myung-gi. "Well, go back home and get it then." He pushed them north with his rifle.

Myung-gi closed his eyes. He hadn't thought this through.

That was when a thought popped into his head. This man didn't know where they lived. He didn't know where they were heading. For all he knew, their home could be in Haeju—one of the southern-most cities in North Korea.

"Sir," Myung-gi said, his voice shaking, "that is exactly where we were going before you stopped us. We were going back home to Haeju to get our travel permit to see our grandmother up north in Chagang Province."

The soldier raised his chin and studied him. After a long minute, he said, "Fine. You can continue home to get your travel permit."

Myung-gi tried not to grin.

"But," he said, "I will accompany you."

This man was willing to accompany them for a hundred miles? But then Myung-gi saw the smirk, and he knew: the soldier was calling his bluff. Myung-gi tightened the jacket around his waist to keep his insides from trembling.

Uhma smiled. "Oh, thank you so much, sir," she said with false cheer, the way she spoke at those communist women's league meetings she sometimes had to host. "You don't know what a relief it is to know that you will accompany us for a hundred miles through sweltering heat and monsoon rains."

The man frowned.

"It fills me with a feeling of security knowing that you will escort us. With you by our side, no other soldier will accuse us of being traitors to our great Fatherland! And I can tell you all about my mother's ailments, like her dead feet. Perhaps you can recommend treatment—I'm sure you would know better, given your position in the army."

He squinted and scratched the back of his head.

"You see, she has black fungus under her big toenail—even

tiny maggots. It wouldn't have happened if it weren't for those imperialist American pigs who started this war! The only doctor in her village had to leave and fight against them. Now, after you accompany us to Haeju, perhaps you could then escort us up north to my mother—and maybe you could even administer treatment? The necrosis under her nail is—"

"Ai! Stop! You go by yourselves! I can't listen to this yammering for a hundred miles," the man said, cringing. He spat once on the ground, then left.

Myung-gi looked at her, his mother, who once stood fashionably beside his father—no, slightly behind him—her white teeth always catching the light like pearls. She had done it! She had gotten rid of the soldier.

But when she looked back at Myung-gi, she took a shuddering breath and slumped over, her smile gone.

CHAPTER 25

July 1950: Myung-gi, Age 14

It was safer to travel at night—that was what they decided. In the dark they could avoid roaming soldiers. They could run from cars' searching headlights. They could sprint across open bridges, the summer's swollen waters rising below their feet.

After three days of walking through fields and over foothills, they stumbled onto a large town under the light of the stars. There were hard-packed roads, tall electric poles, wooden storefronts. Squinting, Myung-gi tried to read the signs in the dark: dentist, cinema, bookshop.

"Uhma, I think I've been here before . . . with Ahpa," he whispered, picking up his pace. "Over here is where the bus dropped us off. Down there is a ghetto. And over there is the bookstore we went to." Myung-gi ran up to the shop, wanting to peek through the windows at those stacks of books, those shelves packed tight, half hoping to see his ten-year-old self inside with his father. He could almost hear it: *Where's the bookstore, Ahpa? Right there, that little storefront with the wooden awning!*

But it was boarded up. Through the glass, he could see only empty shelves, broken tables.

Myung-gi blinked back his disappointment. He didn't want to think of what might have happened to the old shopkeeper who had given Ahpa all those banned books.

"Yah, there's no time to stop and explore. Let's keep moving. Hurry," Uhma said, clutching Yoomee's arm. Their rubber shoes pitter-pattered against the sidewalk.

Myung-gi ran to catch up. Of course, Uhma was right. This was no time for slowing down and dwelling on the past. He had to forge ahead, make it to Busan, where Ahpa would meet them. He couldn't let his guard down, and he couldn't forget—just because it was the middle of the night, that didn't mean no one was around.

They scurried down the street like rats. But even so, their bodies cast huge shadows against the buildings under the streetlights. Myung-gi couldn't stop staring at those enormous silhouettes—he moved one arm up and down and watched it touch the rooftops.

Behind them, the light in the bookshop flicked on.

"Wait! Please, I won't hurt you," someone shouted hoarsely.

Myung-gi stopped and turned. The bent shadow of an old man was heading toward them. Uhma and Yoomee gasped. The three of them watched him hobble up the uneven road, wheezing; by the time he reached them, his balding head glistened with sweat.

"You," the old man said, pointing at Myung-gi. "I remember you. You're the boy that came into my bookstore years ago. Your father is Kim Junho, principal of the boys' school in Chagang Province."

Uhma gripped Myung-gi's arm, but he nodded.

The old man chuckled. "You look just like him now that you've grown up a bit—not as sturdy, but pretty close."

"Excuse me, but please leave my son alone," Uhma hissed, frightened. "We don't have time to chitchat. We must go on our way."

"Ah, my apologies," the old man said, coming closer. "Let me get to the point. I am part of an underground resistance group. Your husband was a great man and extremely valuable to our efforts. He was brilliant, well-connected, and tough. He knew how to scope out recruits, make negotiations, spread our message, and manage our finances. It's a huge setback for us now that he's gone."

"What does that have to do with my son?"

"I want him to join us—take his father's place."

Myung-gi tried hard not to tremble. He didn't have the slightest idea how to do any of those things. He wasn't like his father. He didn't know how to manage anything. All he was good at was reading lots of books and collecting useless information—the iambic pentameter in poems, the unique characteristics of Korean pottery.

"Are you crazy? My son isn't capable of such things."

"What do you mean? Isn't he his father's son?"

In that instant, Myung-gi knew—as if a searing light had cut through the darkness—that he was *not* like his father and never would be. Not even close.

The embarrassment of it all—standing there on that uneven road, his mother saying it so plainly—outweighed any rational thought, any fears of getting hurt or even dying. He could feel shame rising in his chest, bubbling up like lava, burning him.

Before he could think, it came out: "I'll . . . I'll do it."

Uhma smacked him hard on the shoulder and started walking. "Aigoo . . . stop talking nonsense. Come, let's go."

"*Sahmoneem,*" the old man said, addressing Myung-gi's mother respectfully as an esteemed wife, "the boy said he would join us. He could start small—drawing maps and pamphlets, smuggling banned books. Anything."

"Children, let's *go.*"

"Wait, do you take girls too?" Yoomee managed to ask before Uhma dragged her down the street.

Other lights flicked on, this time in the ghetto. A door to a shack slammed shut. The three of them walked faster.

"We must never use roads again," Uhma said, eyes facing forward.

But Myung-gi looked back at the old man who had pinned such high hopes on him—the son of a resistance fighter—and hung his head low.

CHAPTER 26

October 1952: Myung-gi, Age 16

As it happens, the wall between us
is very thin. Why couldn't a cry
from one of us
break it down? It would crumble
easily,
it would barely make a sound.
—Rainer Maria Rilke, *The Book of Hours*

Myung-gi sits and waits for the enemy to stop laughing. But he won't stop. That high-pitched tittering. It keeps echoing. As if the tunnel has turned into the long corridor of an insane asylum. If the man has lost his mind, then he's even more dangerous than any enemy.

"Cut it out!" Myung-gi says, but that only makes the man laugh harder.

If he could back up farther, he would, but Myung-gi's spine is already flat against the rock wall. He tries to swallow, but his mouth is dry. Fumbling in the dark, he unclips the canteen from his belt and shakes it. There is only a small sloshing—not even a cupful. He unscrews the cap and tilts his head back. He thinks of those drunkards in the city who have been away from the drink for too long.

A cough and sputter from the other side, and the cackling finally subsides. The enemy clears his throat. "So you're not trapped. And I'm not trapped. And that's why we're here together, to have a little chitchat, and maybe some tea?"

Even in the dark, Myung-gi can feel his face reddening.

"How old are you?" the man asks.

"Sixteen."

Silence.

Myung-gi squirms.

"I've never killed a kid before," the man says.

The rhythm in Myung-gi's chest goes wild. Myung-gi can't breathe. He can't breathe!

Rollicking laughter, once again.

"So, seriously, though. What's a kid like you doing here, in the middle of a war, stuck in a tunnel?" the man asks.

This is the part that Myung-gi knows will tickle the enemy's sides, make him lean back and kick his feet in the air, roar with more laughter. But he hears himself say it anyway: "I joined the army to find my father. He was abducted in the North."

To Myung-gi's surprise, the man doesn't laugh, only grunts. Maybe he's not so bad.

Myung-gi skims his hand against the wall and bits of dirt and gravel fall. It's like from *The Book of Hours*: *Why couldn't a cry from one of us break it down? It would crumble easily, it would barely make a sound.* And for a second, he almost wishes it.

Until eventually the man speaks. "Joining the army to find your father . . . well, that was a pretty bad plan. Because now you're going to die in this place."

CHAPTER 27

July 1950: Myung-gi, Age 14

The journey stretched out, day after day after day. They walked through rice paddies, swam across rivers, trekked over hillsides. Overhead, fighter jets roared by, though Myung-gi did not actually see any fighting—at least not yet, not in the North. Most of the battles raged in the South, where they were heading.

"We're running out of food," Yoomee said, digging through their bags.

They huddled under an overturned oxcart in the middle of the afternoon, the bright sun streaming through the wooden slats. Sweat drenched the back of Myung-gi's shirt; his glasses were steaming from everyone's humid breath. Not until dusk could they start walking again—and breathing.

Uhma sighed. "I know. We have only a few black beans left."

Myung-gi swatted at the flies buzzing near his face. A pile of cow dung sat only a few feet away. The stench overwhelmed his nostrils. But whenever he tried opening his mouth for air, the bugs flew in.

"We could steal some of the farmers' crops," Yoomee said, peering through the slats. "Look, they have corn!"

"Quiet! Do you want someone to hear us?" Uhma said, closing her eyes and rubbing her temples. "It's not right to steal, you know that, don't you, children? But under these circumstances . . ."

"Uhma, I can go get the corn," Myung-gi said, knowing that it was what Ahpa would've done.

His mother's eyes flew open. "No."

"I'll go at night. No one will see me," he insisted. Who did Uhma want him to be, anyway? The eldest son who stepped in for his father? Or the coddled son too precious to risk? Because she seemed to be treating him like both.

"I'll go with you, Oppah. It'll be faster that way," Yoomee said. The ends of her stick-straight hair, uncut for weeks, looked sharp and spiky.

"Aigoo, whatever, whatever." Uhma lay on her side for a nap, her face slack with fatigue. "Just wait for the sun to set."

Uhma was still asleep when Myung-gi lifted the bottom edge of the oxcart and pushed his way out, holding it up long enough for Yoomee to slip out too. Looking out across the wide cornfield in the cool darkness, he pushed up his glasses. "Do you have your bag?" he asked, clutching his own satchel.

"Yes," Yoomee said, her eyes darting left and right.

Noticing the way she scanned the entire countryside, Myung-gi looked around too. Since when did his little sister know how to do such things?

The cornstalks towered over Myung-gi, and when he waded through the densely packed stems, the leaves closed above his head. He shut his eyes, then opened them and tried not to think about drowning.

"What do you think the South will be like?" Yoomee asked, as they waded deeper and deeper in search of the fattest ears of corn. "What about Busan? Do you think the kids will be nice?"

"If you're nice then you will attract nice people. That's how I see it," Myung-gi said, trying hard not to rustle the stalks.

"That's not true. There was a quiet girl in my class who was nice to everyone, but all the kids ignored her."

Myung-gi sighed. Maybe things *weren't* so black and white. What about those boys who had beaten him under the willow tree? He hadn't done anything to them. And what about the madmen ruling his country? What about this stupid war? What about the war before this one, when the Nazis slaughtered the Jews?

"I don't know . . . the kids in Busan might be nice or they might not," he said finally. "You can't control the people around you. All you can control is yourself."

Fingering the leaves, Yoomee nodded, listening.

Myung-gi searched for the ripest corn, but the ears were all skinny and green, the silk hairs on top still moist—not ready for picking. But no matter; food was food. He snapped one off its stalk.

The twilight started fading, and Myung-gi stuffed the last ear of corn into his satchel. Looking around, he noticed the field growing dimmer and dimmer. He knew how dark it could get in the countryside—without any car or city lights to brighten the sky—and how quickly, too.

Oh God, they should've headed back sooner. "Hurry, let's go," he said. "Before we lose our way."

But it was too late.

They stood in the middle of the pitch-black cornfield, only the sound of swishing leaves around them.

"Which way did we come in?" Yoomee asked, turning around and around.

"I don't know. I thought you knew," Myung-gi said, his breaths short and heavy.

"What? You're the older one!"

"You know I'm horrible with directions!"

Another wind blew, rustling the stalks. They both fell silent.

"Uhma is going to worry," Yoomee said, her voice wavering.

This was what scared Myung-gi most—the idea of their mother, all alone, panicking under the oxcart. What if she left to search for them? How would they find each other? "Let's go this way," Myung-gi said, because they couldn't just stand there forever.

For the next hour, they walked. Myung-gi thought they must look like mice going in circles. He imagined the stalks getting taller, the leaves growing wider. He pictured Yoomee and himself stuck in this maze forever. He pointed his chin up so he could breathe.

"Oppah, we should've paid more attention going into the cornfield—or at least not gone in so deep."

She was right. And since he was the older one, it was his fault. Why couldn't he pay better attention? He should've known better. "Yoomee, which direction do you want to go?" he asked.

"Me? You're asking me?" Yoomee's eyes glistened. She looked up at the stars. "Okay, I think we should go this way." She pointed to the northeast.

"Fine, let's go."

Maybe she had better instincts—those hard-to-pin-down feelings that somehow told you how to act, how to survive—something you couldn't learn in books, something Ahpa had plenty of.

Together they pushed through the stalks, the leaves scratching at them as if trying to hold them back, like some languishing army. At first Myung-gi forged ahead, then Yoomee, then the two of them side by side, for once no longer bickering.

"This must be it," Myung-gi said. "I can feel it. We're near the edge!"

"Yes, Oppah! I think you're right!"

And they stepped out of the cornfield, into the darkness, every footfall an act of faith, a prayer that they would be safe—at least while they were walking together.

CHAPTER 28

July 1950: Myung-gi, Age 14

Back to the oxcart they went.

A match from Myung-gi's pack somehow lit itself—or was it Yoomee's?

Uhma lay on the ground in the flickering light.

Myung-gi rushed to kneel beside her, that rancid stench rushing in too. The rest he saw only in flashes:

Skirt ripped, face bruised, hair pulled from its bun.

Uhma, what happened? they said, or he said, or she said.

A fluttering hand in the air, delicate and listless, like broken butterfly wings.

Nothing, children. Some people found me hiding here, that's all. I'm fine.

What did they do to you?

Nothing.

Where does it hurt?

Nowhere.

Who was it?

No one.

All because he'd gotten lost in the cornfield. No directional sense. Walking aimlessly under the twilight. Bringing back some skinny corn that wasn't even worth the picking.

And now someone had hurt Uhma.

Rage rose into his bent back, against the wooden slats, splintering the floor that was really the ceiling—the whole blasted world turned on its head.

Someone moved the match. Higher and closer. To his face. As if to get a better view of the animal inside him, of his hot eyes staring into the flame.

In the light of that flicker, he saw:

Yoomee's mouth, a perfectly round hole.

Uhma's wincing face, bracing behind outspread fingers.

It was how they would stay forever—frozen in horror—their faces captured in the flash of the camera in his mind.

CHAPTER 29

October 1952: Myung-gi, Age 16

My eyes closed;
Memory looms near
Beyond the rim of sight.
—Kim Sangyong, *The Harbor*

You're going to die in this place. That was what he said. Wasn't that what he said?

What would Ahpa do in this moment?

He would say something wise, something strong, something courageous. He would be a man and knock down these walls to face the enemy. But Myung-gi has to get out of here. Now.

Turning around, Myung-gi starts heading back down the few feet of corridor to where he first entered. Yes, it's still blocked, but maybe he can try digging again.

Back hunched, feet scraping against dirt and gravel, he rakes. Bent double, he must look like Quasimodo. A hideous thing.

But he had a courageous heart, son.

Yes, Ahpa, but his name means half-formed. And right now, I don't feel fully human.

"Why didn't I stop them from taking you? Why didn't I run to the Paks' house and get help? Why did I have to pick up that stupid book and start reading?" Myung-gi cries, because if he's going to talk to Ahpa in his head, he may as well do it out loud too.

"What could you have done to stop them? You're just a kid, right?" the man says.

Myung-gi drops his head between his knees. "I'm not a little kid anymore."

"But how old were you when it happened?"

For this, Myung-gi has to stop and think. Has it already been two and a half years? "Fourteen. I'd just turned fourteen," he says, slowly. That was Yoomee's age now. "But . . . but it's hard to remember. . . ."

The man whistles long and steady. "*My eyes closed; memory looms near beyond the rim of sight*," he says, reciting a poem Myung-gi knows. "Hey, you're right, it is hard to remember. Memory is a tricky thing."

Confused, Myung-gi sits up taller. "Those words you said. How do you know them? They're by a Korean poet."

"Why wouldn't I know a poem? You think I wouldn't know such things?"

"Who are you?"

"Who do you think I am?"

"Stop fooling with me!" Myung-gi cries, wrenching the front of his shirt with both hands. "Fourteen is old enough to be man of the house. It's old enough to get married off. It's old enough to walk alone, at night, when wolves prowl, even Siberian tigers!" That last bit makes Myung-gi's mouth turn dry, and he realizes that he hasn't had more than a few drops of water in a long, long time. The darkness starts spinning.

"When I was fourteen," the voice says, "I liked to play board games with my brothers and sisters. Even hide-and-seek. I bet you did too."

"Shut up. I don't believe anything you say."

Myung-gi starts digging, again, at the sandy grit under the rocks. His fingernails bend backward, even though they're short. Pain shoots through the ends of his fingers. But at least the voice has stopped talking.

CHAPTER 30

August 1950: Myung-gi, Age 14

Uhma never talked about it. And Myung-gi didn't want to know. Which was how every mother-son relationship was, Myung-gi thought, as they reached the Yesong River region. It was evening, but he could see the river from the top of the hill: it wound around a mountain like a black mirror, only its rippling silver edges catching the light of the stars.

Mosquitoes buzzed in Myung-gi's ears, in his nostrils, around his swollen ankles. Hot, itchy bumps covered his body. He scratched hard all over, anxiety tingling across his skin.

He stared out at the water. They all did—Uhma's bruises now turning yellow, Yoomee's voice now growing quieter. They were near the South Korean border. This was where Ahpa had promised them there would be a boat waiting, a boat piloted by his former student Ko Jusung. Everything was planned: they would sail into the Yellow Sea and make landfall in the South.

But even so, there was no thrill running up Myung-gi's spine, no awe at being so close to freedom. Every step only took them farther from Ahpa.

They headed down the hill toward the water.

There were others like them, huddling and waiting and looking over their shoulders at the river's edge. They had been so careful to avoid people that Myung-gi hesitated at the sight of them.

"Where are the border guards? Has anyone been shot?" Uhma asked a woman. Myung-gi thought she might be local—the cooking smells of her house still clung to her clothes.

"No, not yet. That's why we're leaving now." The woman's breath smelled of pungent daenjang and garlic. "Most of the soldiers are being sent down south. This is our only chance to escape."

They walked toward the mouth of the river—the woman with them, and many others—where it emptied into the Yellow Sea. The roaring waters gleamed under the moon.

"There!" Yoomee said, pointing near the shore.

There were fishing boats—just like Ahpa had said there would be!—but only three, not nearly enough for the fifty people already crashing into the water. Mothers, grandmothers, children, babies. So many of them crowding the small boats, like frenzied fish, desperate to escape the North.

Ahpa had arranged passage for them, he'd said—a spot on the boats. But there was no organization here, no order to this chaos. It was every man for himself.

"Hurry!" someone shouted, which set them all running.

They stomped into the cold waters, splashing waist-deep, struggling toward the wooden boats bobbing on the waves. Shouting and crying, thrashing and falling, pushing and pulling.

"Ko Jusung!" Myung-gi hollered into the crowd. "Is there a Ko Jusung here? Hello? Anyone?" But how could he hear Myung-gi over the splashing and screaming? And what did it matter? Ko Jusung, whoever he was, wherever he was, couldn't save them now.

"Get on! Get on!" Myung-gi shouted, pushing Yoomee through the hordes, then lifting her onto a boat. Then he boosted Uhma halfway over the edge, swinging her legs over.

"Oppah! Grab on, let me help you!" Yoomee shouted, her thin arm reaching. But her hands were small, and there were others crowding in front of him.

"It's okay. I'm coming!" Myung-gi yelled back.

That was when someone yanked the back of his collar, jerked him away, and pushed his head underwater.

It was muffled under there, but still loud, the currents churning. He squirmed and kicked, his breaths leaving him in screaming bubbles above his head. Finally he twisted away, freeing himself from the person's grip.

His face breached the surface, and he gasped a mouthful of air—eating it, drinking it, sucking it into his body. Uhma and Yoomee's boat had drifted away from him. Only a few feet, but still!

An old man stomped past him, water splashing, arms flapping. He knocked the glasses off Myung-gi's face. And the world vanished.

"No. No. *No*," Myung-gi cried, his hands frantically sweeping the waters.

He'd always taken those spectacles for granted, but he could do nothing without them. Where were Uhma and Yoomee? Were they still on the boat? Every blurry face looked the same. He had to find his glasses. What if they had settled to the bottom and someone stepped on them? What if they got buried in the sand? What if they floated out to sea?

Then he felt a thin wire frame catch on his fingers. He snatched it, set it back on his face, and pushed through the water.

"*Oppah!*"

"*Myung-gi-ya!*"

He heard them, their voices straining, like rubber bands ready to snap and break.

Pushing through the crowd, Myung-gi grabbed the splintered edge of the boat, hoisted himself up, tumbled onto a woman's lap, rolled off, and sputtered, "Sorry."

Uhma lunged forward to grab him. "Myung-gi-ya, are you okay? Did you get hurt?"

He shook his head. But he was limp and heavy.

"There's nowhere to go anymore!" a young woman cried, her eyes glowing like a wolf's in the light of the moon.

Nowhere to go? Worry flashed through him. "What do you mean?" Myung-gi asked, coughing and sputtering. "We're sailing to Inchon, South Korea. We're escaping!"

"Haven't you heard? It was just on a man's radio! The Reds have taken almost the entire peninsula. The South is almost all under communist control. They've even taken Inchon! We have nowhere to go! Nowhere to go!"

"What? What did you say?" Uhma demanded, gripping the woman's arm.

All Myung-gi's fears came rushing in. There would be no relief in the South. The Reds were everywhere. There was no escaping them now.

An engine revved. The boat started moving. They were sailing out to sea.

Those who couldn't get on began falling away, splashing into the water. Myung-gi watched their heads growing smaller and smaller, until he could no longer see the blackness of their hair; watched the shore shrinking to a tiny line, until they were surrounded by nothing but deep and roiling waters.

No one spoke.

He looked around. There were twelve of them in the boat. What was the point of their escape if the Reds had taken over the South? What was the point of any of this? He spat once into the murky water.

That was when Yoomee said it—words that hurt, like a finger digging deep into a sore. "We never should've left home."

And Myung-gi nodded, sitting motionless on this boat to nowhere.

CHAPTER 31

August 1950: Myung-gi, Age 14

"Are we still going to Inchon?" an old woman called out from the back.

The captain steered the boat into deeper water and said, "Yes, of course we're going." Though it was dark, Myung-gi could see the whites of the man's eyes, bright against the dark leather of his face.

"But it's under the control of the Reds now!" shouted a middle-aged woman, the one whose lap Myung-gi had tumbled onto. She was so skinny that the bones of her face protruded.

"You think I don't know that? What do you expect me to do? Keep sailing forever? You got on *my* fishing boat. I'm heading where I need to go, and I'm doing you all a favor, letting you catch a ride with me."

There were rows of benches in the hull. Myung-gi sat with Yoomee, Uhma in front. He stared hard at that empty space beside his mother and pictured the back of Ahpa's head there—the comb marks in his hair, the breadth of his back, the deepness of his voice.

Ahpa, what if you can't make your way south? What if we can't?

Ahpa would reply with the right answer, as he always did. *We have to at least try. We are not animals. We cannot live imprisoned in our own country, never able to speak our minds.*

But we're leaving you behind.

Son, I already told you. Don't be afraid to go on without me.

For hours, everyone stared toward the mainland where mountains stretched along the shore. Myung-gi shuddered and looked over the edge of the boat, but the black and swirling water seemed close enough to swallow him.

With nowhere else to set his gaze, he watched Yoomee braid a little girl's long locks, her own hair disheveled. He listened to her telling the girl all about Ahpa—how they were going to meet him in Busan, how strong and clever and brave he was.

"You know, the radio said the Reds have taken nearly every city but Busan," the skinny woman said. "In fact, I heard they moved the capital of South Korea there for now! We should sail *there*."

Murmurs of *Yes, yes,* trickled throughout the boat.

"Are you crazy? You know how far that would be? We'd never survive that long at sea," the captain said, steering closer to shore.

"Besides, I've got other plans. I'm dumping you all off once we get to Inchon, and then you're on your own. Just blend in with the masses."

"But the masses are getting massacred out there!" the woman cried.

At that, the captain didn't say a word.

A buzz swept across the boat. *How will we get to Busan if we have to cross a war zone? Will we be walking right into bombs and gunfire?*

Myung-gi glanced at Uhma, wondering what they ought to do. But he couldn't see her face—only the back of her head, lowered as if in prayer.

Myung-gi started tapping his foot, thinking what to do. It had always been the plan to reach Busan—and Busan was still free, unlike Inchon. But getting there wouldn't be easy.

"Sir," he said to the captain. "Where will you go?"

The whites of the captain's eyes turned to him, fierce and bright. "I'm going to the nearest recruitment center to enlist in the South Korean army."

Enlist in the army? Myung-gi could feel his lungs squeezing, as if the tentacles of recruitment were wrapping tighter and tighter around him. In the moonlight, he could see the silver in the captain's hair, the droop of his jowls, the lines around his mouth. First Byongho for the North, now this old man for the South?

"I know what you're thinking," the captain said. "You're thinking, how's an old guy like me going to fight in the war?"

Myung-gi nodded.

That was when the old man leaned in close and said, "Truth is, they're desperate for anyone. So they'll take a washed-up old fisherman like me. They'll even take boys not much older than you." Then he pulled out a photo from his pocket and showed it to him—a young soldier in a South Korean uniform.

Myung-gi stared at the photo, at the badge by the shoulder—yellow field, red marking—nearly the opposite of the North Korean badge, yet so similar. "Was that you?" he asked.

The captain chuckled. "No. That's my son. He joined the South Korean army."

"Is that why you're joining? To help him?"

But the man only shook his head, sadly.

"Then why?" Myung-gi asked. "Why would you want to join? You could get yourself killed."

There was a long pause. "My family," was all the old man managed to say, his lips quivering.

That was when Myung-gi knew that something terrible must have happened. Did his son die? Was he out for revenge? The captain looked toward shore, his chin trembling.

Myung-gi lowered his head in his hands, wishing he'd never asked about it. The salty night air stung his eyes, but squeezing them shut did no good. They kept tearing anyway. Hopefully no one would notice.

He was too busy wiping his face to brace himself when the boat lurched to a sudden halt.

CHAPTER 32

August 1950: Myung-gi, Age 14

Everyone screamed. Myung-gi hung over the bow, winded and gasping.

They'd landed.

But there was mud everywhere—mud for miles. It must have been low tide; the boat had run aground on the tidal flats. Under the starry sky it looked like burnt earth, as if they'd reached the underworld.

"This is where you get off! Inchon, South Korea," the captain said, shutting off the engine. "Best of luck to each of you."

People began climbing off the boat.

Uhma grabbed Yoomee and Myung-gi by the arm. "Children,"

she said, "let's stay in Inchon and hide. Going to Busan will be too dangerous. We would have to pass through the front lines."

"What? How can you say that?" Yoomee cried, squirming from their mother's grasp. "Ahpa told us to go to Busan! If we're not at home, that's where he'll look for us! We'll miss him if we stay and hide here!" She writhed and pushed, and when people stepped past, they shook their heads and clucked their tongues.

"Stop it!" Uhma tried to hold Yoomee still. "If we travel to Busan, we'll run into more North Korean troops along the way. And they'll take Myung-gi. I know they will. Do you want that to happen to your brother?" she demanded, the end of her sentence turning shrill.

Yoomee stopped.

Something broke inside Myung-gi: he felt like a door fallen off its hinges, hanging askew and useless. It wasn't worth abandoning Ahpa's plan just to keep him safe. He had to protect Uhma and Yoomee—not the other way around.

Busan was still free. It was their only hope.

"We've already come all this way. We *have* to go to Busan," Myung-gi said. "We can't just hide in Inchon—it's not safe here, and it's not free, either. Besides, it's what Ahpa wanted. It's where Sora's family is. It's where our new house is."

Yoomee smiled gratefully at him. Uhma looked at her children, then yanked a handkerchief from her pocket and snapped it in the air before patting her forehead and letting out a deep sigh.

They took off their shoes and began to climb out of the boat.

Myung-gi put his foot into the thick brown muck. At first the silt felt soft between his toes. But when he stepped all the way down, squelching into sucking mud up to his knees, sharp razor clams cut the bottoms of his feet.

He lifted one foot, his leg as heavy as a tree trunk, then toppled over—the bulky jigeh on his back threw him off balance. His arm shot out to brace his fall, but it sank up to his elbow.

Myung-gi-ya! Oppah!

The mud was cold and thick. He took a deep breath, rose slowly, and regained his footing. Sludge covered his sides and filled his ears, but he trudged forward.

Sand crabs crept past, each pointing its one giant pincer, bigger than its body, right at him. Yoomee froze at the sight of so many of them, but Myung-gi forced her from behind to keep moving, while Uhma grabbed her hand and pulled her along.

Sudden screams reached them. Rolling in from far away.

Myung-gi looked around. Behind them, farther out on the mudflats, a silver line of water was rushing in. High tide, like a wall. Heading straight toward the last ones off the boat. They couldn't run, couldn't unstick their feet fast enough.

"*Run!*" Uhma shouted.

But Myung-gi's legs wouldn't budge in the mud. Uhma and Yoomee struggled too, both of them teetering. At their backs, the tide was mowing others down, ramming them into the thick sludge—plugging their noses, stealing their breath, suffocating them.

Uhma fell forward, face-first into the mire. Yoomee tumbled backward, collapsing into the muck.

"*No!*" he yelled, reaching for his mother and sister. Desperate, he could only move toward them slowly, picking his knees up with both hands as if they were things to be carried.

Reaching down, he pulled Uhma from the mud, her mouth opening at the surface, gasping for air. Behind them, Yoomee rose on her own, heavy clumps clinging to her hair, and grabbed Uhma's hand.

But the tide came too fast.

Cold water smacked the back of Myung-gi's knees, knocking him down, knocking them all down. It rushed over his head, roared in his ears, stung his eyes and mouth. He pressed his glasses over his nose, silt and water whooshing like a freight train around his lenses.

Finally the surge eased.

Myung-gi dug his foot into the silt and got up slowly, his hair and clothes drenched. Foamy crests lapped against his sides. Cold mud slid down his back. A grittiness filled his eyes.

As he wiped his face, he saw Uhma struggling up, too, still clutching Yoomee's hand—thank God they were alive! The water was up to her waist, and up to Yoomee's ribs.

They started walking with the tide. Myung-gi focused on the shore, only a hundred feet away, lifting one leaden foot at a time, the distant roar of waves mingling with human screams. A body floated past him—its open mouth full of mud, a small crab crawling out of it.

He squeezed his eyes shut, concentrating only on the sound of his breathing until the ground under his feet began to harden.

When he reached the shore, he bent over, hands on his knees, and looked around. There were others who had made it, but they were already skulking into the trees and disappearing, not wasting a minute. Yoomee and Uhma were at his side, panting.

Myung-gi shook the mud from his head and then straightened his back. They stood together—the three of them—frozen in the moonlight.

Three. Only three.

He couldn't help noticing how wrong it looked, as if they were missing a limb—a limb ripped away from them by this rotten war, by those evil men, by their power-hungry leaders playing God with their lives. What right did they have to take away his country, his home, his books, his father? His father!

He looked at Uhma, her once-powdered nose covered in tarry mud. But she was still standing tall and dignified. And Yoomee, the girl who had once fretted about her too-short bangs, made no move to wring her filthy hair dry.

It was then—right before they had to disappear into the trees like the others—that a love shot through Myung-gi so fiercely it stung the back of his eyes. And in that instant, he understood the captain when the only words he could choke out were "My family."

"Are you ready?" Uhma asked, the front of her jacket heaving.

Myung-gi nodded. "Let's go."

CHAPTER 33

October 1952: Myung-gi, Age 16

Why do they never tell us that you are poor devils like us, that your mothers are just as anxious as ours, and that we have the same fear of death, and the same dying and the same agony—Forgive me, comrade; how could you be my enemy?

—Erich Maria Remarque, *All Quiet on the Western Front*

"Hey, kid, do you have any food or water on you?" the man asks.

Topics like food and water—simple things—Myung-gi does not mind. "No," he answers, his stomach churning on cue. "My box of rations got soaked on the way here, fell apart. Lost all my cans."

"Well, that was dumb of you. You got to keep that stuff covered from the rain."

Myung-gi's lips turn down. "It's not like we can share food through a boulder anyway."

"Yeah . . . I've got nothing. And I drank my last bit of water that first day I got stuck, which was probably two days ago."

"Well, that was dumb of you," Myung-gi counters.

At that, the man laughs. "Fair enough. I would call a truce, but we're at war."

Myung-gi blinks in the dark. He remembers reading about some German and British troops in World War I who made their own unofficial cease-fire on Christmas. They came out from their trenches, shook hands, played soccer, even sang carols before going back to killing each other. After reading about this, Myung-gi couldn't decide which was more absurd—that these enemies stopped in the middle of fighting to exchange gifts? Or that they were even fighting in the first place?

Regardless, it gets him thinking . . . couldn't they do this, the two of them? Declare their own unofficial truce, right here in the tunnel? Who says this man has to be his enemy? Myung-gi opens his mouth to speak.

"Listen, I'm going to go now," the man says.

Myung-gi's eyes fly wide open, even in the dark. "What? Where are you going?" Usually Myung-gi likes being left alone, but if this man leaves, he will have no one to talk to. And then his own mind might start leaving him too.

"I'm checking out. Going to take a rest in the inn of my mind and think about all the foods I want to eat once I get out of here."

"So . . . you're not leaving?"

The man snickers. "Maybe. Maybe not. Got to keep the enemy on their toes."

The enemy—that was Myung-gi. This makes him wince.

When he touches his empty canteen, his mouth turns dry. "What foods?" Myung-gi asks.

"Huh?"

"What foods are you going to eat if you get out of here?"

"If? If?" the man says, his voice rising. "Don't you mean 'when'?"

But Myung-gi doesn't say anything, because he himself has uttered those same words before—telling Yoomee *when*, not *if*, Ahpa comes back.

"Soup dumplings," the man says, audibly shifting his weight against gravel, as if making himself more comfortable. "The kind my mother used to make. You know, she was the greatest cook in my province, maybe in all of China. No joke, really. People from all over would come to eat at her restaurant."

"Wah, really?" Myung-gi says, nearly forgetting that the enemy would have a mother too.

"Yeah, and my father, he was a military hero in the war with Japan. Saved a bunch of lives, carrying fallen comrades over his shoulders while bullets were whizzing past his ear."

And a father, Myung-gi thinks. The enemy has a father. A familiar line drops into Myung-gi's head: *Forgive me, comrade; how could you be my enemy?*

The man blows his nose.

"Did you ever do something brave like that?" Myung-gi asks.

The man clears his throat. "Yeah, I have."

"Oh. My dad was brave too—is brave; he is brave too. Did you know, he once—" but Myung-gi stops talking because his stomach starts hurting. "Tell me what other foods you're going to eat once you get out of here," he says instead.

Which sets the man talking about pork buns and chive pancakes, oh, and Russian borscht with kebabs and cabbage soup. He talks about black-bean noodles—the savory aroma, the way the black sauce coats the starchy noodles and glistens against cubes of meat. He talks about twirling the noodles on his chopsticks for that perfect-sized bite, then slurping it into his mouth where the springiness of the noodle and the tenderness of the meat come together perfectly when he chews. Oh, and can't forget the almond cookies and glutinous rice cakes and sesame balls. The man's voice trembles at the exquisiteness of it all.

Myung-gi simply settles into a groove in the rock wall, starts chewing a mouthful of air, and listens.

CHAPTER 34

August 1950: Myung-gi, Age 14

Myung-gi stopped and listened as the wind whistled through the towering fortress. They had reached the entrance of Suwon, a city thirty miles south of Inchon. It had taken them three days walking from where the boat had landed.

Parts of the fortress had been bombed and were crumbling. Myung-gi's gaze traveled up the centuries-old brick walls, three stories tall. The hip-and-gable roofs were still smoking.

"Wah . . . a castle," Yoomee said, looking up.

"No, it's Hwaseong Fortress," Uhma said, reading a sign. "From the Joseon dynasty."

Walking through the massive archway of the Janganmun Gate, Myung-gi thought it looked more like the jaws of a giant beast.

The other side of the gate opened to a main road, lined with electric poles and merchants selling wares underneath canvas roofs propped up with thin wooden posts. Blue buses with yellow and orange stripes stopped at the corner depot where crowds were beginning to form. Myung-gi looked at Uhma who put a finger to her lips, warning them all to be quiet. They retreated through the gate and scurried off the road through the brush, looking for a more hidden path to travel. There were more people in town than they had realized.

"Did you hear that?" Yoomee whispered. "Someone's coming after us through the trees!"

Leaves rustled. Color flashed between branches. Something clanked against tinny metal.

Uhma grabbed the children by their sleeves and yanked them behind a bush, tearing a seam on Myung-gi's shirt. Yoomee stumbled and fell; Myung-gi tripped over her legs. Uhma halted, her eyes wide with horror.

The rustling grew closer.

They froze, their bodies like petrified wood, their eyes fixed toward the noise. What if it was a Red soldier? What if it was a leopard or a lynx? If given the choice, Myung-gi would choose the wild cats, because at least he could understand them.

Then he saw it. A metal laundry bin. An old woman with tissue-paper skin.

He stared at her as she emerged from the trees, his mouth agape.

"If you want to wash all that mud off your clothes, there's a stream down this hill. It's where I just did my laundry," the grandmother said. "And if you need a place to rest, my house is right here, too."

Uhma didn't move.

"Aigoo, loosen your shoulders, woman. I'm not here to hurt you—only help."

Myung-gi looked at Uhma, who was keeping a steady gaze on the old lady.

A man's voice suddenly sounded through the trees, close, barking orders to keep watch along the streambank.

"Quick, hide!" the grandmother whispered, motioning them into a thicket.

They crouched and waited, everyone's heads close together. Myung-gi didn't move, didn't blink. Even the old woman seemed to be holding her breath. Only when the soldier's voice began trailing farther and farther away did the grandmother signal them up.

It was only then that Uhma was willing to follow her.

The old woman led them to a thatched-roof house. She marched in first, the rest of them trailing behind. Inside the door, slippers were lined up in perfect rows.

"Sit, sit," she said.

Myung-gi stepped over the shoes, then sat on the floor of the main room where there was a low table, floor cushions, and a piano in the corner. He tried to tuck in his muddy limbs, not wanting to dirty the old woman's neat and tidy home, but they seemed longer than before. He hunched over slightly.

The old woman went into the kitchen, returning a minute later with clean towels. A skinny girl now followed close behind her, carrying a basin of water.

Uhma washed her hands first, her eyes cast downward. "We are nothing but strangers to you, yet you help us. Thank you."

A deep-throated chuckle came out of the old woman. "I have no family except for my granddaughter, Haewon, here," she said, patting the girl on her bony shoulder. "How meaningless life would be if we never reached out to others!"

Uhma's head snapped up. "No husband, no son to take care of you?"

The grandmother shook her head. "No, Haewon and I have been on our own for twelve years. Before that I had been taken care of all my life by my well-to-do parents, my businessman husband, my professor son. But when tossed into the deep end of the ocean, you start kicking to the surface. I've found ways to manage—and I survive on my own."

Myung-gi rinsed his hands. Haewon, who looked to be around his age, wouldn't stop glancing at him. Was it all the mud on his clothes? But Uhma and Yoomee were caked in it too, and she wasn't staring at them. Maybe there was something wrong with him. He felt his face and checked his body, but nothing. When he finally looked straight at her, she turned bright red.

Uhma and the old lady disappeared into the kitchen together.

"My name is Yoomee, and that's my older brother, Myung-gi," Yoomee said to the girl. Then, leaning toward her, she whispered, "Lots of girls like him, but he's clueless."

Haewon chuckled and covered her mouth. That reminded Myung-gi of Sora, of the way she hid her teeth when she laughed— but always a second too late, as if it was something she kept forgetting she was supposed to do. He had always wished she would move her hand away; Sora had the widest grin and straightest teeth he had ever seen.

"So . . ." Yoomee said, leaning forward, her tone turning serious. "Do you know how to play that thing?"

"The piano? Yes, I do," Haewon said, warily.

"How much for a lesson?"

"Oh, I don't give lessons."

"Why not? Aren't you any good?"

"Yoomee!" Myung-gi said, his voice sharp and scolding. Sometimes she had no manners.

But Yoomee ignored him. "Well then, can I just play it?"

"Yes, I'm very good. And no, you can't play it. *I* don't even play anymore—not since the Reds came. If music started coming out of the house, it would only bring attention to us. It might attract them. Then they would know I was here."

"Are you hiding?" Myung-gi asked.

Haewon looked at him and blinked. "Of course I'm hiding. The only ones the soldiers don't bother are the very old and the very young. But you and me, well, we're right in between."

He nodded, a sick feeling washing over him.

The grandmother set three bowls of red-bean porridge and slices of plum on the table. "Go ahead and eat," she said. "You must all be starving."

Myung-gi took a bite of porridge, and his taste buds ached at the savory sweetness. Though he tried to mind his manners and not eat too fast, he inhaled his lunch in huge clumps, then sucked the plum slices like a bat feeding on blood.

He wondered what Ahpa was eating. The last meal they'd had together was bean-sprout soup and rice. Ahpa had complained that the bean sprouts looked like tapeworms, and that it might not be the best food the day before their journey. Uhma had smacked him play-fully on the shoulder. And the two of them had laughed.

Just one more day, and they would have left together—all four of them.

The plum in Myung-gi's stomach was beginning to sour. He wiped his mouth with the back of his hand.

After their meal, Haewon's grandmother brought the empty

dishes into the kitchen while Uhma and Yoomee went to the stream to wash their clothes. Myung-gi wasn't allowed out.

Haewon stayed in the main room with him.

"They're out there every day, you know, guarding the stream and the roads," she said, standing beside the closed windows. She kept crossing and uncrossing her skinny arms, the ball of her elbow jutting out. "There's a ford near here. They march up and down the water, watching it."

"How many soldiers are there, you think?" Myung-gi asked.

"Two," she said. "I think they're North Korean combat police—I saw those uniforms in the paper, you know, before everything. They arrived a few days ago to patrol, and to block the road and the crossing. I hear them shouting sometimes about blasting the imperialist American pigs off the face of the Earth. One of them moans loudly about missing his mother's cooking. The other boasts to the high heavens about his girlfriend."

He looked at her over the top of his frames. "You really know about their lives. Do you sit inside all day listening to them?"

"Well, what else am I supposed to do? I can't play the piano. I don't like to read."

"You don't like to read?"

"Not really. It's such a bore."

Myung-gi looked at her in surprise. Sora had always loved reading together under the trees. Even Yoomee liked a good book once in a while.

He smiled politely at Haewon, as if he'd just discovered she killed a man.

But when she frowned back, he remembered *that day*: sitting behind the fence, lost in a book, not seeing those four men marching up to their house. . . .

"Yeah, I don't like reading either," he said.

She stopped frowning.

"Since you know them so well, what else is there to these soldiers?" he asked.

"Their names are Kiyoung and Byongho. Kiyoung is the one with a girlfriend and Byongho is the one who misses his mother's cooking. They argue sometimes and——"

"Byongho? Did you say one of them is named Byongho?"

"Yes, why? Do you know him?"

Myung-gi shook his head. No—it couldn't be.

But how many Byonghos *were* there, anyway? Probably not that many; it wasn't a very common name. And it certainly wasn't impossible. He got up and headed toward the window.

Haewon grabbed his hand and pulled him away. "What do you think you're doing? Are you crazy?"

"I'm just going to open it a crack, to get a better look. They won't see me."

"You don't know that! They can see your shadow through the rice-paper window."

"They'll think it's your grandmother," he replied, looking

straight into her eyes. They were so dark and glossy that he could see his own reflection. "I need to take a quick look. It's important. Please."

She stared long and hard at him. "Fine. Just don't open the window too much. Only an inch. Promise?"

He looked down at his hand. She was still holding it.

"Oh!" she said, throwing his fist as if it were a hot pile of steaming dung.

His knuckles hit the wall. He rubbed them, his gaze flitting between the mud wall behind her head, the shiny white keys of the piano, the smooth top of the lacquered dining table—anywhere but her.

She tucked the sides of her hair neatly behind her bright red ears and huffed. "Just hurry up, please."

Carefully, Myung-gi unlatched the double windows and pushed them open an inch.

Sounds from the stream rushed in—laundry sounds, mostly: women calling, children crying, water babbling. Opening the window another inch, he craned his neck, and spotted the two soldiers walking along the bank, rifles on their shoulders—just like the men who had taken Ahpa. He jerked his head away.

"Are you okay?" Haewon whispered.

He nodded.

Myung-gi fixed his gaze on the soldiers once more. One was skinny and short; the other broad and thick. And they were close to Haewon's house, now, only about a hundred feet away.

"What's with your face?" the skinny one asked.

"Eh, it's just a few pimples," the broad-shouldered one said, rubbing his cheek.

"Why do they turn purple like that?"

"Why does your breath stink? Just shut up."

That voice. That height. Those thick arms hanging from those broad shoulders. When the soldier looked up, Myung-gi could finally tell—it *was* Byongho.

The boy from class. The one who had sneered with the others, the one who had beaten him with the others, the one whose name he could hardly remember. But he had been reluctant to join that beating. And Myung-gi had helped him with his schoolwork once. And he had accepted Myung-gi's kindness the day he was taken from school.

If he saw him, would he really arrest him now?

Quietly, Myung-gi shut the window and slid against the wall to the floor.

A thought occurred to him: What if Byongho had information about Ahpa? What if he knew where he was? Whether he was alive? He wore the same uniform and carried the same weapon as those who had taken Ahpa. . . .

Myung-gi ran his fingers through his hair, then tugged hard at the roots.

"What's wrong?" Haewon demanded. "Did you see something bad?"

Abruptly, Myung-gi rose to his feet. "I'm going outside."

"*What?* You can't be serious. No! I'm not letting you." Haewon stood in front of the door, her thin arms splayed out like tree branches.

"Don't worry," Myung-gi said, trying to sound reassuring. "They won't see me come out of your house. I'll sneak around back."

"Do you think that's what I care about?" she asked, huffing. "They'll conscript you and send you to the front lines—or worse, they'll send you to a prison back North! That's where you're from, isn't it?"

He couldn't be sure she was wrong. But if there was a chance he could get information about his father, he had to take it.

"I'll be careful. Listen, is there ever a time when Byongho is alone?" Myung-gi asked, leaning closer to her.

Haewon pressed her lips together and glared at him.

"*Please*," Myung-gi said. "I have to know."

"Why? If I tell you, you could get killed. You could get us all killed."

Myung-gi stared at her. "He used to be in my class," he admitted. "Back home, where my father was the . . . the principal." It had caught in his throat.

Haewon unfolded her arms. "Wah, really?—And Byongho, you know him?"

"Yes." Myung-gi lowered his head.

"Around nine p.m., after they've eaten, Kiyoung goes to the outhouse. They use our neighbor's," she said slowly. "He spends half an hour inside, alone, and Byongho waits for him. At least, that's what they've *been* doing."

Myung-gi looked up. "Thank you. I'll never forget this."

CHAPTER 35

October 1952: Myung-gi, Age 16

In the intoxicating moonlight
the sea is a sheet of silver;
heaven and earth lie so still,
just like a dream.

—Kim Yeong-nang, *Intoxicating Moonlight*

There's a moon inside the tunnel. It's not peeking through some crack in the rocks. It's *inside*, close enough to touch. Yes, yes, Myung-gi is sure of it!

"Thank you, thank you, I'll never forget this!" he cries out, thinking this is a miracle from God. But speaking out loud makes his tongue even drier, and when he tries to swallow, he doesn't have enough saliva. How long can a person go without water? He's read this somewhere. Three, four days, was it?

It's so black in here, he can't tell up from down. Doesn't know if he's sleeping or awake, if his limbs are attached or floating. Myung-gi tries hard not to think of himself trapped inside a dark pocket, deep underground. Instead, he tries to imagine himself in an open field under a full moon.

Which is not hard to picture because it's glowing big and round right over his head, as if a giant hand has pulled the lid off this tunnel. It looks just like the sky back home in the North.

"Wah," Myung-gi whispers to himself.

It's the same moon Myung-gi would see from the courtyard, the one that makes the tides rise, that can be seen by people on opposite sides of the world at the same time. And if you don't believe him, Myung-gi will draw the moon and the Earth and the lines of horizons from different longitudes, until they meet to form a connecting dot in the sky. Just give him a paper and pencil, and he'll show you. . . .

"Ahpa, are you looking at it now, too? The same moon that I'm staring at? Can you see it?" he calls out. Because it's intoxicating. Just like a poem he once read, and he tries to recite it, though he can't remember all the words: *In the intoxicating moonlight, the sea is a sheet of silver . . . just like a dream . . .*

"Why are you babbling? Save your energy."

Myung-gi sits up taller. "Ahpa, is that you?"

"Shhh . . ."

"There are so many things I want to tell you, so many things I want to know. Where have you been this whole time? How can I get to you? What am I supposed to do with my life? What is my purpose in this world? Of all places to have been born, why here, why now?"

And all at once, Myung-gi can see stars.

The lights are twinkling, like Uhma's shimmering pearls, like the shiny beads on her best dress, like the look in her eye when Ahpa would tease her. In summer, Uhma would set out dinners in the courtyard, under the stars, where the air was cool and breezy. Yoomee would plop down next to Myung-gi. Ahpa would sit at the head of the table. And they would eat to the sound of a radio playing outside—only it's not the Kim Il-sung song anymore, it's the "Mountain Bunny" song from when Myung-gi was little:

Mountain bunny, bunny
Where are you going?
Hopping, hopping while running,
Where are you going?
Over the mountain pass, pass
I will climb it alone.
Plump, plump chestnuts
I'll find and bring some home.

The stars are so clear, Myung-gi reaches up and swipes at them. He wants to snatch one and put it in his pocket. *I'll bring you home, I'll bring you home*, he whispers.

But, of course, they're too far.

And Myung-gi's stomach is now digesting itself.

Even in this state, Myung-gi knows this could all be a hallucination. After all, how many times does the top of a tunnel come off like a lid? He's read enough books to know that strange visions can occur under extreme isolation, dehydration, and starvation. But he doesn't care, and he chuckles to himself. If this is a delusion, he wants to stay in it, revel in it, never leave. Because in the dark recesses of his mind, he's found something glittering.

Myung-gi slumps onto his side, feels something fuzzy and small and warm by his face. Without thinking, he hugs it close.

CHAPTER 36

August 1950: Myung-gi, Age 14

Later that evening, everyone hugged their good-byes after Myung-gi had packed the jigeh.

"I don't know how I can ever repay you for your kindness," Uhma said, bowing to Haewon's grandmother. Both of them cried, and Myung-gi looked away, digging his nails into his palms until nothing was wrong and he was fine.

Haewon's grandmother wiped her eyes and pulled away, saying, "You can repay me by living a good life. Take care of yourself and your children. You can do it; you are stronger than you think." She waved a hand in front of her face. "Now enough of this sappy talk. You must go. Hurry."

But Uhma hugged her one last time, the thin bones of her shoulders poking through her white blouse.

Haewon jotted down her address and told Myung-gi to write to her after the war, then promised Yoomee a piano lesson once this was all over.

"You will write to me, won't you?" she pressed, looking right at Myung-gi.

He nodded, though he couldn't be sure about anything anymore.

"Because I think you're probably good at it—writing, that is. I can tell by your smooth hands and that writing lump on your fourth finger," she said.

He stopped fidgeting with the jigeh.

"And don't think you can fool me about reading. I know you like to read, even though you said you didn't."

At that, Myung-gi let out a brief laugh.

She handed him the small piece of paper with her address. He took it, tucking it carefully inside his pocket.

The small clock on the piano read 8:40 p.m. Myung-gi lifted the jigeh, which had grown weightier after Haewon's grandmother filled it with rice and dried cuttlefish and sweetened black beans.

"That doesn't look too heavy. I bet I could carry that," Yoomee said, grabbing for it. But she ended up yanking it off his arm, back onto the floor.

Myung-gi sighed and lifted it onto his shoulders again.

The three of them stepped outside into the early evening air.

Myung-gi looked back at Haewon and her grandmother, standing just outside their doorway: the old woman's long skirt and Haewon's straight hair flapped in the wind like broken sails. He worried for their safety.

They headed southeast through tall grasses. Myung-gi counted his steps in seconds, his distance traveled in minutes. He had a plan to double back.

But what *if* Byongho arrested him for being a traitor to their country? What *if* his old classmate forced him into the Red Army? What would happen to Uhma and Yoomee then?

Myung-gi turned his face upward. The light was almost gone. There was no more time to think.

He stopped walking.

"Uhma, I forgot our money. I left it at Haewon's house," he said, trembling. "I'll go get it. I'll be right back."

"What? How could you leave that?" Uhma cried, her head snapping around so quickly he almost took it back. "Where is it? I'll go get it. You two wait here."

"No! It'll be easier if I go. I know exactly where I left it. And I can run faster than you. I'll be careful. No one will see me. I promise," Myung-gi jibbered, his palms turning slick.

He ran off before she could argue.

Dusk had set in. It was probably 8:50 now, and it would take ten minutes to get back. Which meant arriving at Haewon's by nine o'clock—the time when Byongho would finally be alone.

Thorny bushes whipped his arms. The rough hemp of his pants chafed his skin. But he hardly noticed, sprinting all the way back.

There. Byongho stood near the stream in sight of the outhouse, a rifle in his hand.

He was alone.

Myung-gi walked toward him, not knowing how to pace his steps. Too fast and Byongho would think he was going to attack. Too slow and he would think he was trying to sneak up on him. If only Byongho would recognize him right away and remember him! Myung-gi always read books during break time, while the others played games of war; he was no threat.

But Byongho's rifle suddenly flew up. It was aimed at him.

Myung-gi froze. His classmate looked bigger up close; he must've grown a few inches. "I'm from the same village as you." Myung-gi raised his arms. "I'm Myung-gi from Comrade Hong's history class. I sat in the front row to your right. My father was once the principal of the boys' school."

Byongho squinted at him for a long moment, then slowly lowered his rifle. "Myung-gi? . . . What are you doing here?"

Myung-gi stepped a little closer. "My mother, sister, and I have been heading south. But my father . . ." He tried to swallow. "My father, we don't know what happened to him. Do you?"

Byongho stared, his face steady. Myung-gi shifted his weight.

"Why are you here? You should be back north where you

belong . . . or in uniform alongside me," Byongho said slowly. He raised his rifle slightly higher.

Oh God, this was a mistake. This was a huge mistake. Coming here, thinking he could trust Byongho. Myung-gi didn't have a single good answer to give.

The sweltering heat made it hard to breathe.

"I'm just trying to do what's best for my mother and sister," Myung-gi finally said, his voice so low it nearly disappeared in the breeze. "Trying to keep them safe, now that my father's missing." He took a deep breath and decided to look him in the eye. "He was taken . . . taken by the secret police. You know what that means. We couldn't stay."

Byongho glanced at his feet, breaking his hard and stony stare.

"Your father was sent to a prison that burned down and killed everyone," he said.

Myung-gi bent over. The air turned thick. He made a strange sound.

"But he was transferred before that happened," Byongho continued. "Our military decided his language skills would be useful to them. Last I heard, they had him somewhere near the border above the 38th parallel." He hung the rifle on his shoulder. "That's what my officer says, anyway. He's from our village too. He keeps an eye on these things."

His language skills! Of course! Ahpa could speak five

languages—Korean, Mandarin, Japanese, English, and Russian. He was the smartest man in the whole world! "Thank you. Thank you so much for letting me know. My mother will be so relieved." Myung-gi bowed then turned to leave.

"Hey, wait."

Myung-gi stopped short, all that forward momentum now crashing inside him. So close—he had almost walked away!

"Don't go farther south," Byongho said. "That's where the war really is now. You're better off going back North. Our army is going to win this war, anyway—you're just wasting your time trying to get away from us. They're saying we're going to liberate everyone in Korea any day."

Liberate? Liberate everyone from what? But Myung-gi only nodded, his smile a thin line.

Byongho's face brightened. "Hey, if you ever run into someone from our village, could you ask them to send word to my mother that I'm safe and fine? That I miss her cooking and that I'll be home soon? Could you do that for me?"

"Sure," Myung-gi said, and for a second he no longer saw the rifle on Byongho's shoulder or the red patch on his jacket. He was just that kid from history class whose name Myung-gi sometimes couldn't remember.

Byongho looked up the hill toward the outhouse door that was opening. "You better run. My comrade is coming. He shoots traitors."

At that, Myung-gi turned and tore through the tall grass, faster and faster.

Ahpa was alive! He was just north of the 38th parallel! Maybe only tens of miles away! He leapt over logs and rocks, flying, a bubble of hope buoying him.

CHAPTER 37

October 1952: Myung-gi, Age 16

Like sunlight whispering on stone walls …
my heart longs to gaze quietly up at the sky, all day long.

—Kim Yeong-nang, *Sunlight Whispering on Stone Walls*

Myung-gi startles awake to a sliver of light streaming in through a crack.

Particles of dust float in the dim beam. It isn't like those bright white flashes from grenades and explosives; it's *like sunlight whispering on stone walls*. . . like the light of a sunny morning.

Looking around at his dimly lit surroundings, he picks up the shard of mirror and shoves it into the crack, hoping to reflect more light inside the dark tunnel. He wonders if this is what the Chinese soldiers used for light, if that is why these shards are even here. Myung-gi angles it back and forth. Finally he catches it—a spotlight. It hits the wall, fluttering and bobbling like a dragonfly.

Myung-gi can't stop staring at it. He and Sora used to catch dragonflies along the river, their small hands cupping them. They were royal blue and tickled his palms. And when they grazed Sora's pink cheeks, they looked like jewels on a princess. The day she caught him staring, he glanced away.

The light moves down the wall, and as it grazes the dark nooks, Myung-gi sees something.

Two eyes glowing.

He drops the shard, yelps.

But the eyes come closer.

A pink nose pokes out first, then a furry brown head. A mouse. Just a mouse. Myung-gi lowers his shoulders.

"You found it? The little mouse? With the pink nose?"

Myung-gi's head snaps up. He had nearly forgotten about the voice on the other side—a voice which could be the enemy, or a hallucination, or his father.

"How did you know?" Myung-gi asks, the words coming out slowly, his starving brain having a hard time thinking, judging, talking.

"Well, I know everything." The man chuckles. "Plus, there are cracks, and mice can squeeze through one the width of a pencil."

"Oh. So the mouse has been on your side too?" Myung-gi asks, but the man doesn't reply.

Then, because no one is watching, Myung-gi strokes the mouse's soft fur, scoops it up and holds it close to his chest. It allows this; perhaps the Chinese soldiers fed it. He looks at the small creature and prays it doesn't leave, doesn't just disappear. As if it heard his prayer, the mouse nuzzles deeper into Myung-gi's open palm, and when he closes his fingers, its little heart beats in his hands. For a second, Myung-gi marvels at this living thing, so warm and alive, inside this hard, dark place.

CHAPTER 38

August 1950: Myung-gi, Age 14

It was bad in the South. Fields were scorched. Houses were leveled. And everyone was on the move—hundreds of people. Thousands.

Myung-gi walked barefoot in the middle of the crowd, his rubber shoes having fallen apart miles ago. He looked at Uhma and Yoomee, their skirts hanging loose on their bony hips, and wondered how much more walking they could endure. At least the Buddhist temples in the foothills remained untouched, the pagodas' upward-curving roofs curtseying to all those passing by.

They were moving slowly through Gimcheon, a small city about eighty miles northwest of Busan. It had taken them weeks to travel there from Haewon's house, more than halfway across the

South. Around him, there were crying babies strapped to women's backs, old men with scraggly beards, grandmothers smoking long bamboo pipes. Flies and mosquitoes shrouded them in a cloud—as if these insects knew something they didn't, as if they could smell death.

Oily black smoke billowed in the distance, drifting over rivers and plains and into Myung-gi's stinging eyes and burning nostrils. He spat on the ground, but nothing could get rid of the bitter taste of napalm.

A teenage girl shuffled along in front of Myung-gi, her long hair as thick and wavy as Sora's, and for a second he thought it might be her. He pictured her turning around and asking what books he'd brought today. He imagined the rest of her family appearing along-side her, Mr. Pak even pushing Ahpa through the crowd and saying, "Look who I found!" They would all laugh and cry in astonishment.

Myung-gi continued staring at the back of the girl's head. And even when he caught glimpse of her profile—pockmarked, with glasses—he continued dreaming.

"What are you looking for, Uhma?" Yoomee asked, interrupting his fantasy.

Uhma was searching the crowd, her neck straining. "I'm looking to see if there are any other young men. I don't see many. Even in a crowd, I don't think it's safe for us to travel by day. What if one of those Red tanks comes by and they spot Myung-gi? Ai! We should've stayed off the main roads!"

Except the back ways had turned out to be just as dangerous, and slower too. They had decided they wouldn't be able to survive them with food running low and their shoes wearing thin. Myung-gi hunched lower, the straps of his jigeh digging deeper.

"The Reds do come by in their tanks, but don't worry," a woman said, carrying a basket on her head and a toddler on her back. "Whenever any of us spots one, someone shouts a warning, and we all scatter off the road. And the old people, well, they just stay and continue walking, clogging up the path and slowing them down."

At that last bit, the mothers around her chuckled, one of them quipping, "We all do our part to serve our country."

Another lady patted Uhma's shoulder. "Best thing is to break your son's hand or arm. The Reds won't have any use for a boy who can't hold a rifle. I heard that some families with sons were doing this." The woman seemed older than the others, her hair streaked gray. At her side, her husband pushed a bullock cart loaded with luggage and furniture, his skin a deep tan—the same color as the tree trunks alongside the road. Neither of them even glanced at the fresh rows of roadside graves.

Myung-gi flicked his gaze to Uhma, who seemed to be thinking.

"But wouldn't they take him anyway, knowing it will heal?" Uhma asked.

"Well, some are doing something more permanent than a simple breaking of bone. But nothing too serious that would ruin a boy's life," the gray-streaked woman said. "All you need is a heavy rock."

Oh God, no. There had to be a better way. It wasn't even the pain that scared Myung-gi; it was the idea of permanent injury. What if he couldn't write with a pencil anymore? Or hold open a book?

Uhma held closed the ripped front of her blouse tighter. Beads of sweat glistened on her forehead. A worry line creased right between her eyes. She looked at Myung-gi, then at his hand, just dangling there like a piece of meat on a hook. "No, no, no," she said, shaking her head. "I couldn't possibly do it. I wouldn't be able to. Crush my own son's hand? No."

That was when the gray-streaked woman offered up her husband to do the job. The man stooped to pick up a large rock.

Uhma watched—and didn't object.

"It's better to lose a hand than lose a life," she said tremulously, turning to Myung-gi. "And you wouldn't even lose the hand; you would still have it."

Myung-gi fixed his gaze straight ahead. If this was really what other sons were doing, then he shouldn't be afraid to do it too.

"What do you want to be when you're older?" the large man asked Myung-gi.

What did he want to be when he got older? What did that have to do with anything? Myung-gi blinked at him. Though this man didn't look anything like his father—not even with the blinding sun casting a fuzzy light around his face—Myung-gi said it anyway: "I want to be a principal, or a professor, or even a businessman."

The things Ahpa had wanted for him. Anything but a writer.

"Oh good," the man said, "then your hands won't be your money makers—not like a farmer." He pulled his cart off to the side of the road, and Myung-gi and the rest followed. "Put your hand down on this stump," he instructed.

Myung-gi did, the splintery wood rough against his palm. He tried to imagine his hand detached from his body, belonging to someone else. The man raised the rock, and Myung-gi looked away—only to see Yoomee cringing.

He closed his eyes and held his breath.

CHAPTER 39

August 1950: Myung-gi, Age 14

Although Myung-gi half expected Uhma to step in or Yoomee to let loose a blood-curdling scream—anything to stop it from happening—in the end, his hand got smashed. Hard.

But it wasn't enough. *Only bruises*, the large man said apologetically.

No matter. Myung-gi had bigger worries than bruises. They had run out of food. Their feet were blistered and sore. And the blazing sun—the temperature close to a hundred degrees—was slowly killing them.

Uhma's sunburnt forehead crusted and bled. Yoomee's dry lips cracked open, bloody and raw. The old and infirm had given up under the oppressive heat, and now sat on the roadside beside the makeshift graves, where they would soon lie too.

Hours had stretched into days when they finally reached the bridge at Waegwan on the west bank of the Naktong River. This was the edge of the Busan Perimeter, but it was still nearly seventy miles to the city itself.

There were even more of them now—many thousands of refugees converging at the bridge—and everyone was pushing and shoving, desperate to cross to the east bank. That was the American side, the side the American and South Korean soldiers holding the bridge would soon retreat to.

"Hurry, children," Uhma said. "We must get across the bridge!"

But the crowd surged. Pulled them apart. Swept them off their feet. Soon, Myung-gi could no longer see his family in the press.

"Uhma! Yoomee!"

Someone cuffed him on the head. *Pay attention! Keep moving! You're going to slow us all down!*

Up ahead, steel girders stretched across black waters. The bridge, like an arm extending to him. All he had to do was reach it! Cross it! And he would be safe. They would all be safe. On the American side.

The crowd rushed forward in a wave, pushing Myung-gi until he was at the entrance of the bridge. The metal reverbated underfoot. So many feet pounding. He hoped Uhma and Yoomee were nearby and moving east, too.

But midway, the American soldiers guarding Waegwan began

yelling, blowing whistles, waving them back—back toward the west bank.

Why? Weren't they here to save them?

Pushed close to the men, Myung-gi could see veins bulging, faces reddening, the US Army First Cavalry Division patch on one man's sleeve.

"Get off the bridge! We're gonna blow it up! Back off *now!*" the soldier shouted in English.

But the crowd had morphed into an eyeless, earless, swarming thing, hell-bent on nothing but survival. Even if they had understood the English words, they did not obey. The soldiers cleared the bridge, pushing the refugees back to the west end, then running to the other side, ready to detonate—only to have the throng follow on their heels, filling the bridge again and again.

Where was his mother? Where was his sister?

That was when he saw it—the edge of Uhma's torn blouse, the side of Yoomee's pale face. They were there, revealed by the crowd—and in arm's reach.

"Uhma! Yoomee!" Myung-gi shouted, grabbing for them. "They're going to blow it up! They're going to blow up the bridge! We have to get off!"

"Why would they do that?" Yoomee shrieked, still pushing forward.

"I don't know!" he cried. "To stop the enemy from crossing into Busan? But I heard them! Listen!"

At that, Uhma looked as if she'd awoken from a spell. "Myung-gi is right. We mustn't go on!"

Together, they tried wriggling backward out of the crowd, but they were caught in its rushing wave. It was run forward again or be trampled.

The American soldiers were standing. Watching. Waiting. To push a button. But the bridge would never clear. Then one of them shook his head. Gave an order. Started walking away.

"Get off the bridge!" Myung-gi tried warning those running alongside him, but he couldn't penetrate the panic plastered onto their faces. "They're going to detonate it!"

"What do we do?" Yoomee screamed, bright red circles forming on her cheeks.

"Into the water!" Uhma yelled, gripping her children's shoulders and shoving sideways through the press.

They reached the edge of the bridge—and all fell into the river. The brown, murky current dragged on their sleeves and pant legs, almost as if some drowned spirit was trying to pull them down into the underworld.

"*Swim!*" Uhma shouted.

Myung-gi plunged down and forward, his glasses forced off his head. This time he reached out and snatched them.

It was quieter with his head under the surface. The whoosh of water plugged his ears. Arms sweeping, legs kicking, the jigeh pressing heavy on his back, he didn't want to come up for air, didn't want to hear all the screaming, didn't want to see the bridge blown to pieces, all those body parts come raining down.

Distantly, muffled through the water, he heard an enormous detonation.

But he needed air, and after a minute his head jerked above the surface. Gasping, he turned to see a man floating past him, dead.

Why? Why? Why?

"Uhma! Yoomee!" he shouted, swallowing mouthfuls of reddened water. Arms splashed everywhere, refugees like so many sea turtles swimming toward shore, but everyone's heads looked the same. It was impossible to find them.

Just then, a bullet pierced the river right beside him. And he dove *deep*, as deep as he could go.

Was a battle starting? Were the Reds here?

When he reached the bottom, his glasses still in one hand, he could see only swirling silt, straight shafts of bubbles from bullets whizzing through the water surrounding him like long spears. He swam madly until he knew he had reached the east bank, the sandy slope rising before him.

He dragged himself out of the river, algae clinging to his body. More bullets whizzed past, this time through the air. But exhausted, he didn't flinch.

What will be will be, he thought.

He just had to find Uhma and Yoomee. Maybe they had gone ahead of him. He ran toward the rice paddies where everyone was heading. Behind him, the bridge was gone. A military truck rumbled past—South Korean soldiers.

Can't see them! I can't see them! Uhma, Yooomee!

Myung-gi's feet moved on their own—zigzagging here, there, left, right—his brain not knowing where to step between bullets. There were others too: long skirts flapping, rice-paddy hats falling, babies wailing, tall back carriers bobbing. Running in all directions.

A silent mortar shell sailed suddenly overhead, like a flying fish.

Its long body and fin-like tail glided through the air. Left to right in a smooth arc—heading right for a boy soldier at the end of its trajectory.

The soldier's too-big helmet hung low over his eyes. His pimples flared bright red against his cheeks. His neck looked thin in his gaping collar, like so many of the boys at school. Myung-gi couldn't stop staring at him—standing straight as a reed, one hand down, the other reaching under his nose so he could wipe it.

Up! Up! Myung-gi wanted to scream at the boy. *Look up! Run!*

But time slowed, thick and heavy as tree sap, and when Myung-gi tried to move his body, he couldn't—not even his mouth. If only he could've reached up and snatched that flying fish before it hit the soldier. Before it exploded like a fiery geyser. Before it blew a small crater in the earth. Before it whipped the air into something solid, knocking him to the ground.

He lay waiting for the smoke to clear, his head turned and watching.

But the boy soldier was gone, snuffed out like a candle. One hand down, the other reaching under his nose, getting ready to wipe it. Myung-gi put his own hand up, the other one down—yes, that soldier had done it just like that. He couldn't stop seeing.

A bitter smell flooded his nostrils. Burning hair and searing flesh and blistering fat. Fire and smoke filled the air. A metallic taste coated his tongue.

Myung-gi got up and stepped closer to where the soldier once stood. But there was nothing now. Just a scorched space. And bits and pieces, random parts—only the suggestion of something human.

He stared and stared. Here one minute, gone the next. That boy soldier, reaching under his nose, getting ready to wipe it. His dirt-smudged fingers. His big, round nostrils.

The boy could have been from his village. From his school. One of Ahpa's former students. But who *was* he, exactly? He wasn't Byongho, because he was too short. And he wasn't Myung-gi, because Myung-gi had already patted his chest to make sure he was still there. But maybe this soldier *should've* been him—it seemed like everyone else his age was picking a side and risking their life for it, while he couldn't even keep watch outside the house like he was supposed to. Myung-gi circled the spot. Again and again. Like a dog tracking a scent. Because the boy had to be there. How could he be gone?

Myung-gi-ya! Oppah!

A faint cry. Was someone calling him?

He blinked and blinked at the burnt ground. How could someone get taken like that? Where was he? He had to find him.

There! There! I see Oppah over there!

Myung-gi-ya! What's wrong with you?

Someone was tugging his arm. He pulled it away. People
shouldn't just disappear. Because now there was a hole in the world
where that person used to be. It wasn't right. It wasn't right.

Myung-gi-ya!

Someone slapped him on the cheek. He hardly felt it. As if his
face had turned to rubber. He moved his mouth, pulled on his ear—
all rubber. Which was strange for a boy once made of blood and
bones and a beating heart.

Myung-gi-ya! Look at me!

If he had known he was going to turn to rubber, Myung-gi
would've jumped in front of that flying fish and saved the boy soldier. But he didn't. Just like he didn't warn Ahpa, didn't even grab
the shovel on the side of the house.

Myung-gi stared at his own hands, front and back, wondering
if they were real.

CHAPTER 40

August 1950: Myung-gi, Age 14

Three days later, they finally reached Busan.

At a checkpoint just outside the city, soldiers pumped a chemical called DDT into their hair, up their sleeves, down their shirts to get rid of any lice. Myung-gi squinted, fanning the noxious fumes from his face as the crowd was treated. Then another soldier went down the line of refugees and stuck them with a needle—the same one!—from arm to arm. *To prevent disease*, someone had said.

But Myung-gi no longer cared what they stuck him with or why. They were all nothing but ghosts, neither dead nor alive.

It was late afternoon, and no one seemed to notice when they actually entered the streets of Busan, except the wig merchants on the corners and the recruiters shouting at passersby. The sun blazed on the back of Myung-gi's neck and dripped sweat into his eyes, but he didn't bother wiping it.

"I think the house is up this hill," Uhma said, checking the paper in her trembling hand. Sora's auntie was the one who had found them a place to stay. *Nothing fancy*, Ahpa had warned them. *In her letter, she said that all the housing had been taken.*

Which Myung-gi now understood. Thousands of people— bloodied and stained—were roaming aimlessly. They camped out in yards. They slept inside cardboard houses. They found shade inside corrugated metal sheds that were too hot to touch. They slept on the floor of the Busan theater, in the storage rooms of the Korean Pottery Company, in the corners of the Taeryuk metallurgy plant, on the pews of the Chungang Church. They stood in endless lines that snaked around buildings—tempers flaring on the tail end, tongues lashing near the front. The lucky ones lived in leaning huts propped up on skinny stilts over the Cheonggyecheon Stream, or in relatives' repurposed chicken coops, or in shacks on "Refugee Hill"—like the one Myung-gi and his mother and sister were going to.

Myung-gi followed Uhma up a muddy slope.

Yoomee slipped and slid backward on a patch of sludge, and when Myung-gi's hand shot out to catch her, he was sure that hand didn't belong to him. Because nothing seemed real, not even his body, which was walking on its own. Under the weight of his heavy jigeh, his feet sank deep into the ground.

The houses stood clustered together. People's hanging laundry fluttered into neighbors' windows. The closeness made Myung-gi seize up: back home, an eavesdropping neighbor down the lane had turned in the family next door for denouncing the Great Leader over dinner. They were never seen again.

"Here we are," Uhma said.

The dwelling was the size of a shed, secured for them with money from Sora's uncle and auntie, which Myung-gi's family would have to pay back. The wooden planks were spaced far enough apart in some places to see right through to the inside. Uhma took a key out of her pocket, carefully guarded over hundreds of miles, and unlocked the door.

It was one room with a kitchen counter in the corner. A hot breeze blew in through the cracks in the wall, kicking up dust on the dirt floor. Uhma and Yoomee wore blank stares. There was a charred charcoal burner on the floor, and in the corner, a yoke with two buckets. A low dining table and wooden chest stood in the middle of the room—and even though they were splintered and cracked, Uhma took a rag out of her bag and started wiping them.

Myung-gi unhooked the jigeh off his shoulders and decided to unpack. Because he was pretty sure that was what he was supposed to do. Looking at the bundle strapped into the wooden carrier, his brain told him to untie, open, pull items out. And so he did. Pots and pans. Cotton jackets. Underwear.

And then he pulled out one of Ahpa's undershirts and stared at it until his eyes turned hot and watery.

He could picture his father wearing it, cross-legged on the floor on a Sunday morning, a newspaper in front of his face, the summer's heat already turning everything sticky. But when he and Yoomee had tiptoed up behind him—their small hands poised like claws, their giggles smothered—and lunged for their father's back, Ahpa's skin was smooth and cool and dry.

Why hadn't they packed any old photos? How could Myung-gi ask people if they had seen his father if he didn't even have his picture?

"Sit and rest," Uhma said, motioning toward both her children. She set her heavy bag down, then collapsed on the floor and took off her shoes. Her feet were blistered and raw. She rubbed them.

Yoomee plopped herself on the floor and sprawled out like a spilled bag of squid. But when Myung-gi sat beside her, his back stayed rigid, as if the jigeh were still on it.

"So . . . what do we do now?" Yoomee asked, scratching her greasy hair.

At that, Myung-gi almost jumped up and started moving. Because they had to run, wasn't that right? That was what they'd been doing for so long.

Uhma sighed. "There is so much to do. I don't know where to begin. We need water. We need food. We need to wash. We need to clean this place." A rat scurried across the floor and out the door.

"What about Sora's uncle and auntie?" Yoomee asked. "Should we go see them? Maybe they can help us settle in."

"No. Our family has burdened them too much already. They

are not our kin. We've only ever seen each other through Sora's family pictures. They are relatives of a friend—nothing more." Uhma reached into her bag, hunched herself over the only money they had, and counted the bills carefully. Myung-gi could practically see the worry creeping up her spine and stiffening her back. "Besides, I feel bad enough about having to work at Sora's uncle's fish stand for a little while."

Sora's uncle was just being nice out of pity. Ahpa had said as much when he was planning their journey. *That man never had need for a hire before. Now he's offering our family a job. I don't want to be a burden,* he had said, before folding the letter from Sora's uncle and auntie and tucking it away. No one wanted to be a burden.

Uhma's cheeks turned pink.

"Eventually, though, I can start my own business," she said, as if trying to convince herself. "I was thinking of knitting blankets and scarves and selling them. What do you both think?" She stood and walked toward the one small window, her arms crossed as if trying to hold herself together.

But Myung-gi wasn't sure. Ahpa had always been the breadwinner, and now Uhma would have to do it. She'd never worked a paying job in her life. Neither had Myung-gi.

"I can help out, Uhma. I can earn money," he said, knowing that was the right thing to say. But his voice sounded strange when he said it—like a puppet's, someone else's words coming out through his moving mouth.

Uhma stared out the window. "You and Yoomee need to go to school. You should not have to worry about such things," she said, as if she were reading a script. And for a second, Myung-gi wondered if his mother had also turned into something rubbery and strange and without feeling.

"Hey, I want to earn money too," Yoomee said, suddenly attentive.

"No, Yoomee," Uhma said.

"But I want to help!"

"Please, just listen. I'm too tired to argue."

"Listen to Uhma. You're too young," Myung-gi said without thinking.

Yoomee turned to him, her loud voice pushing harder. "You always think I'm too young, but I'm almost thirteen!"

Even though the rest of Myung-gi had turned numb, his brain could still count. "You turn thirteen in ten months," he said.

Yoomee sat on the floor and flung her socks. "I could be a hundred years old, and you would still tell me I'm too young!"

"Stop, that's enough," Uhma said, wiping her eyes. She put away the money and began untying her bag. "Let's unpack the rest of our things."

Which they did in only a few minutes—their three pots stacked in the corner, utensils poking out of their blue-flowered cup; their pink and yellow blankets folded on top of the dresser; their clothes put into drawers. How strange to see all their belongings in this unfamiliar, dirt-brown place, lined up like such good little things—sitting patiently, waiting to go back home.

After unpacking, they sat around the low table, their hands folded like visitors, knees tucked in tight. Because this *couldn't* be home, not with these plank walls and mud smells and the empty space at the head of the table.

Myung-gi looked left, right, up, down at the strangeness of this new place, where even the light streaming through the window cast an eerie glow, as if they were in an old sepia photograph, all of them set down in the wrong time and place.

Outside, a dog barked. Women walked past, chatting. The smell of spicy seafood stew wafted in through the window. These were not the sounds and smells of war. Then why wasn't Myung-gi letting go the breath he'd been holding?

Flashes of the Busan Perimeter flickered in his mind. Rice-paddy hats trampled on the ground. A metallic flying fish sailing overhead. That boy soldier standing there one second, gone the next. They had been lucky to make it out alive, but what about the others left scattered on the ground, their arms and legs bent into impossible positions? What about the people still trying to make their way south? What about Ahpa?

And then he knew—as sure as the sepia light and this dirt-brown place and their things sitting so patiently, waiting to go home—that nothing would be right, that *he* wouldn't be right, until Ahpa returned. But when would that happen?

CHAPTER 41

October 1952: Myung-gi, Age 16

"What you need," the Savage went on, "is something with tears for a change."

—Aldous Huxley, *Brave New World*

Myung-gi sits and waits for it to happen. For the mouse to disappear—squeeze through a pencil-thin crack in the rock wall and leave him for good. But it doesn't go; it stays. He knows this because he can feel the mouse's warm body pressing against his arm in the dark.

"Thank you," Myung-gi says, his eyelids drooping, head leaning against rock.

"You're welcome," the voice on the other side of the wall says.

"No, no. I'm talking to Mouse, not you." Dizziness overtakes him. The voice is silent.

"Wait . . . unless it's you, Ahpa," Myung-gi whispers. When he blinks in the darkness, his eyelids rub against his pupils like sandpaper.

"I waited and waited for you to come. Put my life on hold . . . Because it didn't feel right for things to change without you there—not even the seasons. Now I hate fall and spring."

"You can't stop change," the voice says, though now it sounds as weak and low as Myung-gi's.

Myung-gi knows this to be true. He couldn't stop those four men with rifles; he couldn't stop that flying fish from hitting the boy soldier. He can't stop his own body from wasting away right now. But he doesn't want to think about it, and he curls on his side, the mouse nestling against his chest. "Mouse is the only good thing," Myung-gi says.

He pets the mouse behind the ears, strokes its soft back, grateful that no one is watching. Its nose wiggles into Myung-gi's hand.

"I miss my wife. I wish I could hold her. I wish I could take back all the angry things I've ever said to her," the voice says. "What about you? Who do you miss back home?"

Everyone. Myung-gi misses everyone.

But he says nothing, only stares into the void and thinks of all the times he never told his mother anything, never let Yoomee get too close, never reached back out to Sora. It wasn't that he wanted to be alone; he was just afraid of what might happen if a person could look inside him.

Myung-gi cups the mouse in his hands. It's warm against his skin. He knows mice are intelligent beings with a range of emotions: happy, scared. Myung-gi wonders what Mouse is feeling right now—what he himself is feeling right now. Because everything is numb—his mind, his heart, his foot.

If Yoomee were here, she would tell him what to feel. She would tell it straight, too--*What you need is something with tears for a change*—like in Huxley's book. But the tears won't come, at least not for Myung-gi.

At best, he can pet Mouse's soft fur and hold him close and ask him not to leave. And if he presses Mouse too tightly in his hands, he can unfurl his fingers to give him a little air. Because there's no risk in opening up to a mouse, no risk in showing it all that he's feeling, especially here in the dark where no one can see.

Standing on Myung-gi's open palm, Mouse sniffs, his body elongating. He crouches back down on all fours, as if poised to jump off.

And Myung-gi holds his breath. "I can make a cozy bed for you," he says, just as Mouse leaps from his hand and into the void.

CHAPTER 42

September 1950: Myung-gi, Age 14

For days, the feeling followed Myung-gi wherever he went, like a voice whispering in his ear that he wasn't right—a single rotten kernel in an ear of yellow corn. It made him fidget and spill things and not eat. It kept him up at night. When he sat on the sidewalk and watched the bustle of the outdoor market—people chatting, children laughing, families walking—it was as if he were seeing them through a long, narrow scope from deep inside himself, that layer of rubber that encased him growing thicker.

"Is this the right way to school?" Yoomee asked, walking past a large church turned refugee center. Hundreds of people crowded the lawn, and Myung-gi scanned the crowd as he walked past. None of them were Ahpa.

Myung-gi sighed. "Yes. I think the school is up this road."

But when they reached the address, there was no school building in sight—only refugees, military convoys, tents, and soldiers.

"Are you sure this is it, Oppah?"

An American soldier walked past, and Myung-gi ran up to him. "Excuse me, sir," he asked in English, "can you tell me where I can find the Busan Provisional School?"

"It's right here," the man said, a strange drawl in his words, as if he had a mouthful of marbles.

Myung-gi looked around. There were no hard walls, no floors, no student desks—only the large military tents.

A hint of disappointment must've shown on Myung-gi's face, because the soldier said, "Well, what did you expect? We're in the middle of a war," then left.

He was right. These were temporary tents with temporary teachers and temporary students—hundreds of them. Myung-gi went to the boys' tent. Yoomee went to the girls'.

Inside, there was a long folding table, boys clothed in tatters crammed shoulder to shoulder. They wriggled and shifted in their seats like squirming larvae. Myung-gi took a seat beside them. A breeze fluttered the canvas walls. A rat scurried by his feet. The youngest boys sat on the floor.

"Quiet down, everyone," an old man said, not even looking

up from his desk at the front of the tent. He was gray: his hair, his button-down shirt, his cotton pants, everything. "I'm not here for my health or for fun or to babysit," he continued, "I'm here because you need a teacher, makeshift school or not. So don't expect me to coddle you. You put in as much as you want to get out of your education, and that's it. None of us are victims here."

Myung-gi stared at the dead fly on the edge of the table.

"Today, we are going to continue with our English lesson by reading *A Tree Grows in Brooklyn*, a favorite among the American GIs who have kindly donated a few copies. Who would like to start us off by reading out loud?" He waved the book in the air—all the boys straining their necks to see—then set it back down before anyone could make out the front cover. Everyone looked at one another and shrugged.

Though Myung-gi had never read that book, he knew about it. It was an American novel about an Irish Catholic immigrant girl in Brooklyn, New York. Why would the teacher assign that for their reading when they were a bunch of Korean boys in Busan, South Korea, during a war? An absurd laugh almost broke out of him. Because in his soundproof head where everything was so far away, this book was even farther.

Myung-gi's gaze traveled around the room. It was like watching a movie—the boys' and teacher's voices floating on the other side of a screen. The old man kept talking, his words in slow motion. One boy nodded, his ruddy face curved like a fishbowl. Myung-gi wanted to reach out and poke that boy's rounded cheek, but when he lifted his hand, it felt detached. Was any of this real? Maybe he could scream, and no one would notice. Like at the Naktong River.

Myung-gi tried to make sense of it all. That boy soldier—here one minute, gone the next. Ahpa—here one minute, gone the next. Even Yongshik on his way home from school. Soon Myung-gi would be here one minute, gone the next too. Maybe that was the only real thing: the certainty of being here one minute and gone the next.

A scream rumbled deep in Myung-gi's throat. He started to open his mouth.

"Any volunteers?" the teacher asked again.

No one spoke. Everyone's squirming had stopped. A few boys stared at their feet. Others looked right at the teacher like a dare. One younger boy put a tremulous hand up and asked to go to the bathroom, to which Teacher Chun snapped, "Go and hurry back!"

Myung-gi simply sat and watched.

"You," Teacher Chun said, pointing at him. "What's your name?"

Clearing his closing throat, he said, "My name is Kim Myung-gi, sir."

"Take out your copy of the book and start reading."

"Uh, I don't have a copy of the book, sir."

"Why not?"

"This is my first day, sir."

"You're new?"

"Yes, sir."

"Eh, I can't keep track of all of you. . . . " Teacher Chun muttered. "Do you know how to read English?"

"Yes, sir."

"Then come up and read from this copy."

As Myung-gi rose from his seat, everyone stared, their eyes judging, as if the classroom were a tribunal.

"Hurry," Teacher Chun said, sitting high in his chair of authority.

Myung-gi wondered if this old man even cared about books or teaching or kids. He was probably like Comrade Hong from back home, hiding cigarettes up his sleeve. But when Teacher Chun handed him the book and told him not to bend the spine or fold the pages, Myung-gi wasn't so sure.

The novel's cover felt as smooth as the oiled paper that used to line the floor of his room. That familiar musty scent of wood pulp rose from the pages. He brought the book closer to his face, and when he breathed in, it was as if he were back home, the dresser pushed aside, the hole in the wall staring back at him. And Ahpa . . .

How about this one, son, did you like it?

Yes, Ahpa.

Write me an essay on it.

What?

Just kidding!

Myung-gi started blinking behind his glasses.

Teacher Chun tapped his pencil against the papers he was grading. "Start."

Myung-gi began reading—his voice low and quiet—about the Tree of Heaven that grows anywhere, especially in hard and poor places. As he read, he glanced up at the tent full of boys—all of them now leaning forward in their seats, their eyes turning bleary—and he knew all too well that they were beginning to forget themselves and this place.

Though he would never again allow himself to get lost in a story, he would at least let them enjoy it.

He continued reading about this tree that can grow out of cement and sewer gratings. "It would be considered beautiful, except that there are too many of it." He looked up again, at the "too many" of them. Tall and short. Skinny and gap-toothed. Dirt-smudged and hair-mussed. Barefoot and callused. How many of them were from the North? How many were still coming? An urgency coursed through him. He had to stop by the refugee church right away. To see if Ahpa had come through. Maybe it was still possible. Maybe—

A heavy hand thumped him on the back. Myung-gi jumped.

"Alright, that's enough. Nice job," Teacher Chun said, already passing out graded papers. "Oh, hold on to that book. But you have to share it in groups of five because there aren't enough copies to go around. Who here is not part of a group of five?"

Across the room many hands rose slowly, each one like a blade of grass—enough to fill an entire yard.

"Pick four boys at your table and share the book with them. Take turns reading it. Now go back to your seat," he said, squinting at the names on the papers and then at the sea of boys.

Myung-gi went back, his hands numb and tingly. The last time he'd read anything was on that day . . . under the twin pines, behind their stone wall, where he was lost in that book, the one about the tiny Earth and the vast universe and the insignificance of this all. . . .

"Do you guys want to share this book with me?" he asked four boys at his table.

They all shrugged and squirmed and half nodded.

"Okay," Myung-gi said, "who wants to take it first?"

No one answered.

"Because I don't want it," Myung-gi added.

One of the boys, spiky-haired and spindly, said, "Well, none of us can read English, so you might as well keep it."

"Oh, okay." Myung-gi didn't want to carry it, didn't want to read it. There were more pressing things to do. He stared at the book expressionless, but an ache welled in his throat. Sweat prickled across his scalp. And suddenly the book felt so hot in his hand that he dropped it, down deep, into the dark abyss of his bag.

CHAPTER 43

September 1950: Myung-gi, Age 14

After school, Myung-gi wove through the crowded streets and headed to the refugee church. Cars honked at slow-crossing oxen. Customers haggled up and down market rows. Solicitors on street corners called out to passersby. Street urchins crashed into stacks of pots.

Once Myung-gi could see cardboard houses covering the front lawn, he knew he'd reached the church. They were made from US military C-ration boxes: a few had BEEF SLICES & POTATOES W/ GRAVY printed on a side wall.

Myung-gi stared at the church. Nothing about this place looked real—not the white steepled top, not the bloody cross in the window for all to see, not the pastor walking around wearing his pulpit robe. The whole scene made him uneasy, even here in South Korea where church was not banned. And he swiveled around, about to say how strange it all looked—forgetting for a second that Ahpa wasn't right there to talk to.

A dry, dusty wind swirled.

Stepping between cardboard houses and sticking-out feet, Myung-gi waded through the crowd of refugees crammed on the front lawn.

"Excuse me," he said, his quiet voice no match for the chatter and commotion. "Have you seen my father, Kim Junho? He was the principal of a boys' school in Chagang Province, North Korea."

A few people poked their heads out of their boxes, looked up, then pulled themselves back in, like turtles not wanting to be bothered. But one man stuck his finger at Myung-gi and accused him of being a communist. *You're a Red! From the North! President Syngman Rhee will execute all the Reds!* he cried. Which Myung-gi knew could be true, having heard about the South Korean president's growing obsession with routing out all the communists—real or imagined. But even so, Myung-gi would much rather take his chances here than in the North.

Why was it so hard to live in peace?

Myung-gi looked around at the sea of faces. Maybe more people would help if he had a picture of Ahpa, or if he could tell them how brave his father was. Like the time he had walked in on Comrade

Lee interrogating a boy in her class about his older brother missing the communist youth meeting. The boy's hands were trembling on top of his desk when Ahpa told Comrade Lee to stop. *This child's family affairs are not your business,* he'd said, staring straight into her glaring eyes.

Maybe if people only knew things like that, they would care enough to help find him.

"Is there something I can help you with?" a woman holding a clipboard asked.

Myung-gi straightened his shoulders. "I'm looking for my father, Kim Junho. He was a principal at a boys' school in Chagang Province, North Korea. He is kind and wise and—"

"Do you have a photo?" she interrupted, checking things off with a pencil.

He shook his head, shoulders slumping.

"Don't worry, dear," the woman said, already moving on to help the next person. "Just keep checking back."

And so he did, every day, several times a day. Because just waiting wasn't good enough.

CHAPTER 44

September 1950: Myung-gi, Age 14

Though a few boys from class had asked Myung-gi to stay after school to study and eat together, he always went home alone and did his homework. Because that was what he was supposed to do—divide the numbers, fill in the blanks, his arm moving like a seismograph and his pencil like the recording tip, scribbling nonsensical lines on the page. But Uhma would look over his shoulder and tell him he had a good brain.

Myung-gi barely slept. Most nights he would light a small candle after Uhma and Yoomee fell asleep. He would lie on his side, watching that blue flame wrestle with the wind blowing in through the planked walls. He would stare at it until his eyes began to tear, thinking of his father's bruised face, of his eye swollen shut. Then he would pull the covers over his head, as if a thin blanket could do anything to muffle his whimpering. There was still no sign of Ahpa at the refugee church. And he still hadn't read *A Tree Grows in Brooklyn*.

"How is this blanket so far?" Uhma asked one day, holding up a square of knitting. The radio blared on the floor beside her—clips of General MacArthur's voice, President Syngman Rhee's voice, Premier Kim Il-sung's voice—all imposing their orders.

Myung-gi tuned down the radio. The blanket was green and yellow and full of uneven lumps. The combination of colors made Myung-gi cringe, but he smiled hard, pushing all that rubber up into the balls of his cheeks.

"Have you sold one yet, Uhma?" Yoomee asked, plopping back into her corner where there were all things Yoomee, things she'd gotten from school—her charcoal pencils and drawing pad and disheveled pile of papers, all the edges poking out and bent.

Uhma sighed. "Not yet."

"I will get a job after school. I saw some boys delivering water," Myung-gi said, as if reading instructions on how to survive: earn money, buy food, eat, repeat. He knew Uhma would object—insisting that he focus on his studies instead—but he offered again anyway.

"I want to go with you, Oppah," Yoomee said. "I can help you carry stuff. I can help you do things. I can—"

"No," he replied. He knew she would only make things harder.

But she pretended not to hear and drew in her notepad instead.

"Myung-gi-ya, when can you start? Can you work every day after school? Maybe weekends too?" Uhma asked, the words rushing out as if she'd been long holding them back.

Myung-gi's face turned bright red. Of course his mother needed help from him. He was the oldest son. Ahpa was gone. He wasn't a little kid anymore; he should have insisted sooner. Even though he didn't really know how to get a job or how to step into that empty space Ahpa left behind, he would try—he had to. "Yes. Yes, of course I can work. Every day," he said, nodding too vigorously. "I don't know when I can start, but I can go and see tomorrow."

Uhma let out a sigh of relief.

It was fine. In fact, it was better. Yes, yes, it was definitely better. Because Myung-gi couldn't focus on his studies with Ahpa gone, couldn't think about a future. None of that mattered anymore, and besides, books made his stomach hurt. Myung-gi sat very still, thinking about this.

CHAPTER 45

October 1952: Myung-gi, Age 16

> I discovered the head of a mouse peeping out … and I was surprised to find that it did not run away, but suffered me to advance quite close … saying, "Will you write my history?"
>
> —Dorothy Kilner, *The Life and Perambulations of a Mouse*

That sunny morning light has since faded. Now Myung-gi sits very still, alone in the dark.

"Mouse, where are you?" Myung-gi asks, his voice low and quiet. "Hey, how about you? Are you there?" he tries, this time to the rock wall. "Do you want to talk about food again?"

But there's no answer.

Myung-gi doesn't stir or slump or sit up taller; in fact, he doesn't move a single muscle. There's no need when there's nothing to react to, nothing to do. All he has are his thoughts, which are filled with all those useless books he's read.

A small shadow appears at the far end of the nook. "Mouse?

You're here! Were you here all along?" But Mouse only wiggles his whiskers against the palm of Myung-gi's searching hand. He strokes Mouse's soft fur gently.

"What? Why are you looking at me like that? I'm not really a loner. I can be friendly."

Little eyes blinking.

"Don't listen to those boys at school. I never talked to them because they were cruel. And I had to keep to myself, for Ahpa . . . because I didn't want him to see them bully me. His only son."

At this last part, he snorts, listening intently to the scritch-scratching of mouse feet.

Turning to the air, he says, "I'll tell you what's so funny. I'm the son of a military hero, a successful businessman, a fearless principal, the grandson of a judo master." He turns his foot, and sharp pain shoots through his ankle, straight up to his gritting teeth.

Mouse only stares.

"Stop being so obtuse. Do I really need to spell it out for you? You're an intelligent creature, right?"

Myung-gi waits, but Mouse starts nibbling on something.

Lifting his arms and gesticulating wildly, Myung-gi shouts, "I'm stuck in a hole! An ROKA recruit, stuck in a hole! I came here to save Ahpa, and I got stuck in a hole! That's me, living up to my name and legacy!"

And now it begins in earnest—the walls pulsing, visions floating, voices crowding inside his bandaged head. "Who says I'm a scholar? And what good is one anyway? I was so busy with a book that I didn't keep watch! *I didn't keep watch!*"

Swiveling around only to face a different wall, he says, "What? How can you say that? That may be what you think. But I know books wouldn't do me any good."

Mouse moves away from Myung-gi's hand.

"Oh, I know what this is about. You're like the mouse from that old English fable—you know, the one about having good virtues. I didn't like that one—didn't like being preached at. You want me to write your history, don't you? Just like in the book. Well, I won't do it. Sorry."

Mouse scurries to the edge of the nook.

"So then that's it? You're just going to leave?"

Mouse sniffs the air.

"I'm sorry," Myung-gi says, his voice breaking. "I said I'm sorry. I'll consider it, really. The books. Writing your history. Just please don't go."

But maybe Myung-gi has gone too far, said too much, shown a side of himself he shouldn't have. Or maybe it's just time to eat. Mouse jumps down, scurries across, and disappears through a crack.

CHAPTER 46

September 1950: Myung-gi, Age 14

Myung-gi sat outside their house on top of the hill and stared down at the streets below. He watched water delivery boys teeter up and down the city blocks, their arms wrapped around oil drums splashing over with water, their hands blistered and red. They wore caps and sweat-stained shirts. And when someone called out to them, they would thrust their chins out and holler back.

After studying them for hours, Myung-gi grabbed his yoke and two buckets and headed down the slope.

Blurry heat rose from the streets. He tugged on his collar. Though it was early autumn, the sun was blazing, as if summer was reluctant to move on. Which was fine with Myung-gi, because he wasn't ready to move on either.

The line for the public water tap wound around two buildings. The city supplied water to people's homes only every two to three days, if that, and with the huge flood of refugees coming into Busan, water was becoming scarcer and scarcer. People had to stand in line for hours.

Myung-gi knew the rules: families of five or more could have three buckets of water a day, while families with fewer than five could have two buckets. The larger families would need to send at least two people to carry back their allotment—two people who could be doing other things, like earning money, instead of waiting for hours. Maybe Myung-gi could be of service to them—or to old people who couldn't easily carry heavy pails. He walked up and down the line in search of likely customers.

"You cut in front of me!" a woman shouted at the man beside her, her sleeves pushed up to her armpits.

"What? No, *you* cut in front of *me*!" the wiry man shouted back. "I was standing here all along!"

"*Uh-muh*. . . ." the woman said, shaking her head in disbelief. "You expect me to believe that? You think I'm stupid? I've been standing here for two hours! I know who's been here all this time!"

A water-line skirmish. Myung-gi's head throbbed.

"You're a hypocrite!" the man shouted back. "I saw you cut this line the other day!"

At that, the armpit woman let out a war cry and rammed into his chest. The wiry man pushed her back, yanked her hair bun. She grabbed his face.

Cries shot up from the crowd. *Cut it out! You two are pathetic! Shame on you!*

A police officer stepped between them, and the man and woman disentangled, their hands still snapping like pincers.

The sun beat down on Myung-gi's neck full blast, ruthless and unrelenting. Around him, everyone's faces were red hot. They fanned themselves, their lips pursed. They checked their watches and groaned loudly. A few even heckled passersby, warning them not to cut in front. How could he get any customers from this angry crowd? What should he say? Just ask if anyone wanted water delivery? He'd never even started conversations with his old classmates back home. Those boys always seemed to know things he didn't—the rules of sports, how to crack a joke, ways to lift a few extra potatoes from the landlords. One time Myung-gi had tried talking about the philosophical underpinnings of his favorite poet, and the boys in his class had just stared.

But he had to do this. So he adjusted his glasses and cleared his throat.

"Water delivery. Water delivery," he said, walking up and down the line. "I can go to your house." But his voice was quiet and thin. Inwardly, he cringed.

One woman looked at him, then held her purse closer to her body.

"Water delivery!" he said, louder, his voice cracking. He tripped on the uneven sidewalk.

Children pointed and giggled. Men looked right past him; ladies chatted, ignoring him. Myung-gi flushed, knowing that he sounded fake—a bookish boy trying to act street smart.

"I could use a water delivery. And so could some of my friends in the old people's group at my church," a grandmother, her back hunched, said suddenly. "But are you a good boy?"

"Uh—yes, sahmoneem," Myung-gi said, addressing her respectfully.

"Do you study hard and go to church?"

Sweat tingled on his scalp, but he nodded.

"How about your parents? What do your parents do?"

He seemed to be shrinking—or maybe she was growing. Either way, she seemed taller than a second ago. "Uh, my father was a school principal, and my mother is starting a knitting business," he managed.

She twisted her neck out from under her hump and peered up at him. It was like coming eye to eye with a whale in the ocean; he prayed she wouldn't hurt him.

"Oh, wait a minute—you're the boy my friend at the fish stand told me about! Kim Myung-gi, right? The son of a school principal. He said I should ask you to deliver water for me because I'm too old to carry it," she said, her gaze softening. "He owes me a game of baduk, by the way."

Friend at the fish stand? Oh, Sora's uncle! "Yes, yes, that's me!" Myung-gi said.

She took out a piece of paper from her purse and scribbled some addresses on it. "Here," she said, handing the paper to him. "Deliver water to these houses. But I want you to start at my house first."

He thanked her and bowed.

CHAPTER 47

September 1950: Myung-gi, Age 14

Hours later, Myung-gi's yoke had dug deep into his shoulders. The water buckets sloshed on either side. After standing in the public line for hours, he was finally able to fill his pails before the tap went dry for the day.

He headed to his first delivery, a hot wind blowing in his face, sweat drenching his shirt. Up the dirt road he walked, carefully, one foot after the other. But no matter how slowly he went, water splashed over the sides of his pails.

He peered into them. Nearly half the water was gone.

Sighing, he squeezed his eyes shut. Sweat dripped down the sides of his face. He reached up to wipe it, then felt the yoke tilt.

More water spilled from the buckets. Ai!

By the time he reached the address, there was hardly any water left. Myung-gi set his yoke down and poured one bucket into the other. One full pail seemed better than two half-empty ones.

He knocked on the wooden gate. The humpbacked halmoni opened the door. She looked at her watch, then at the buckets.

"What took you so long? I thought I told you to deliver here first."

"I'm sorry, sahmoneem, it took me longer than I expected. But you're my first stop."

She shook her head. "And what about my water? I see only one bucket."

"Uh, yes, about that . . ." He adjusted his glasses, then looked straight at her. "I spilled some."

That was when she called him a donkey in Russian—and he told her that he wasn't one. Which led her to call him a dumb cow in English—and he said that wasn't very nice either.

"You understand all those languages?" she said, peering up at him again.

He nodded.

"Well, what are you doing this job for? You should be studying, using the God-given talents that you have!" she said. "And let me tell you—delivering water isn't one of them."

Myung-gi shifted his feet.

"Obviously, I cannot pay you for two buckets when I only got one," she said, fishing through her purse.

"No, of course not," he said, wondering what the going rate was for delivering water—something he hadn't thought of beforehand. *That's because you have a great mind, son. Great minds don't quibble over details. Great minds think in big pictures.* But he knew Ahpa had only said that to make him feel better when he didn't understand game point deductions in chukguk.

"Here you go. Two hundred won and a few coins."

"Thank you," he said, taking the money and stuffing it into his pocket.

But a coin slipped from his pants, hit the ground, then started rolling.

Down, down the hard-packed dirt road.

In a straight line, not slowing or stopping.

They watched it, heads turned, mouths agape, as it rolled right in front of an old man, who picked it up and stuck it in his pocket.

Too afraid to move, Myung-gi just stood there, still watching, even after the old man had gone.

"Aigoo . . . you're the type of person who looks at the sky while walking by a cliff's edge," the halmoni said, shaking her head. "Be careful."

CHAPTER 48

October 1952: Myung-gi, Age 16

Nothing is so necessary for a young man as the company of intelligent women.

—Leo Tolstoy, *War and Peace*

Be careful, be careful, always be careful! That's what they all said to him—the humpbacked halmoni, Uhma, Yoomee, Sora, even the piano girl. God, why can't Myung-gi remember her name?

Oh yeah, that's right, of course. He knows why he can't remember. It's because his brain is starving, drying up like a prune. And he's buried in the dark, deep in the earth, where no one will ever find him.

But, you know, he should've listened to them. Really, he should've. And Myung-gi claws at the front of his shirt in regret, shouting, "*Nothing is so necessary for a young man as the company of intelligent women!* Leo Tolstoy! *War and* blasted *Peace!*"

Yah! Myung-gi-ya, watch your language. What has happened to my son?

"Uhma? Uhma, is that you?" He knows she's here because he can see the glow of red, of peach, of sparkling jewels.

War has changed you.

"I know, and I'm sorry. I wish there were no wars, no evil governments, no power-hungry madmen. Why are we always being held hostage by the loudest, the ugliest, the most egotistical—"

Careful, watch your language.

"You know, if everyone stood up to the Japanese—and then the Soviets—maybe things would be different. If all the good people of the world united—and I don't mean just *saying* we stand together, but actually coming out of our houses and *standing* together—what couldn't we do? But everyone is too scared to speak up. Except Ahpa; he wasn't scared. But because he did it alone, because no one stood up beside him, he got taken away. And I'm as angry at our cowardly neighbors as I am at our oppressors!"

Now you're sounding like your father.

"But I'm angriest . . . at myself," he adds, quietly.

Still just like your father.

"Really? Because I don't think I'm anything like him. In fact, I think you're in for a big disappointment, Uhma. I want to be a writer one day; did you know that? Not a professor or a principal or even a businessman. A writer. And did you know I probably won't make enough money to support you and Yoomee? I'm not capable of that."

Myung-gi-ya, I don't need you to support me. My knitting business is doing well.

"Oh good, Uhma. That's really good. But . . . a part of me thinks you're just saying that."

Her colors darken to blood red and burnt peach. *I'm not just saying that. I'm stronger than you think. You just see what you want to see, but if you really looked, you would notice that I've expanded my display of knittings, and that I have more orders than I can keep up with.*

"Sorry, Uhma. I just want to support you in any way I can. . . ."

I could sure use some support, Oppah. How about supporting my art? How about letting me help you sometimes? Do you think you're the only one who can be head of the house?

"Yoomee? Oh, little sis, how have you been?" Myung-gi swivels around to face her.

You shouldn't have left, Oppah.

"I know, but I had to try to get Ahpa back."

But it was a bad idea. What made you think joining the army would solve anything?

"I already told you. I thought with a weapon in my hand and a division at my back, I could get up north and I could find him. That was the plan."

Well, that was a dumb plan.

"Yes, that seems to be the consensus around here. But it was the least I could do . . . to try to make up for everything."

But what happened to Ahpa wasn't your fault.

Myung-gi chuckles. "Oh, but it was. Trust me . . . you don't know."

At that, Yoomee stomps up the side of the rock wall and hangs upside down, arms crossed. *"You don't know, you don't know, trust me"—that's all I ever hear, and I'm sick of it.*

Something flits across the other wall—a spotlight, dancing like a dragonfly—and Myung-gi's cheeks grow warm.

"Sora? You're here? Thank you for coming," he says quietly, lowering his head. She is beautiful.

Oh, please! Yoomee rolls her eyes. *Just tell her you like her already.*

Myung-gi glares at his sister in the dark.

Myung-gi Oppah, what books did you bring today?

"Books? I . . . I don't have any books, not anymore. I stopped reading a while ago, Sora."

Why?

"Because books . . . are a waste of time."

You think I'm a waste of time?

"What? No, I never said that."

But I am what I read. You know I read all the time.

"It's fine for you, just not for me, okay? I'm a water delivery boy now, not a scholar."

Sora begins floating away, disappearing in a swirling mist. *I thought I knew who you were, but I don't.*

For some reason, this hurts Myung-gi more than anything.

Oh, how he throbs and aches. So exposed, stripped bare and unprotected. In front of the girl he loves. He is a pink and hairless thing, surrounded by pointed rock walls that threaten to crush him from every quivering side.

CHAPTER 49

October 1950: Myung-gi, Age 14

Weeks passed of going to school, delivering water, and stopping by the refugee church. Myung-gi had gotten better at not sloshing water out of his pails, though he was still not as skilled as the men who kept a running pace, their buckets so steady not even a ripple showed.

Morning fog covered the top of the church steeple. By now, all the church workers knew his name.

"Hey, Myung-gi!" one of the custodians said, sweeping leaves from the front steps. When he grinned, his toothless gums showed, like a roll of Vienna sausage from one of those American C-ration cans. "Back again so soon? Weren't you just here this morning?"

Myung-gi's face turned hot, even in the cool autumn wind.

He always hoped no one was keeping track of the number of times he stopped by the refugee church every day—which was five, to be exact.

"Oh, I just stopped by for a second this morning, that's all," Myung-gi said.

"Aren't you supposed to be in school right now?"

"It's my lunch break."

The custodian nodded. "Still haven't found your father yet?"

Myung-gi shook his head.

"Well, I'm sure he'll turn up one of these days," the custodian said, his smile half closing.

The church lawn was especially crowded. There was an old grandmother missing two front teeth. A crying baby bouncing on a mother's knee. An old man with a long, scraggly beard and a cane.

Myung-gi threaded his way between the cardboard houses, calling out his father's name. A few times, someone popped out of one of the boxes saying that his name was Kim Junho. But they were never his dad.

Before he left, he asked the lady with the clipboard if she had seen his father, and when she shook her head sadly, he just stood there, the whole world telescoping out until he was nothing but a single black dot in a sea of brown cardboard. He turned to leave.

"But you've heard about the good news on the war front, right?" the clipboard lady inquired.

Myung-gi turned around.

"General MacArthur made a surprise landing at Inchon and cut off the Reds—he forced the North Korean troops to retreat. UN soldiers have taken back Seoul—even captured the capital of North Korea! I think they're going to push the Reds all the way up to the Yalu River on the border with China. In fact, I think we're going to win this war," she finished.

"Really? Then all of Korea would be united and free?"

She nodded and grinned.

The war had flipped. The South was now winning! It was the kind of hope that was too important, too fragile to hoist up high, so he tucked it deep inside his head, where it pulsed slow and steady in its nest of thick rubber.

"Thank you, miss," Myung-gi said, bowing and running back to school.

His bag bumped against his body as he pelted down the street, that book still heavy inside. He hadn't touched it, even though he hadn't been able to fall asleep the night before, and reading was the only thing that could've soothed him. At most, he let himself listen to passages being read out loud in class—and only because he had no other choice.

Myung-gi ducked inside the school tent. He sat at the long table and didn't join in with the schoolboy chatter, voices floating around his head like a fog. *Got paid this week. Gonna deliver water tomorrow. Saving up to go to America, one day.* A few boys were staring off into some dreamy distance, but when he followed their gaze, he saw only mud splatters on the canvas wall.

"Boys, settle down," Teacher Chun said, flipping through some papers. "Lunchtime is over. I have an announcement to make."

The tent quieted.

Teacher Chun held up a piece of paper. "The school director asked me to recommend several students to take the specialty high school entrance exam next month. So I made a list based on recent test scores." He waved the paper in the air. "The exam is once a year, and it is difficult. If you get in, you will attend one of the most prestigious high schools in Busan, starting this February. Then you'll be on your way to bigger and better things—a bright future."

Bright future.

A buzzing started inside Myung-gi's head. Teacher Chun was getting smaller and smaller. Myung-gi's hands were turning numb and tingly. Because the idea of applying to a specialty high school felt a lot like moving on . . . which felt a lot like giving up on Ahpa. His body erupted in a cold sweat. A wave of nausea swept over him.

Teacher Chun proceeded to write the names on the chalkboard.

Myung-gi tried not to look. Because he didn't want to, except he did. But not really. So he just sat there, not knowing where to set his gaze. He wasn't ready to start something new without Ahpa. No, he was not.

Murmurs rose across the room. Students strained their necks to see. A few shouted in joy.

That was when he saw it. On the chalkboard: KIM MYUNG-GI.

His head was still abuzz when Teacher Chun pointed at him and asked, "Did you finish reading that book yet?" The teacher looked faraway and blurry—nothing but a skinny gray matchstick, his red face the fiery tip.

"Book?" Myung-gi repeated. No. There was no time for something as frivolous as reading, especially when he had water deliveries to make after school.

Someone snickered.

"No, sir. I haven't finishing reading it," Myung-gi said.

"Hmm . . . well, then pass it on to the next boy. You've had that book for two months now. Better not to waste anyone's time. If you're not going to read it, I can't help that. Like I said, you get what you put into your education."

CHAPTER 50

October 1950: Myung-gi, Age 14

Myung-gi shuffled through piles of leaves on his way home. Gazing up at the bare trees, he wondered when the seasons had changed. It didn't feel right. But against the orange evening sky, the blackness of empty branches stood out like painted calligraphy, prettier than any scroll, and he couldn't help but stare.

That announcement about the specialty high school entrance exam already felt like days ago, but it had been that afternoon. Since then, Myung-gi had already gone home, switched out his school bag for his yoke, delivered water, stopped by the refugee church two times in between deliveries, and was now heading back home. But first, he wanted to visit the church one last time.

"Any word on my father?" he asked the clipboard lady, who was now putting on her coat, picking up her purse.

She sighed. "No, dear. Why don't you go home and do your homework and have some dinner?"

Myung-gi pushed up his glasses and nodded. He was probably annoying her.

It was darker now. He headed up the hill toward his house.

Why did he and his family have to be born at this time and place? Were there boys in the world who would never live through war? How much control did they really have over their own lives? If Ahpa were here, he would know.

A sharp pang shot through Myung-gi, the kind that made it hard to breathe, his chest moving up and down like a wounded animal's.

Ahpa always had the answers, even when the questions were hard. Myung-gi had asked him once how Comrade Lee could run in front of a jeep to save a little girl, but also turn in a family to the secret police for hanging a picture of the Great Leader crookedly on their wall. Was she a hero or a monster? Was she good or evil? Could he trust her? They were walking to school, Ahpa's principal's suit jacket flapping in the breeze, when Ahpa told him that Comrade Lee was *all* those things. This disturbed Myung-gi greatly, but he continued listening when Ahpa told him that trusting her depended on who you were. If you were that little girl, then you could trust her with your life. But if you were the son of a principal who was an anti-communist dissident, then you should not trust her. Not at all.

Myung-gi pushed open the front door of their house. No one was home. Uhma had tried to make their one-room shack as cozy as possible——a woven mat on the dirt floor, neatly stacked pots and bowls on top of a small round table, an iron fire pot in the corner—— but it never quite felt like home. A brisk wind blew in through the cracks in the wall, and Myung-gi kept his coat on.

Yoomee's disheveled heap of papers, sketchpads, pens, and pencils were on her low work desk. He picked up a pen and one of the drawing pads. It was still blank inside. Without thinking, he turned to the clean first sheet and wrote his name on top: KIM MYUNG-GI.

Oh, no. What had he done? This was one of his little sister's favorite things. He couldn't erase pen, couldn't rip the sheet out from its sewn binding without her noticing!

Sighing, he told himself that he would buy her a new one as soon as he could. But for now . . . for now he would keep putting words down on this crisp sheet, words that had been inside him for so long that they were clogging his chest. If he didn't let them out soon, they would probably burst like an appendix and spread infection throughout his entire body.

For the next hour he wrote, his hand moving feverishly across the page, the world falling silent all around him.

He wrote everything he knew, everything he felt, everything he could never say out loud. The words kept coming, and he kept writing as if possessed. He didn't even notice when Yoomee came through the door.

"Oppah! What are you doing with my sketchpad?"

When Myung-gi looked up and saw his sister's crumpled face, he felt sorry—really, he did. But he had to find a way to hide his writing. Because no one could read it. No one. "Sorry, Yoomee. I promise I'll buy you a new one. You know I'm making money delivering water. Don't worry, okay?" But nothing could appease the wailing siren that Yoomee had somehow managed to swallow. "Shhh! Quiet! The whole city is going to hear you!"

"*The seller at the market said that was the last one!*" she shrieked. Not even the thick scarf around her mouth could stifle her cries.

"It's just a drawing pad. I'll find another one somewhere else, okay?" he said, even though he wasn't sure whether he really could.

"Drawing is the most important thing to me!" Yoomee managed between hiccups.

"What? You never told me that. How was I supposed to know?"

"Well, it's true," she said, shuddering.

Myung-gi dropped the notepad, no longer caring whether anyone read it. He looked down at his hands as if they had committed a serious crime. Sometimes he could be so selfish. What was he thinking, taking his little sister's notepad?

They faced each other in the dimming room. Yoomee turned on the kerosene lamp. "Well, can I at least read what you wrote?" she asked, sniffling.

"What? No. It's private."

"Please, Oppah? It's the least you can do for stealing my

notebook and ruining my dreams." She always seemed to know how to hit her big brother's softest spot.

"Fine." He sighed, then handed it over, and she snatched it from him and scurried into the corner to read by the lamp.

Myung-gi opened his bag and stared into the abyss. He should probably start his homework, but when he opened his math book, the words and numbers blurred. He knew she would probably hate what he wrote and maybe say something mean about it. But no matter, writing was stupid anyway. After this, he would never do it again.

Five math pages later, Myung-gi dared to glance toward his sister, who had been sitting too quietly in the corner.

She looked up at him, her mouth twitching strangely. "Is this . . . about our family?"

He nodded.

"What's going to happen next?"

Myung-gi looked right at her. "I don't know."

CHAPTER 51

October 1952: Myung-gi, Age 16

> Even a mouse can help a lion.
>
> —Aesop's Fables

Mouse is gone. Usually he comes and goes, but he's gone. A cold dankness settles into Myung-gi's bones, and he wishes Mouse's warm, soft body were there to hold.

"Hey, are you there?" Myung-gi says toward the rock wall.

No one answers.

"Hey! I'm talking to you!" he says, his voice raspy.

Silence.

"Mouse is gone," he continues.

And for some reason, saying the words out loud puts a crick in his throat, and now he can hardly swallow. Myung-gi curls up into a ball.

"You don't know where he is, do you?" Myung-gi asks.

When the voice doesn't answer, Myung-gi curls up even tighter—his chin touching his knees, his knees touching his chest—as if crowding himself will make him feel less alone.

He never lets me hug him anymore, never tells me anything. Myung-gi hasn't stopped thinking about Uhma's words since the day he overheard them. It wasn't that he didn't love his mother . . . or Yoomee . . . or Sora . . . it was just that he was afraid. Because when someone gets too close—you start saying things, and feeling things, and before you know it they're chipping away at the stone pit in the center of your being, the one that you've grown your flesh around.

But not with Mouse; he can tell him anything without worry.

Myung-gi grinds his heel into the ground. It's just a mouse, isn't it? A dumb little mouse. But something brushes his hand, and Myung-gi's breath catches.

It's Mouse. He's back!

"Where did you go last night?" Myung-gi asks, his voice trembling.

A faint light seeps in through the cracks overhead, and now he can make out Mouse's shape. When Myung-gi squints and looks through his cracked lenses, he sees fractals and lines cutting across the mouse's body. And a third eye—he sees a third eye. Myung-gi smothers a laugh.

Mouse's whiskers twitch.

"Listen, I'm sorry about the things I said earlier. You're more like the mouse in Aesop's Fables—the one that helped the big silly lion. I'll consider writing your history. Just please don't go. You're the only one I can talk to," Myung-gi pleads.

But just speaking out loud sharpens the dizziness in Myung-gi's head—a sign of advanced dehydration. He has read enough books to know. It is only a matter of days now.

CHAPTER 52

December 1950: Myung-gi, Age 14

Sunday. Though they hadn't attended church since arriving in Busan, Myung-gi knew Uhma would say something eventually. And eventually had arrived. *We must find a church. We must start attending,* Uhma had told them the night before.

Myung-gi tugged on the sleeves of his white button-down shirt, which were now too short. Yoomee put on her best red dress that she'd brought from home, even though it had faded. They sat in silence, waiting for Uhma to return from an errand. Myung-gi couldn't bring himself to talk much to Yoomee, not until he could buy another drawing pad for her. But supplies were scarce, and there never seemed to be any extra spending money.

A cold wind was whistling through the slats of the wall when Uhma finally came through the door—with all her hair chopped off.

Myung-gi jumped to his feet at the sight of her.

"What happened to your hair?" Yoomee cried.

Chunks were missing. The back and sides were jagged. It was as if someone had taken a knife and just sawed it off all at once. A long, thick ponytail swung in Uhma's grasp like fresh kill. Myung-gi half expected it to drip blood.

Uhma touched the nape of her neck where the shortest strands stuck out. "What?" she asked, chuckling weakly. "It was bothering me, so I cut it."

His mother had always twisted her shiny hair into a bun. Everyone had always said she looked so elegant. Now Myung-gi could hardly recognize her. And he wondered whether Ahpa would either.

"Uhma," Yoomee said, running over to the dresser and fumbling for a comb. "Let me comb it. It'll look better if I comb it."

But Uhma leaned away from her daughter's hands. "It's okay, it's okay. Why? Does it look that bad?" she tried to joke, her eyes drooping. When she looked at Myung-gi, he couldn't look back. "Listen, we have to go to church now. We're going to be late."

Myung-gi and Yoomee put on their shoes and snuck nervous glances at each other. Uhma picked up one of the knitted scarves she was always trying to sell at the market, examined its uneven holes, sighed, and wrapped it around her neck. Then she stuffed her ponytail into her bag and stepped out the door.

They all headed down the hill.

※

It was the refugee church. Myung-gi had thought that Uhma might've chosen a different one. Not that it was a problem—in fact, it gave him another chance to look for Ahpa's face in the sea of exiles on the front lawn—but he hoped none of the church workers would recognize him and comment on the number of times he stopped by every day. Uhma and Yoomee didn't need to know.

Walking up the path toward the double front doors, Yoomee turned back to look at the lawn full of cardboard houses, the clipboard lady walking between the rows.

"Come on, Yoomee, let's go," Myung-gi said forcefully, pushing her from behind.

"*Myung-gi! Yoomee!*" someone called.

Myung-gi turned around. It was Sora's auntie! He recognized her from Sora's old family pictures. *She's the one!* Sora had once told him, pointing to her auntie's photo. *She's the one who got married at sixteen.* Then, folding her arms and blinking fast, she had said, *I'll never do that. Not ever.*

"How are you all doing? I was so happy to have your note, Mrs. Kim. How is the house?" Sora's auntie asked. "Is it comforta—"

That was when Sora's auntie stopped short. Her eyes flitted up toward Uhma's hair, then away. "Oh! You look so . . . strong and healthy," she said, patting Uhma on the arm.

Uhma's eyes lit up, and for a second she looked the way she had back home when having tea with Sora's mother. "Thank you again for finding that house for us. It is just the right size."

"Wah, look how tall Myung-gi has grown! Where have you been?" Sora's auntie cried, pounding him hard on the back.

He coughed.

"He's busy delivering water, thanks to your husband, who helped him get customers," Uhma said, smiling.

"Oh, no, it was nothing." Sora's auntie waved a hand in front of her face. "Your son would've taken care of you anyway. Such a good boy, so strong and handsome too. Aigoo, I can only hope one day I should be as lucky, but I'm getting older and soon my childbearing years will be behind me."

This talk of sons always seemed to brighten Uhma's mood, and she nudged Sora's auntie playfully on the arm. "You still look like a teenager! Why are you talking about getting old?" she teased, her voice growing lighter. "But I have to admit, it does give me great comfort and security knowing that I have my son by my side to take care of me and Yoomee."

Sora's auntie nodded to that. She might've even said "Amen." But Myung-gi stood there, feeling like a charlatan on the brink of being exposed. He was trying to be the head of the household. It was what his father would have expected. But sometimes he still cried like a baby under his covers at night—couldn't fall asleep thinking of that deep blue bruise, that eye swollen shut . . .

Uhma patted Myung-gi on the shoulder. When she looked at him—her proud gaze the only thing holding up the tired lines on her face—he knew he would have to do more, do better.

Inside, crowds of people filled the sanctuary. A wooden cross hung up front. Dusty benches sat in rows. Nearly every spot was taken. The preacher walked up to the altar, but everyone in the front row kept sneaking glances over their shoulders.

Myung-gi followed their gaze to Uhma's chopped hair. And something flared like matchsticks inside him. What was their problem? Hadn't they ever seen a haircut before? Didn't they have any manners?

He stopped and assessed the other women's hair—something he'd never done before—and noticed that most of them had hair that was long and drawn into a bun. Even if their clothes were tattered and their faces haggard, that smooth, neat bun seemed to pull everything together. A few ladies had short cuts, but they were fashionably styled, curling on the ends and sides.

His gaze returned to Uhma. Why did she have to chop it so close to the nape of her neck, so short that her scalp was showing? It made her look sickly—or crazy. And everyone seemed to think the same, leaning away from them as if they were carrying a disease.

On the way home, Uhma told Myung-gi and Yoomee to wait on the corner while she took care of an errand. She checked inside her bag and held it close, then started walking.

Yoomee kicked at the pebbles on the ground, seeing how close she could get to the side of the brick building without touching it. But Myung-gi didn't play. Instead, he adjusted his glasses and watched his mother go—across the street, past the outdoor market, then around the corner, where he knew the wig merchants stood, bidding for hair as shiny and pretty as Uhma's.

CHAPTER 53

December 1950: Myung-gi, Age 14

After Uhma cut her hair, they all got new shoes. Myung-gi's were leather and rubber-soled. Yoomee's were canoe-shaped and powder blue. And Uhma's were flat and plain, the same as the grandmothers and widows wore.

Yoomee slipped her shoes on and kept admiring them from the front and sides. But Myung-gi could hardly look at his, knowing the price Uhma had to pay to buy them. He needed to work more hours to earn more money. But there was never enough time.

He'd stopped by the refugee church and was now running late for school. His feet pounded the frost-covered pavement, and by the time he reached the tent, class had already begun.

"So glad you could join us," Teacher Chun said, his lips pursed.

Myung-gi hunched his shoulders and sat low in his chair.

Teacher Chun turned to the rest of the class. "The specialty high school entrance exam is this Saturday. If you were on the list, I hope you've been studying."

A few boys crossed their arms and leaned back in their seats. If they'd been wearing suspenders like Westerners, they would've hooked their thumbs through them, snapped them confidently.

But Myung-gi sat motionless. He still hadn't decided whether to sit the exam or not. If he passed, it wouldn't mean he *had* to go to the high school; it wouldn't mean that anything *had* to change. He could stay in his holding pattern, keep working, keep waiting for Ahpa to return—couldn't he?

But he hadn't even studied. More and more, he felt he didn't belong with the eager, shining, test-taking boys at the top of the class, whose eyes gleamed so hard Myung-gi wondered if they could see through them.

For the rest of the afternoon, Myung-gi could hardly concentrate on Teacher Chun's science lesson. *The atom is the basic building block of matter. Our bodies are made up of cells, which are made up of molecules, which are made up of atoms, which are 99.999999 percent empty space. Therefore, all the matter of the human race can fit in a baby's spoon.* Teacher Chun had said this with a mad gleam in his eye, but all Myung-gi could think was that he could be crammed shoulder to shoulder at this table, jammed inside a tiny house, crowded in this overflowing city, and *still* feel alone. He truly was made up of empty space.

A microscope sat on a table up front, and Teacher Chun had them line up and take turns looking through it. Myung-gi got up and stood behind that spiky-haired, spindly boy—one of the students in his book-sharing group.

"Hey, do you want the book now? Teacher Chun said I should pass it along," Myung-gi said.

"Nah, I'm never going to read it—none of us will. I'm not even planning to graduate. I've got more important things to do."

Myung-gi nodded, waiting silently for his turn at the microscope. He'd never used one before, and he wondered whether it could really help him see better.

At the front of the line, one of the boys pressed his eye to the scope. *"Wah! This is amazing! I want to see what my hair looks like under this thing,"* he shouted, then plucked a strand from his head.

Which reminded Myung-gi of Uhma's hair . . . of her shabby knitting . . . of the measly amount he earned every week delivering water after school. He looked down at his new shoes. There was never enough time.

That was when he stepped out of the line and grabbed his bag, then headed toward the teacher, his hands numb and tingly.

"Is there something I can help you with?" Teacher Chun asked, marking papers on his desk.

Myung-gi stood there, not knowing what to say, not even sure exactly why he'd come. He opened his mouth, but nothing came out—only a cloud of white breath.

Teacher Chun continued grading.

"I don't like losing myself in a story. There are more important things I should be doing," Myung-gi said, a sick feeling washing over him.

"Hmm . . . maybe so," Teacher Chun said, not even looking up.

Myung-gi dug into his bag, and when he pulled out the book, it flopped open to where they'd last left off in class. "And I don't want to read this. I don't even like reading," he said, his eyes fighting not to see the words:

She loved books. She loved them with her senses and her intellect. The way they looked and smelled; the way they felt in her hands...Everything there is in the world, she thought, is in books.

He slammed it shut. A vein pulsed hard on the side of his neck.

Teacher Chun glanced up for a second. "What's so wrong with losing ourselves in a story? Don't we always find our way back a little wiser?" He returned to his papers. "But if you don't want the book, you can pass it along to the next boy. I already asked you to do so."

Something tore inside Myung-gi's chest, but he said it anyway. "The other boys don't want to read it either."

"Then set it here." Teacher Chun pointed to a basket on the corner of his desk, his eyes still fixed on those papers.

Myung-gi was sure his teacher had heard the tremor in his voice, the catch in his throat, but he'd told him to return *A Tree Grows in Brooklyn* anyway. Wiping his eye underneath his glasses, Myung-gi set the book on the desk, then walked out and left, for good.

CHAPTER 54

October 1952: Myung-gi, Age 16

> Deep beneath the ground
> there is a soul imprisoned.
> It seems always to be looking down
> at the distant sky.
>
> —Kim Yeong-nang, *The Clear Well in Front of the Yard*

Myung-gi can't stop worrying that Mouse will leave again. Which is silly, because Mouse is just a field mouse—the kind Sora's mother would brush out with her broom.

A dim light hits the wall where Mouse is sitting in a nook.

Too tired to move, Myung-gi leans against the wall, shifting only his gaze to look at Mouse. Such a little thing, sitting so recklessly there, like a human heart unprotected outside a body. "You can go, you know," he mumbles, because he can't go on like this— worrying and worrying and then worrying some more. But as soon as he says it, a small panic rises in his chest.

Mouse flattens his ears back. Maybe he doesn't like what Myung-gi said.

"I don't need you. I just need my father," Myung-gi says. "So go . . ." And he nudges Mouse from his nook. Better to beat Mouse to the punch.

Mouse scampers down the wall, onto the ground, then stops in front of the boulder where there is a tiny crack along the edge—just wide enough for him to squeeze through.

An ache throbs inside Myung-gi.

"Are you trying to get rid of the mouse?" the voice says.

Both Myung-gi's and Mouse's heads turn toward the sound.

"Where have you been?" Myung-gi asks. "I thought you were dead."

The voice chuckles. "No, not yet. But maybe in another day or two."

Myung-gi starts trembling.

"So is the mouse bothering you?"

"No."

"Do you just hate mice?"

"No."

"Are you scared of the mouse?"

"What? No." Myung-gi scoffs, though it sounds like a feeble cough.

"Then what are you scared of?"

"Nothing."

"Nothing? Wah . . . I wish I were scared of nothing."

Myung-gi huffs. "Now you're just making fun of me."

"No, I'm not. I just think you're lying and that you're so scared that the little mouse will leave you that you're trying to get it to leave first. Pretty twisted."

"What? I'm not."

"Instead of looking on the downside, why not try looking up sometime? Don't torture yourself."

Myung-gi suddenly wishes the voice, the mouse—*everyone*— would leave him alone. Because when there's someone to talk to, there's a chance of saying too much, feeling too much, hearing things he doesn't want to hear.

And in the end, they're just going to leave him anyway.

Mouse stands on his hind legs and sniffs the air, as if trying to figure out where to go by the direction of the wind. But there's no wind in here, and Myung-gi lets out a tired chuckle.

If only the lid would come off the tunnel again, and he could see that night sky full of stars—stars just like the ones back home. He stares overhead at the rocks, trying to picture the moon, but he can't.

So he stops straining and drops his gaze instead, where *deep beneath the ground, there is a soul imprisoned . . . looking down at the distant sky.* Oh, he gasps softly, picturing the back of someone's head staring into a clear well, someone who never looks up. He hasn't read that Kim Yeong-nang poem in so long. Myung-gi lets out a small breath. The words come without warning, faster and faster all the time.

That's when Mouse gets down on his haunches. Sniffs the crack in the wall. Turns once to look back. Then squeezes through and disappears.

CHAPTER 55

January 1951: Myung-gi, Age 14

Quitting school was what Myung-gi wanted, so why couldn't he stop looking back at the tent classrooms?

He shook his head, walking toward his first water delivery. Dropping out was easier than he'd imagined. Even Uhma hadn't given him the hard time he was expecting when he told her—now he would be able to work more hours and earn more money, he'd explained, and the school was just a provisional one, anyway.

She had nodded slowly. *Just a provisional school. And these are unusual times. I suppose you can always go back and finish next year.*

In his first week of a full work schedule, he'd earned enough to buy a new kettle to replace the one with the broken handle. Though he felt strange not going to school and learning new things, he grew used to keeping his head down and carrying water up and down the streets.

⚜

In this way, the weeks passed, nothing changing.

Except for one thing.

It was Sora's uncle who told them. Myung-gi had just filled his buckets and was on his way to the humpbacked halmoni's house. A cold wind blew, and he shivered inside his cotton coat. As he passed the fish market, already bustling early in the morning, he heard Sora's uncle shouting to Uhma and Yoomee at the fabric shop. "Hey! I have great news!"

Uhma and Yoomee headed toward him, and Myung-gi followed.

"They arrived last night," Sora's uncle began, wiping his eyes with the back of his hand. "The two of them just showed up at our gate. We were all amazed that two kids could travel here on their own! You should've seen the look on my sister's face when she saw Sora and Youngsoo standing there in the courtyard. Her children, safe with her, at last!"

Sora! Here! In Busan! Though Myung-gi hadn't started his route, he was already out of breath.

"But it was a hard journey. They're both a little thin. Young-soo's a little sick," Sora's uncle continued, and then he couldn't say another word, his chin quivering.

How did Sora know which way to go? Did she have to dodge

bombs and bullets? How had she managed to trek across mountains and rivers in the freezing cold, all alone? And wasn't Youngsoo only eight or nine now? How did he manage without his parents and only his sister? Last Myung-gi remembered, Youngsoo was so little, playing with his spinning top, and then copying the way Myung-gi sat.

Myung-gi suddenly thought of that girl, Haewon, hiding from the soldiers—and that same queasy feeling washed over him. What had Sora endured? Grimacing, he wished more than anything that he could've been there to walk beside her.

Uhma clasped her hands and cried at the news. Yoomee insisted on going to visit them right away. But Myung-gi still had water deliveries to make.

"Wait," Myung-gi said, realizing just then that Sora's parents had arrived before Sora and Youngsoo, and that no one had told him. "Sora's parents have been here in Busan? For how long? When did they arrive?" After all of Mrs. Pak's worrying and fretting about leaving, they'd made it here.

"Didn't we tell you? They've been here for about two weeks— Mr. and Mrs. Pak and baby Jisoo. I'm sure we told you," Yoomee said, her forehead crinkled. "I don't know . . . you've been in your own world lately."

"Oh."

"Well, it doesn't matter. You know now. So let's go see them," Yoomee said, already hooking her bag on her shoulder.

"You go without me," Myung-gi said.

She turned around. "What? You're not coming? But Sora and her whole family will want to see you!"

He could picture it—both their families gathered inside Sora's uncle's house. Baby Jisoo opening and closing drawers. Youngsoo following Sora around. Sora spilling soup and accidentally breaking things in the kitchen. And all the adults sitting around talking—all except for one.

That father-shaped hole at the table would suck all the air out of the room. Besides, it was enough to know that Sora was here and safe. He didn't need to see her.

"I'll try to stop by some other time. I have water deliveries to make," he said.

Yoomee sighed. "We'll see you later at home."

Myung-gi started on his first delivery, cold water splashing out of his buckets, but then he turned to watch Yoomee and Uhma walk down the dirt road—past the ragamuffin boys stealing fruit, alongside the endless lines for water, right in front of the wig merchants eyeing Yoomee's long, shiny hair. He watched them until they disappeared in the crowd, and even long after that.

"Hey, you're blocking the whole sidewalk!" someone shouted.

But he just stood there, still watching. Sora was alive. Her parents and siblings were alive. His own mother and sister were alive. And Myung-gi too. It was more than he deserved.

Ducking into an alley, he set his yoke down, then slid to the ground—just for a minute—and let his face break into a million pieces.

CHAPTER 56

February 1951: Myung-gi, Age 14

Over the next few days, Myung-gi noticed something strange.

At first he thought it was his imagination. But no—in the cardboard labyrinth of the snowy churchyard, it seemed there were fewer and fewer refugees from the North. It was always Kangwon Province or Seoul or Kyonggi Province—all of which were in South Korea. Where were the North Korean refugees? Where had they all gone? Why weren't more coming?

"When are we going to win the war?" Myung-gi asked the clipboard woman.

She sighed, a white cloud of breath obscuring her face. "Things have changed over the past few months, you know that. The Chinese joined in on the Reds' side, and now they've retaken Seoul. Look, Northern refugees can't cross the 38th parallel anymore. I'm sorry."

A sharp wind blew down the mountainside and staked Myung-gi to the ground. That fragile hope, once pulsing slow and steady, was now shriveling up in the cold, dry air.

"But what about my father?" he asked.

She didn't answer.

And he could hardly breathe.

"I have to go to a funeral today, and I'm late," he blurted out. He wasn't sure why he'd said it. Maybe because she carried that clipboard around like someone who should be told everything.

"Well then, what are you doing here?" she asked.

※

It was at Youngsoo's funeral that Myung-gi finally saw Sora.

She wore a plain white blouse and skirt. And when the wind blew, her long and tangled hair swept in front of her face, where she left it. He could see that she had grown older and taller.

Pneumonia, Uhma had told Myung-gi the night before. *The journey was too hard for Youngsoo. Sora did everything she could to care for him on the road ... but in the end, it was too much.*

By the time he had run up the mountainside to the grave site, the service had already started. The afternoon light was fading, and the men had already buried Youngsoo's small body deep under the ground.

"I'm glad you came," Uhma whispered, blowing her nose into

one of Ahpa's old handkerchiefs. He'd always kept one in his principal's jacket, sometimes lending it to Uhma to let her wipe the dust from her feet.

"I'm sorry I'm late."

"It's all right." She glanced sideways at him and tugged on the short strands of her hair. "Listen, I was thinking—you have to go back to school. Take that specialty high school exam."

Myung-gi blinked at her. "What? No. I can't. It's too late. I have to work anyway."

"I don't need you to work so much. I can take care of all of us now," she said, her voice thin but steady.

"I like delivering water."

"You're wasting your life."

"I'm waiting for Ahpa."

Uhma dabbed her eyes and stared straight ahead, her lips pursed.

Yoomee stood next to Myung-gi, tear stains on her left sleeve, pencil smudges on her right.

A chorus of hymns rose like shaky scaffolding. Myung-gi only mouthed the words, not trusting his voice. But Yoomee sang out loud.

Finally she turned to him and hissed, "Where were you, Oppah?"

"Working," he mumbled.

"That's the only thing you do these days—all day, every day. You're hardly home. You never even stopped by to see Sora."

How could he stop by and see her? Their families broken, their lives broken? Besides, he didn't want Sora seeing him like this—a scholar turned delivery boy.

Everyone began singing the refrain to an old church song they'd sung before the war, before the Reds, before their lives had turned upside down:

All things bright and beautiful
All creatures great and small
All things wise and wonderful
'Twas God that made them all.

Myung-gi stared straight ahead. A fawn stood between the trees, watching, flecks of sunlight hitting its spotted back. He almost didn't see it standing there, so solemn and quiet, as if it knew this was the funeral of something equally pure and small. No one seemed to notice. If Ahpa had been there, he would've seen it.

When it was all over, Uhma and Yoomee went straight to Sora and her family and offered their condolences, but Myung-gi lagged behind. He could've seen Youngsoo one last time, could've played a game with him, could've done something big-brotherly. What right did he have to be here? He should've gone to see them, the first day Uhma and Yoomee visited.

Now it was his turn to offer his regrets.

He moved closer, until Sora was standing right in front of him.

It was like seeing a character come to life and step off the page. For so long, he'd pictured her only in his mind, but now she was just inches away, Mr. and Mrs. Pak hovering beside her. Her parents' hair had grayed, and a tiredness pulled down on their cheeks; where there was once fullness, he saw only skin and bone.

Myung-gi bowed deeply at the waist. He almost spoke. He almost said how sorry he was about Youngsoo, about not visiting sooner, about the hard time she must have had. He almost told her about Ahpa, about the gaping hole, about how sure he was that his father would've grieved Youngsoo like one of his own.

But nothing came out when he opened his mouth. Because how do you talk to a girl who just lost her little brother?

Sora's gaze traveled up to his eyes, and when she looked right at him, she hid her face and started crying. Which was how he knew—now Sora had a gaping hole like his.

CHAPTER 57

October 1952: Myung-gi, Age 16

We march up, moody or good-tempered soldiers—we reach where the front begins and become on the instant human animals.

—Erich Maria Remarque, *All Quiet on the Western Front*

Mouse is gone. Again.

Myung-gi slumps against the wall. He thought he could make it hurt less by telling Mouse to go before he could leave him, but it hurts just the same.

There's no way to stop things from happening.

A strange cry slips out from deep inside him.

"Sorry, kid," the voice says.

This hits Myung-gi hard, and he curls up, holds his stomach. But it's not until he puts his head between his knees that he goes tumbling in the dark—upside down, right side up—and now he's lost and adrift, floating in space.

"Where's home for you?" the voice asks.

"Busan, I guess," Myung-gi mumbles.

"Then think of Busan and going back there. Think good thoughts."

"But Busan is where time keeps moving forward . . . everyone is trying to move on, get back to normal."

"So?"

"So I don't want time to keep moving. Not without my father."

"And how do you stop time, exactly?"

Myung-gi's head is pounding. "Skip the specialty high school entrance exam? Quit school? Curse the changing seasons?"

"Well . . . that's dumb."

The back of Myung-gi's neck bristles.

"You may be book smart, kid, but you sure are naïve."

On the instant, Myung-gi becomes a human animal—just as he once read in a book. Enough of niceties and conversation. He is ready for that hand-to-hand combat in the dark. Except instead of fists and pistols, he will stab with words. Deeply piercing words. "Actually, I think *you* are dumb—and pathetic. A Chinese soldier stuck in his own army's tunnel, insulting a kid who is—what—half your age? And I bet your wife is relieved you're gone so that she doesn't have to put up with your nasty words and your mean spirit."

For a second, the man says nothing. And Myung-gi wonders if he has gone too far. Then a rasping sound comes through the cracks, and he realizes the man is laughing.

"Good one, that's a good one, kid! Keep it up! You're keeping me alive." The man sighs, and Myung-gi pictures him wiping tears from his eyes.

"See, that's why I don't like talking to you! Or anyone."

"You don't like talking to your father?" the voice demands, sternly.

Myung-gi, cloudy-headed, is confused. "Ahpa, is that you?" he asks.

A hyena laugh echoes against the walls. "Sorry, sorry. No, really. Sorry," the voice says, between breaths. "That was too much. Sorry."

Myung-gi closes in on himself, curling up and covering his ears. None of his plans, none of his ideas, not even his insults are any good. He's ready to give up, until, finally, he feels something warm and soft against his cheek.

It's Mouse. Returning from the unknown. Forgiving Myung-gi for all his foolishness.

"Thanks for coming back to me," Myung-gi says, holding Mouse close.

CHAPTER 58

August 1951: Myung-gi, Age 15

It was August again, and a hot wind blew through the city. Myung-gi tugged on his collar, the seam of his shirt popping across his back. He was fifteen now—his shoulders had broadened from delivering water every day, and he'd grown three inches over the past year.

Which, these days, made him stand out to the recruiters on the corners.

"You! Join the ROK Army. Our country needs you!" a red-faced man shouted, pointing right at Myung-gi. "Yes, I'm talking to you. How old are you? Eighteen?"

"Uh, no, I'm fifteen, sir."

The man snapped his fingers in regret. "Well, no matter.

Between you and me, I'll just pretend I didn't hear that. There are plenty of boys your age serving." He tried to whisper, but it still came out as a shout.

"Me? You want *me* to join?"

"You wouldn't have to worry about food or shelter. You'd have a better life than in this desperate city."

A line of new recruits piled into a military truck. Most of them looked to be around Myung-gi's age. A cry shot out from inside the vehicle: *Tell my mom I'll miss her!*

"Where are they going?" Myung-gi asked, his solemn gaze following the truck down the road.

"To train. After that, most of them will be sent farther north, near the border."

Up north. Where Ahpa was.

At least, that was what Byongho had told him—just north of the 38th parallel was where the Reds were keeping his father, for his language skills.

He could feel something stir inside him, like rusted wheels starting to crank, faster and faster. Maybe this was what Myung-gi needed to do: enlist in the South Korean army and make his way back north with a weapon in his hand, an entire army at his back, and intelligence information he wouldn't otherwise have.

With all these things, Myung-gi *knew* he could find his father.

For the first time in a year, the fog in his head started clearing. The answer had been obvious all along: Myung-gi had to enlist in the army—not on the side of the Reds, like Byongho, but on the side of the South, like the captain from the boat.

But then why was his hand shaking?

Myung-gi glanced at the recruiters on other corners. He'd always walked past them, their shouting voices blending in with the sounds of the city. They all wore different military insignia on their uniforms, carried different clipboards. The red-faced man had ROKA on his jacket; others had KATUSA or MP. Myung-gi had some idea of what the letters meant—Republic of Korea Army; Korean soldiers attached to the US Army; military police—but who knew which was best? Did it matter?

The recruiter shoved a paper in his face. "All you have to do is sign here," he said, rattling the sheet.

Myung-gi stared at the paper, but the words kept blurring. Was he really going to do this? Risk his life to find his father? Wasn't that the least he could do as the eldest son? His trembling hand started reaching for it, closer and closer. But what about Uhma and Yoomee? How would they survive without his water delivery money? Maybe he should wait . . . but he was sick of waiting, and sick of being afraid, too.

Ahpa, tell me what to do.

"Look, I'll even let you go home and say good-bye to your mother before shipping you off to training," the recruiter said, smiling—though it looked more like a grimace.

Please give me a sign, Ahpa. You're the only one who can tell me what I should do. I can't ask Uhma—she would only worry. And I can't ask Yoomee—she's just a little kid.

"You would be doing your country a great service," the man boomed. A second group of recruits shuffled past, one of them crying that he'd changed his mind. His officer pushed him along anyway. Myung-gi's recruiter pinched his lips and glared, shooing them on.

Ahpa, here's the thing—every time I think of you, I see you in our old house, sitting alone with no one to talk to, no one to laugh with, no one to care for you.

The recruiter's voice dropped an octave lower. "Listen, kid, I don't have all day." The forced smile fell from his face.

Going back north would be easy. I know those roads, those mountains, those rivers. I know every thatched-roof house, every low tree branch, every bullock cart in the fields. I could find my way with my eyes closed. And I could make up for all my screwups, everything, Ahpa.

"Hey, snap out of it! Do you have an answer for me or what?" the man shouted, his face so red and pinched it looked ready to pop.

Myung-gi looked the recruiter in the eye. "Soon," he said, his jaw set tight. "I'll have an answer for you soon."

But first, Myung-gi needed to make a plan.

CHAPTER 59

October 1951: Myung-gi, Age 15

Weeks passed, but Myung-gi did not forget his encounter with the red-faced military recruiter. Myung-gi had decided that he couldn't leave until he saved enough money for Uhma and Yoomee to live on while he was gone.

Every day, he went to city hall to look for job postings, but other kinds of flyers covered the walls instead:

Have you seen my wife?

Lost son, birthmark on right ear.

Sister missing since December 5, 1950.

The papers had hung for so long, all the edges now curled like thinly sliced radish. Myung-gi walked slowly, reading every name.

He went to his family's flyer, the one Yoomee had made—*Looking for Kim Junho, Principal of the boys' school in Chagang Province, North Korea*—and touched it lightly. If only they had a photo of Ahpa to go with the flyer. He twisted the tail of his shirt.

Eventually he found extra work shining shoes, and he planned to go see about a translating job at the provisional school. Though his mother started to ask why he was always so tired, he never told her about the extra work. He didn't want her to worry.

But nothing could get by Yoomee.

It was a cool autumn evening when Myung-gi had decided to sit on top of their hill and rest his aching feet. Yoomee stepped outside and sat on a rock beside him.

"Oppah, what do you think of this drawing so far?" Yoomee asked, holding up her sketchbook.

Myung-gi gasped. Ahpa's eyes were staring back at him. It was their father's face—well, part of it, anyway—the eyes, jaw line, one eyebrow. The rest of him seemed to be breathing under the expanse of white paper, just waiting for Yoomee's pencil to bring him to life.

"It's good," Myung-gi said. "Really good." When had his sister become an artist?

"Thanks," she said, studying it at arm's length. "It's taking me forever. I keep drawing and erasing and starting over."

Myung-gi wanted to tell her that she should keep going no matter what, that it was more than really good—it was incredible—but Yoomee jumped up from where she sat.

"What happened to your feet?" she asked, pointing.

He looked down at the bare foot he was rubbing. It was blistered and bleeding from all the extra work he'd taken on—delivering water, walking around the city looking for shoes to shine. He hadn't seen it look that bad since their journey south.

"Eh, it's not a big deal. It just chafes sometimes," he said.

"Why are you obsessed with working?" she asked.

"What? I'm not."

"Yes, you are. I saw you shining those American GIs' shoes the other day—that's a new job. And you barely make it back home in time for curfew!"

Myung-gi sighed. "So I'm working harder. What's wrong with that?"

"Nothing. Except where's all the money you're making? We still only eat two meals a day. And it's still pig porridge made from US Army trash-bin scraps. I don't see any extra rice in our kitchen."

"It's not made from trash bins! We buy those ingredients from the market!"

Yoomee rolled her eyes. "Come on, Oppah. And where do you think the sellers get *their* ingredients from?"

Maybe Yoomee was right. She was like those boys back home who knew how to pilfer an extra potato from the landlord. But if he could match her street smarts, maybe he could get her off his back.

"The price of rice has gone up, you know. It used to be six hundred *won* for just over a tenth of a kilogram. Now it's nine hundred won. That's why we don't we have extra rice. And that's why I'm working harder," Myung-gi said, folding his arms. Even Yoomee couldn't argue with a good answer like that. Now maybe she would stop talking.

She paused and studied her brother long and hard.

Myung-gi glanced at her from the corner of his eye and started sweating.

After a long minute, she finally spoke. "I don't buy it. What are you up to, Oppah? Why are you hoarding all the extra money? Tell me, please! I can keep a secret!"

He closed his eyes and dropped his chin to his chest. Should he tell her? If he didn't, she would never quit bothering him. She might even bring the whole thing up in front of Uhma. He sighed. "I'm working extra jobs so I can save enough money for you and Uhma to live while I'm gone."

"Gone? Where are you going?"

"I'm going to enlist in the South Korean army so I can go back north and find Ahpa."

Yoomee's eyes bulged. "What? You can't do that. You're going to get killed."

"Enlisting in the army doesn't mean you're going to die!"

"Did you tell Uhma?"

"No, not yet."

"What about Sora? Did you tell Sora?"

"What? Why are you asking that?"

"Because you like her, don't you?"

"What?" Myung-gi said, breathless. Sora was the girl he grew up with, the girl he had once caught fireflies with in the dark.

Yoomee bit her lip. "This isn't a good idea, Oppah."

It didn't matter. It was his fault Ahpa got taken—now it was up to him to get his father back. If something happened to Myung-gi in the process, well, that would be the punishment he deserved.

"Just do me a favor. Don't tell Uhma. Let me tell her later. I can trust you, right?" Myung-gi pressed, his eyes turning dark and serious. "It'll be like a secret mission," he coaxed, trying to smile.

Yoomee didn't smile back. Instead, she looked at her brother's blistered feet, then at the worry line creased into his forehead. "Fine, I won't tell her," she said.

CHAPTER 60

October 1952: Myung-gi, Age 16

If only I had known before!
Everything in life
is but a lovely
shadow in the corner of the eye.
—Kim Sowol, *Hope*

A terrible crash rumbles overhead. Myung-gi tries to sit up but can't. What was that sound? More artillery shelling the hill? An avalanche?

Mouse scurries closer, into the crook of Myung-gi's arm.

Another boom. This time long and low. The tunnel vibrates.

And now there's a new sound—a shushing, or maybe a hissing. Myung-gi imagines a dark shadow slithering down the wall. Even the ends of his hair tremble. He sits and waits for the shadow to coil around him. . . .

That's when he feels it, in the dark. Something wet dripping onto his head. He angles his face upward, and the liquid snakes its way into his mouth.

Is he hallucinating? No—he *feels* it. Liquid dribbles down his cheeks. This is real.

"Water! It's raining!" Myung-gi gasps, his voice cracking.

He can picture it: rain coming down in sheets, hitting the mountain, running down its sides. And all he can think is: *If only I had known before! Everything in life is but a lovely shadow in the corner of the eye*—ha, ha! He'll take a line of hope from a poem anytime, anywhere!

Hands fumbling, Myung-gi unscrews his canteen and holds it under the thin stream until it fills to the top. Oh, how he wishes he still had his helmet to store more. Then he remembers the tin cup and gropes in the dark, snatches it off the ground, and starts filling that too.

And he laughs because his cup runneth over—just like in Sora's Bible.

Sora. He should've spent time with her in Busan. Even Yoomee knew better, scolding her big brother for not doing more, saying more. Since when did his little sister get so smart? If he could go back, maybe he would ask her advice about Sora. Maybe he would talk more to Uhma—ask her what she liked to do before she became a mother, what she misses most about Ahpa.

Twisting in the dark, Myung-gi tries to find something else to hold the water, but there's nothing. So he opens his mouth and sticks his head under the stream, letting water spill into his hair, down his face, over his ears. And he laughs, not even wondering whether Mouse could be getting trampled by all his flailing, whether the thunder could have scared him off, whether Mouse is even still here.

CHAPTER 61

February 1952: Myung-gi, Age 15

One season turned into the next, and before he knew it, it was February, and he had saved enough money for Uhma and Yoomee to live on for at least six months.

He couldn't leave before seeing Yoomee graduate from junior high, however—she had made him promise. The afternoon before her ceremony, he signed on, but he made arrangements with the red-faced recruiter to have one last day at home. Tomorrow he would leave for training.

No, he hadn't told Uhma yet.

But he would. After graduation. Uhma and Yoomee had already left so that Yoomee could rehearse songs before the ceremony. But

Myung-gi stayed back. There was something he needed to do before heading to the school, he'd told them.

Alone in the house, he stood in front of the hanging mirror and looked at himself long and hard. At the lock of hair hanging over his right eye, at his wire-frame glasses resting delicately on his long nose. He flared his nostrils, and a white cloud of breath blew out of him.

Who was he kidding? He was no dragon. What if his glasses broke during battle? What if they fell off? What if his hair covered his eyes, and he couldn't see for a second?

Myung-gi picked up the straight razor by the water basin. Tonight was his last night in this house. A cold wind whistled through the planked walls, raising tiny bumps along his arms.

Shivering, he grabbed that lock of hair like a skunk's tail and put the razor to its base. He sawed back and forth, the strands vibrating at the roots, tickling his scalp, sending a quiver down his back. Eventually the blade made its jagged way through, and his hand flew up holding that shock of hair. Staring at it, he thought of Uhma and the time she'd walked in holding her ponytail, the way it swung like fresh kill.

Sometimes you had to do what you had to do.

He touched the freshly shorn tufts on top of his head—as soft as paintbrush bristles—then took the razor and sawed off other sections—quickly, without thinking, no turning back now. Because all that hair would just get in his way, block his vision, make him vulnerable in battle.

Once all the longer strands were gone, he grabbed the bar soap and lathered his hands in the water basin, then covered his head with the foam. Water dripped down the sides of his face, trickled into the back of his shirt. The coldness made his teeth chatter. Bringing the blade to his scalp, he pressed gently, testing the best angle so as not to cut himself. In one steady swoop, he shaved off one section of stubbly hair—then another, and another, until his pale head was speckled blue.

Wiping his shaved head clean with a towel, he stepped closer to the mirror and touched his scalp. By the glow of the lamp, his bare head looked more misshapen than he'd expected. And when he clenched his jaw, he could see the bones of his skull move.

Well, no matter. Myung-gi grabbed his cap and covered his head, then stepped out the door.

CHAPTER 62

February 1952: Myung-gi, Age 15

By the time Myung-gi reached the school, a crowd had already gathered inside the largest army tent. A cold wind flapped the canvas walls. Uhma sat on one of the benches in the back, and Myung-gi hurried toward her, head lowered, shoulders hunched, hoping no one would notice his shaven head.

"Uh-muh! What did you do?" Uhma cried, reaching for Myung-gi's cap.

Myung-gi ducked away. "Nothing."

"Why would you shave your head?"

He shrugged.

"You were so handsome, but now you look so strange!"

"Stop, Uhma. Please."

"Why didn't you tell me first? You never talk. It's no wonder you have no friends. You should've told me you were going to do this," she said, pulling at the edge of his cap.

Without thinking, he threw back the words she'd once said to him and Yoomee: "What? It was bothering me, so I cut it."

He wasn't the only one who never told them things.

Uhma just nodded—her lips clamped shut—and touched the back of her shorn hair, her ears bright red. A pang of regret pierced him.

"Where's Yoomee?" he asked, his head lowered.

"Huh? Oh," Uhma said, blinking, "she is sitting up front with the other graduating students."

Myung-gi strained his neck to see. There they were. Up front. Laughing. Sora and Yoomee, as if they were best friends, and he wondered when that had happened. Yoomee had always envied Sora and gotten into spats with her, and Sora, after her brother died, had walked around as if in a fever dream. Now both their faces were bright, their eyes clear and shining. Where had their gaping holes gone?

He tugged on the sleeve of the blue suit he was wearing. Uhma had borrowed it for him from Sora's uncle. Though it fit better than any of his other outgrown clothes, it was still a little small.

"I am so proud of her, you know," Uhma said, dabbing her eyes with Ahpa's handkerchief.

Myung-gi nodded. He was proud of Yoomee too.

"I'm going to go thank her teacher before the program starts. I'll be right back," Uhma said, hurrying toward the front.

The tent filled with students and families and teachers, and it wasn't long before someone tried to take Uhma's empty seat.

"Is anyone sitting here?" a man asked.

Myung-gi looked up. It was Teacher Chun, holding the book Myung-gi had returned.

His teacher sat down before Myung-gi could answer. "You can have this book to keep. We finished going over it in class. Judging from your moving reading that first day, I think you might want to give it another chance."

"Oh. Thank you, sir," Myung-gi said. It would be rude to decline a gift, even if he had no use for it. Reading was a luxury of the past.

Teacher Chun sniffed once deeply. "So, when will you be returning to class? Usually, when boys drop out to help the family earn money, they return once things have settled."

Myung-gi rubbed the back of his neck. "Sir, I enlisted in the ROK Army. I leave tomorrow morning."

Teacher Chun stared straight ahead and didn't say a word.

Myung-gi clasped and unclasped his hands.

Finally, the old man got up to leave. He looked at the boy long and hard, as if studying an old photograph of someone he once knew. "Well, then, best of luck to you," he said.

Myung-gi wanted to say thank you, but he only nodded, not trusting his voice.

CHAPTER 63

February 1952: Myung-gi, Age 15

Myung-gi watched Yoomee and Sora walk to receive their diplomas. Everyone clapped and cheered, then rushed forward with hugs and tears. But he hung back, just as he had that day of the funeral.

All around, voices cried out: *Yooomee-ya! Sora-ya! Congratulations!* Sora's auntie even swayed to the folk music playing from the loudspeakers. Myung-gi wondered how she could dance like that—as if she were alone, no one watching.

"Oppah!" Yoomee said, breaking through the crowd and slapping him on the back. "Do you want to see my diploma? Pretty neat, huh?"

Myung-gi looked at the paper, then at his sister's beaming face, and wished more than anything that Ahpa could've been there to see this. He started blinking fast. "Wow, that's great. Really great," he said, trying hard to match everyone else's smiles. But his kept quivering.

"Oppah, I'm going to go talk to some of my friends," Yoomee said, turning.

"Wait," Myung-gi said. "Where's Sora?"

"Oh, she left for a walk on the beach."

"That's okay . . . I wasn't looking for her."

"Yeah, okay, Oppah. I'm going now." She scurried off toward a cluster of girls, and Myung-gi marveled at the number of new friends she'd made.

For hours, the tent stayed full. Parents stood in a circle eating rice cakes and laughing. Children ran around, playing games and shrieking. The speakers blasted music.

Myung-gi sat and waited on one of the benches, all of them now empty. Only, he wasn't alone—not really. Ahpa seemed to talk to him more now.

I bet you wish you had a good book, son.

No. I don't read anymore. I don't walk around with my head in the clouds. I try to stay vigilant.

Myung-gi was folding and unfolding his arms when Uhma motioned for him to come. Families were packing their belongings and saying their good-byes. He got up and followed everyone out of the tent.

They headed to Sora's uncle's house.

It was dinnertime. The men and children sat on the floor around the low dining table. Uhma and Sora's mother and auntie went into the kitchen, then brought out trays of rice, stir-fry squid, kimchi, and mung-bean pancakes. It was crowded. Even Sora's uncle's friend the humpbacked halmoni came—sliding open the rice-paper doors and shuffling inside. *We invited her because she lives all alone*, Sora's auntie had whispered when Myung-gi startled at the sight of his customer joining this family celebration.

He looked at the old woman and bowed slightly. She looked back and grinned.

"Congratulations to Sora and Yoomee for working so hard and graduating with such honor," Sora's uncle said, raising his cup of barley tea.

Cheers rang out all around the small room, and though Myung-gi clapped with the rest of them, hot shame crept up his neck knowing that his little sister would soon surpass him in school. Somehow, even not moving on with his life, everything had changed anyway.

Everyone began eating and talking, but Myung-gi could hardly swallow. He would soon have to tell Uhma what he'd done.

"Oh, before I forget," the humpbacked halmoni said, turning to Myung-gi, "can you change my delivery to Monday instead of Wednesday? I prefer the beginning of the week."

How could he have forgotten about all his customers?

A piece of kimchi fell from his chopsticks. He should've told them, should've made arrangements for them. "I'm—I'm so sorry, but I can't. You'll have to find someone else to deliver your water from now on," he stammered.

The halmoni's mouth hung open, and Myung-gi could see bits of chewed-up squid. "What? Why? How am I supposed to get my water?"

All the chatter in the room stopped. Everyone's eyes turned to Myung-gi. Especially Uhma's.

Myung-gi lowered his gaze. "I've enlisted in the ROK Army. I leave tomorrow morning."

A spoon clattered against a bowl. Uhma's hand hung in midair, holding nothing. Her face drained of color.

Someone gasped.

"I'm so sorry, Uhma. I didn't tell you because I didn't want you to worry. And, actually, you don't have to worry, because I saved a lot of money for you and Yoomee. And I promise to be careful. I'm just going back north to find Ahpa. I know the North with my eyes closed, and I know I can find him, and then I'll bring him back here, I promise," Myung-gi said, the words tumbling out upside down and right side up, as fast as an avalanche.

Uhma sat motionless, her lips shut tight. But Myung-gi knew something was coming, as sure as that wall of water on those mud-flats in the Yellow Sea.

"You think I care about money? You think it matters that you know

the North? What were you thinking?" Uhma suddenly shouted, hurling every word across the room.

Sora's mother rushed over, held her shoulders, told her to calm down, please calm down.

But Uhma only scoffed—something Myung-gi had never heard her do. "Imagine all those months of avoiding your only son's conscription, only to have him go and sign up himself!"

Then she crumpled to the floor like a kite that had lost its wind.

Myung-gi fumbled to pour a glass to give his mother, not even sure whether it was water or vinegar, not sure about anything anymore. "Sorry, Uhma, I'm sorry." Then, looking at Sora and Yoomee, whose faces had turned white, he apologized for ruining their graduation. "I'm sorry."

"Wait a minute," the humpbacked halmoni said, her brows crinkled. "Which military unit did you say you signed up with?"

Myung-gi turned to her, grateful to have someone interrupt. "It was ROKA—Republic of Korea Army, I think. At least that was what was on the recruiter's insignia. . . ."

At that, the halmoni frowned. "Not good. ROKA sends their soldiers to the front lines. Their platoon leaders are called 'one-day officers.' That's what my grandson told me. He was fighting at the border until he got sent home with a missing leg."

"'One-day officer'?" Myung-gi repeated.

The halmoni looked down, as if she wanted to take it back. "Eh, you know. They're officers for only one day because . . ."

"Because they don't live beyond that one day, Myung-gi-ya!" Uhma cried, rivers streaming down her cheeks.

The halmoni crinkled her face. "You should've paid better attention! The military police or KATUSA men would've been safer bets! They would've sent you on street patrol or something easy like that."

"Oh." Myung-gi's hands and feet turned cold and numb. He blinked around the room and saw Yoomee crying, Mr. Pak rubbing his neck, and Sora's auntie rocking. Across from him, Sora was wiping her eyes, but she reached over to squeeze his hand. He could almost feel it—her warm palm against his dead fingers.

"Goodness, child," the old woman said. "What made you think you should join the army at all? You can't even manage two buckets of water. You don't even know the going rate for delivery—if you knew, then you would know that I've been cheating you this whole time! And now you're going to try to stay alive at the front?" Now even the halmoni seemed as hot and flustered as his mother.

Uhma's eyes were wild. "Just don't show up tomorrow. Run away and hide!"

"No, Uhma," Myung-gi said, quietly. "I signed a paper. If I don't go, that's desertion. I'll get sent to jail for that—maybe executed. And I don't want to run and hide for the rest of my life."

Sora's father rubbed his chin and cleared his throat. "I will go in the boy's place."

Cries shot up across the room. *No! What about your own children? Don't be ridiculous!*

"Stop, please. *Everyone just stop!*" Myung-gi shouted, raising his arms. "No one is going in my place. This is something I have to do—me."

The room fell silent. Only sniffles punctured the quiet.

"I should leave," the humpbacked halmoni said, getting up and heading toward the door. "Myung-gi, will you walk me back? It's dark now."

Myung-gi nodded, relieved. They stepped out into the winter air, and he sucked it in long and deep.

"Listen, thank you for all the water deliveries," the halmoni said, reaching up past her hump and holding onto his arm. "You're a good boy."

"Okay," he replied, his voice cracking.

They continued walking, both of them looking up at the clear night sky. "Wah, what a pretty moon tonight," she said.

CHAPTER 64

October 1952: Myung-gi, Age 16

The greatest happiness of life is the conviction that we are loved—loved for ourselves, or rather, loved in spite of ourselves.

—Victor Hugo, *Les Misérables*

You certainly usually find something, if you look, but it is not always quite the something you were after.

—J. R. R. Tolkien, *The Hobbit*

It is nothing to die. It is frightful not to live.

—Victor Hugo, *Les Misérables*

Myung-gi tries to picture the moon, a clear night sky. But it's afternoon—a dim light is streaming through the crack.

Mouse isn't here. Maybe all that thunder and lightning scared him. Or maybe Mouse left to get food and will be back soon. But it's been almost a day. Mouse has never been gone this long.

"Mouse!" Myung-gi whispers hoarsely. Squinting, his eyes find nothing.

It's just a mouse, Myung-gi tells himself. But he was smart like a dog and soft like a baby, and when Myung-gi talked, he listened intently, staying by his side.

Mouse stayed.

In spite of sometimes squeezing his little body too hard. In spite of pushing him away. Mouse let Myung-gi hug him, didn't care that he wasn't as nimble as him, made no judgements on who he was.

Perhaps Ahpa loved him—his only son—in that way too, *loved him for himself, or rather, loved him in spite of himself,* just like Victor Hugo once wrote.

Ah, and now more words flood his head and fill his chest, like warm water rushing in.

Myung-gi looks at the rocky walls, so hard and dark and lonely. And that's when he breaks—face twisting, snot dribbling. Because he knows he's not coming back. No matter what he does. He's never coming back.

When Myung-gi curls up and opens his mouth, everything comes out in shuddering heaves. He lets the hurt echo down the corridor, against the walls, so loud and clear. He imagines his cries hurtling through the shafts and flowing right into the enemy's ears, where they will swirl and roar like the ocean inside a conch shell. Which reminds him of that first day in the hole, and he worries that every conversation has been nothing but wind rushing through this tunnel—*like a conch shell, Ahpa, nothing but a conch shell.*

"Hey, you! Are you there? Answer me!" Myung-gi shouts, hoping the Chinese soldier is still alive, hoping he is real.

Because he is through with being quiet and lonely and afraid. He doesn't want to die alone.

Myung-gi waits and listens. Bits of dirt crumble overhead. But there's no answer.

"*Ahpa!*" Myung-gi shouts. "It's been nearly three years since you were taken. And as hard as I've tried looking, I'm not sure I can find you!" His face is slick with tears. "But if you're alive, don't be sad, don't stop living, don't spend your days alone. Find a family you can love, and who will love you back—because we can't be with you anymore. I can't be with you anymore. Be happy!"

Now the words keep coming, words from the greatest writers of all time, each of them whispering in his ear, and he remembers: *It is nothing to die; it is frightful not to live.* So he imagines Ahpa living in their old house—not alone in the dark, wallowing in sadness, but with another family carrying a father-shaped hole in their hearts, a hole the same size as Ahpa. Together they will complete each other like puzzle pieces. There will be a woman who will kindly care for him, and a daughter who will make colorful pictures for him, and a son who will play games with him. And though they are not free, they will make their own freedom inside their house, at their dinner table, within their own little family. They will cobble together some semblance of happiness, which over time will become real.

And suddenly, Myung-gi wants this for Ahpa more than anything.

The irony of it makes him sob and laugh at the same time, and now it's Tolkien inside his head, telling him *You certainly usually find something if you look, but it is not always quite the something you were after.*

He quite enjoyed *The Hobbit*, he thinks back, smiling. Yes, yes, he did.

That's when he takes a deep breath, wipes his face dry, gets on his knees—a sharp pain shooting from his ankle, which is now swollen like a winter melon—and starts digging.

CHAPTER 65

February 1952: Myung-gi, Age 15

By morning, the red-faced recruiter was at Myung-gi's door, ready to accompany him to the collection point where new recruits were shipped off to their training centers.

Uhma's eyes were nearly swollen shut from all her crying the night before. Yoomee's face was pale and drawn. And Myung-gi's body ached from carrying as many months' supplies of firewood and drums of water as he could to stock in their corner kitchen.

"It'll be okay," Myung-gi said, hardly able to look at them. "I'll find Ahpa and bring him back." He hoisted his bag over his shoulder, his head down.

At this mention of finding Ahpa, the recruiter raised his brows but didn't say anything.

Myung-gi lightly hugged his mother and sister good-bye, his arms barely grazing their shoulders. But Uhma yanked him close and held him tight, then pounded his back with an angry fist.

"I will never forgive you for this," she whispered in his ear, without letting go.

Looking away, he dug his nails into his palms until they gouged small crescents, then walked out the door.

The hill had frozen, and Myung-gi slipped on a patch of ice. The recruiter yanked him upright by the collar and told him he better not think about running off, to which Myung-gi told him he wouldn't: he had a job to do. The recruiter laughed.

At the bottom of the hill, the usual crowds were out—families walking, children shouting, merchants haggling—as if this were any day and he were any boy on his way to school. Myung-gi liked that idea and let himself pretend for a little while, pointing his face up toward the sun, imagining his bag full of books instead of his mother's jars of black beans and dried anchovies—*food to give you energy for marching*, she had told him while sniffling.

"Hey, wait!" someone shouted, pushing through the crowds.

Myung-gi turned to see.

It was Sora. Her cheeks were flushed. Her wavy hair had puffed up in the wind, framing her face like a lion's mane. What was she doing here?

His insides started jumping.

"We're going to miss our meeting time at the collection point," the recruiter said.

"I'll make it quick, sir. I promise," Myung-gi pleaded.

The man sighed. "One minute. That's all you've got."

Sora bent over to catch her breath. "I just wanted to say good-bye," she said, her eyes red-rimmed and glossy. It was the way she sometimes looked after finishing a sad book, and for a second, he could picture the two of them reading together under the tree. She managed a smile. "I found all of them, you know."

He stared at her, puzzled.

"The books you left under the willow tree back home. I found all of them. I couldn't believe you went through all that trouble for me."

At that, Myung-gi looked left, then right, then finally settled on studying his feet. He pulled his jacket tighter.

"Also . . ." she said, her eyes turning dark and serious, "I know you crossed the Yellow Sea to reach the South, but Youngsoo and I stayed inland." She took in a deep breath. "I came to warn you."

"Warn me?" Myung-gi said, his head snapping up.

"About what it's like. The bridges. They were all bombed. If you have to cross a river using ice chunks—when you step on them, they dip, and if you fall into the water, your face turns blue and your fingers get frozen." She held his gaze, firm and steady. "And there are wolves. At night. They follow you everywhere—down the mountain, along the road, even into your dreams."

Sweat soaked the back of Myung-gi's shirt. In the cold air, it left him shivering.

"And there are enemy soldiers everywhere. You have to be on the lookout for them all the time," she said, looking him dead in the eye.

Myung-gi hoisted his bag higher on his shoulder. He couldn't let his fears get in the way of finding Ahpa—besides, it was too late. The recruiter was checking his watch and glaring at him. Nothing could change his fate.

"I don't want you to go," she said.

"What?"

"It's a bad idea."

"What?" he said again, standing at full attention.

"I could come and help you. I've been through it. I know what to do."

"What? No! Why are you telling me this now?" Myung-gi asked, her words prying open a door he'd held tightly shut for so long.

"Because . . ." Sora said, her eyes crinkled in worry, "you're my friend."

At that, Myung-gi let go the breath he'd been holding. He smiled faintly, trying not to show his disappointment. "I'm lucky to have such a good friend," he said, meaning it.

Then he hollered to the recruiter that he was ready to go.

As they headed down the street, Myung-gi took one last look over his shoulder at the girl who no longer covered her teeth when she laughed. He thought of how they'd grown up together, then grown apart, only to come back to being friends again—and how that was more than good enough.

The red-faced recruiter grabbed his arm and marched at a quick pace. "You ready for this?" he asked.

Myung-gi stopped looking over his shoulder. "Yes, sir. I'm ready."

CHAPTER 66

February 1952: Myung-gi, Age 15

They sat in rows atop the military truck rumbling down the dirt road. Myung-gi looked at the other recruits, their heads bobbling, teeth rattling. They were pimpled and baby-faced, hairless and smooth-skinned. Their arms were thin and lanky. Their shirt collars circled their skinny necks like rings tossed onto sticks. Some of them had been "night boys," stealing cigarettes, gum, and candy from the US Army, then selling them on the streets. Others were country bumpkins, their cheeks still ruddy from the fresh air. Some of them talked about Frank Sinatra and Marilyn Monroe and James Dean, wishing for some Coca-Cola to quench their thirst. Others sat quiet, staring at the passing sights, including a burnt refugee center where a kid had forgotten to put out a campfire.

Among these onlookers were the oldest boys, watching solemnly and swallowing, the huge knobs in their throats bobbing up and down. Without thinking, Myung-gi put a hand to his own throat, but there was only a bump of a mosquito bite where his Adam's apple would soon grow. What if he really *was* too young to be here? What if the three inches he'd grown wasn't enough? What if he'd made a terrible mistake?

The truck came to a halt, and everyone climbed out.

They headed inside an old elementary school that had been converted into a training facility. Myung-gi peered into the classrooms as the recruits walked down a hall: some had been repurposed as offices for company commanders, some as medical examination rooms, but others remained untouched, still full of tiny school desks and chairs and chalkboards. He could almost see it—students chatting, a teacher writing on the board, Myung-gi himself sitting at a desk. And then Ahpa poking his head inside to check on the class.

Ahpa, Ahpa!

No, son, you should call me Principal at school.

Principal Ahpa.

No, Principal Kim.

But you're my ahpa.

That's right, son. He chuckled. *I'll always be your father. Just call me Ahpa.*

A chalky smell wafted into the hallway, and Myung-gi breathed it deep into his lungs.

They entered a room where there were boxes of recycled uniforms. A man sitting at a table handed Myung-gi a top and bottom, but they were too large when he held them up. The man then gave him a different set, but the pants still dragged past the soles of Myung-gi's feet.

"That's all we've got. Figure out a way to make them fit," the man said. "Now go to the medical examination room and undress for your physical."

"Yes, sir! I'll cuff the bottoms," Myung-gi said, the uniform's long pants dragging on the floor.

One of the other recruits snickered. "What, are you twelve years old?"

Myung-gi wasn't, but he felt close.

"How old are you, really?" the army doctor asked when Myung-gi stood naked and shivering for his physical exam.

"Almost sixteen, sir."

"Go home. You're too young," the doctor said.

But the recruiting officer beside him disagreed. "It's fine. He's big enough."

"What? He's just a boy."

"Doctor. I already said it's fine. He's big enough. Next."

Though the army doc gaped at the officer—as if this still surprised him—he gave Myung-gi's papers the stamp of approval, shaking his head.

After Myung-gi got dressed, rolling his sleeves four times on each arm, he followed everyone outside to a tent. There, they listened to rousing speeches by sergeants and lieutenants about how they were there to save this great nation, a nation worth giving their lives for. Afterward, everyone clapped—except one boy who was picking gum off the bottom of his boot. And Myung-gi watched, mesmerized by the line of gummy gray stretching thin like rubber.

Ahpa, I don't really care about all this patriotism. That's not why I'm here.

"Why are we here? Why are any of us here? To make this world a better place: to leave an indelible mark that makes a positive difference in people's lives."

Ah, I remember that speech you gave. That was a really good one, but I was worried the whole time. Comrade Lee was listening so intently for you to say something that could get you in trouble.

Another sergeant was speaking—face red, spittle flying, finger wagging. But by now that gummy gray was off that boy's boot and being molded into balls and triangles and cubes.

"I believe that most of us want what is best for all people. The only disagreement we have is how to make this happen—the process."

Yes. You were right, Ahpa. We all want the same things, but we have different ideas of how to make them happen. Uhma just wants to wait for you to come. I want to find you.

Gum Boy tossed the tiny rubbery ball in the air.

"Never be afraid to speak out against injustice. Never be afraid to do what is right. Never be afraid to take the hard road."

That was your last speech, Ahpa. I thought of it often after you told me to go on without you if I had to. And that's what I did.

"Psst . . . hey, do you know what the sergeant's talking about?" Gum Boy whispered.

Myung-gi looked at him and blinked. "I have no idea."

After the officers' speeches, Myung-gi stood in line for dinner inside the tent. It was rice and murky seaweed soup. Though it smelled as fishy as the ocean, his stomach gurgled anyway.

"Ooh, food fit for a soldier," someone muttered. Another boy snickered.

"And why do you think all your mothers ate this after giving birth to all you pig brains? It helps with circulation and digestion and is full of vitamins and minerals!" the cook shouted, pointing his ladle at them like a finger.

Myung-gi hadn't eaten all day. He didn't care that the soup had the consistency of silt; he would take it.

But when the cook handed Myung-gi his portion, it was smaller than everyone else's. Just like the rifle he received later that day. Why? It wasn't until he received the rest of his gear and ammunition—fifty pounds worth—that he actually welcomed that small-size weapon.

The officers sent the boys out to an open field for evening

target practice. Trudging under the weight of all his gear, Myung-gi hoped he would never have to use the bullets or his knife.

"Hit that tree," one of the officers told Myung-gi.

He tried—and missed. He didn't like the volume of the rifle or the way it recoiled against his shoulder—and he worried it might kick back against his eye and break his glasses. He had to think very hard about which hand to put where, too.

"Perhaps I could get a book or instruction manual on how to operate this thing, sir?" he asked the sergeant, who laughed and laughed and laughed.

There was the time when one of the recruits lost his footing and fired toward Myung-gi and the lineup instead. But on that frigid morning, Myung-gi's head was wrapped so thickly in a scarf and helmet that he couldn't hear the bullet whizzing past his ear, couldn't see the periphery of the great wide field, couldn't believe any harm could come to him when he was so snug in there. That afternoon, his life was spared by only a few inches.

After just ten days, they told Myung-gi that he had completed his basic training, even though he had not fired more than one clip and had not successfully hit a single target.

"I passed?" Myung-gi wondered aloud. *He's not old enough. Can't even aim and fire. What's he even doing here anyway?* He had heard the drill sergeants say these things over and over.

"Yes, of course," one of the sergeants answered.

Just like he'd passed the age requirement and the physical and everything else that required only a stamp of approval and a look the other way.

After that, the recruits lined up inside a tent to receive their assignments. They fidgeted, bit their nails, stepped from side to side. Finally they heard where they were going: Suwon.

CHAPTER 67

March 1952: Myung-gi, Age 15

Back to Suwon. Haewon and her grandmother had welcomed Myung-gi and Uhma and Yoomee there, as if they were family.

Myung-gi sat inside a truck beside other skinny-necked recruits, the vehicle rumbling up a snowy road toward the entrance to the city. Though it had been nearly two years since he was here, something glowed warm inside him, like a bed of bright orange coals. He imagined Haewon's and her grandmother's faces lighting up in surprise at the sight of him. He would tell them about his encounter with Byongho and about his plan to go north and find Ahpa. Haewon's grandmother would offer him a home-cooked meal that would make his mouth water.

An entire section of the Janganmun Gate was now missing, as

if a giant had bitten off a mouthful. On the other side, morning had come to the city, but there were fewer shopkeepers setting up their stands, fewer villagers coming out to buy scraps and soup bones. He wondered where all the people had gone.

The truck rolled to a stop, and at the sergeant's order, everyone scrambled out—Myung-gi's helmet hanging over his eyes, his rifle slung awkwardly over his shoulder—and headed toward town. He looked around for Haewon's house.

Suddenly, he could see it: the window he'd once looked out of, the door where Haewon and her grandmother had stood saying good-bye . . . but the door was wide open, the home dark.

He broke ranks and ran inside.

The piano stood in the corner. All the keys had yellowed. Water dripped from the ceiling onto its buckling wooden top. There was a long crack down the middle of the low dining table. All the blankets and mats were strewn across the floor.

Tiny drops of blood trailed over them.

He remembered what Haewon had once told him—*The soldiers, they don't bother the very old or very young, but you and me, well, we're right in between*—and he gripped the piano to steady himself.

"*Haewon!*" he called, but no one answered.

What had happened to them? Where had they gone? Were they alright? Myung-gi leaned against the mud wall. He wished he had written to Haewon at least once. She had been a friend, and he didn't have many of those. Why did everyone always disappear?

"Hey, what are you doing in there?" It was Gum Boy. "The sergeant sent me to get you."

Myung-gi wiped his eyes. "Nothing."

"Wah! Is that a piano?" Gum Boy ran over and started pounding random keys. "Look at me, I'm a fancy piano player," he said, grinning.

"Stop," Myung-gi said, heading out the door and onto the road by the stream.

There was only the sound of water trickling over rocks and ice.

How strange to patrol where he had once hidden, to return to a place where everyone was now gone.

CHAPTER 68

October 1952: Myung-gi, Age 16

It was fall when Myung-gi was sent to the front lines in the Osong mountains, right by the 38th parallel.

The day had come. He and his platoon were preparing to enter the battle. The words *one-day officer* popped into his head as the voices of fellow soldiers were droning in his ear. What was the lieutenant saying? Something about heading to the main line of resistance, fighting in the trenches? The hills here had all been assigned strange numbers—597.9, 537.7. How was he supposed to keep track? All the hills looked the same.

"Chinese troops have dug intricate tunnels under the mountains and fortified their positions. We believe it's a fan-shaped system made of three sections, about twenty to thirty feet underground. But we must not be timid. We must take the hill!" the lieutenant said firmly, squinting at Myung-gi and the other skinny-necks, the shadow of the numbered foothills towering behind him.

Gum Boy looked at Myung-gi, and Myung-gi looked back, at the tiny ball of gum rolling between the boy's fingers.

Myung-gi was hardly listening now. He couldn't believe that he was finally by the border, so close to home that he could taste it in the back of his throat—that familiar scent of pine and earth. When could he break away to go find Ahpa? After this mission? Before?

It was a cool autumn night, the kind that sharpened your senses, let you finally breathe after a long, stifling summer. They were marched into position and told to ready arms.

Myung-gi took in a deep breath, and the crisp air stung his nostrils, shot up right behind his eyes. His scalp tingled inside the plastic liner of his steel helmet, which was trapping all the heat coursing through his body. He wanted to rip off his gear and run into battle screaming. Like the old man from his village who had gone crazy and run out of his house naked, clanging a metal pot with a stick. Uhma said he'd crumbled under the pressure of having to watch what he said and did all the time, but Myung-gi had spoken to that old man afterward and found him completely reasonable. Maybe he hadn't been crazy—maybe he had just been sick and tired of feeling scared.

Myung-gi understood. It had been nearly three years since Ahpa was taken. Three years of waiting for him. Three years of constant fear. He'd had enough too. He straightened his glasses, pressed them firmly onto the bridge of his nose.

This was it. This was it. The moment that would change everything.

Bodies flying, mortar shells dropping, the lieutenant's mouth moving—everything in slow motion.

Advance forward! To the top! Go, go, go!

Chest heaving, sweat dripping, Myung-gi charged up that hill.

A scream rose from his gut, blasted out his mouth, joined the roaring of others.

God, it was almost beautiful. Like the swell of so many instruments tuning before the grand performance. The cacophony of war.

Until the flash of a grenade sent him reeling.

No! Myung-gi!

Tumbling

down,

down,

down.

Without a weapon. His helmet gone. He touched his bare, exposed head, then scrambled into a hole, the kind where animals burrowed deep. And when he tried to crawl back out, there was a terrible crash—walls caving, earth falling—burying him alive.

Of course, it wasn't a hole for burrowing creatures.

It was a tunnel, an enemy tunnel. Where his greatest fears awaited him.

CHAPTER 69

October 1952: Myung-gi, Age 16

> Death was a friend, and sleep was Death's brother.
>
> —John Steinbeck, *The Grapes of Wrath*

The rainwater has given Myung-gi a burst of energy. And now he's digging, hard, in the dark.

He finds the edge of a boulder, a gravelly spot where he can loosen the earth and try to break through. A piece of rock falls to the ground—as big as his fist—and when he reaches down to feel its mass, his hand slips into Mouse's nook.

For a second, he expects to feel Mouse's warm little body, his tiny beating heart. But, of course, he's not there.

Myung-gi keeps digging. Then it dawns on him that he has chosen to dig on the side where the enemy is, not the side of the opening where he first crawled in.

"I have water! Just hold on! I have water!" Myung-gi shouts at the wall, while clawing furiously. But no one answers.

One of these days, he'll have to tell Yoomee all about Mouse and the way he would sit in his cupped hands. She will probably want a pet mouse afterward, and then go out into the fields to trap one herself. Myung-gi chuckles out loud.

In this way, he passes the hours from night to morning—thinking of everyone he hasn't seen for so long. Sora, and the way she looked at him the day he left, as if she wanted to hold him back. Uhma, her knitting needles clicking so fast, the radio droning on about war and politics and the men who tell her what to do, tell everyone what to do. Someday, Myung-gi will tell her things too—not what to do, but about the son she raised. And Haewon, the girl from Suwon who doesn't like to read but knows how to play the piano . . . he wishes he could've heard her play.

Morning light streams in stronger, the crevice now slightly wider. His hands are sore and bloody, and he allows himself a rest against the wall. Soon, his eyelids grow heavy; he can hardly keep them open. He shimmies a quarter turn to the left, and—as if he's lived here all his life—finds a familiar groove to cradle him. His limbs feel weighted down, as if they've transformed into rocks and become part of the tunnel. Which is probably why he can't move—even though he keeps telling himself to wake up and dig—because Myung-gi and the lifeless rocks are becoming one. He imagines his body breaking down into a primordial soup, then melding into the walls of this mountain which has been here since the beginning of time.

Even now, the books whisper to him. *Death was a friend, and sleep was Death's brother.*

When it is all done, he will sleep.

CHAPTER 70

October 1952: Myung-gi, Age 16

Mom and sis, let's live by the river;
In the yard the glistening golden sand;
From over the back gate the song of the reeds.
Mom and sis, let's live by the river.

—Kim Sowol, *Mom and Sis*

Myung-gi tastes it before he hears it—bits of dirt crumbling into his mouth from footsteps pounding overhead. He sputters and coughs at the grit catching in his throat.

Muffled voices speaking in Korean and English trickle in from above. *He's in there! I know he is! I heard him the other night!* someone says, cracking gum.

Myung-gi blinks and squints. The ray of light streaming through the crevice is flickering, the way sunlight dances between trees when you're in a moving car.

He scrambles onto his knees and presses his face up to the crevice. "*Help!*" Myung-gi screams. "*I'm trapped!*"

A loud commotion on the surface—voices rising, tools clanking. Pieces of rock start falling, and he crawls out of the way, his foot dragging at a strange angle.

"They're here! They're here to rescue us," Myung-gi says to the rock wall. But there's no answer.

Boulders are moving, light is streaming, the sky is opening up above him. Cold air rushes in. He squints through clouds of dust, which are now filling the tunnel and erasing the walls, as if this place was nothing but an illusion.

Is this really happening? Is he really going to get out of here? Will he get to go home?

He tries to contain all the bouncing and skipping and ricocheting inside him. But his body won't stop shaking, even though he has curled himself into a tight ball.

"What's your name?" someone shouts down.

Son, your Korean name, your real name, is Myung-gi. Kim Myung-gi. Do you understand?

"I said, who are you?" someone shouts again.

Blinking, Myung-gi wets his cracked lips and looks up. This, he knows he can answer. "My name is Myung-gi, Kim Myung-gi. Soldier of the ROK Army, Second Division, sir."

An arm appears from above. "Grab my hand," a man says.

Rubbing his eyes, Myung-gi just blinks and stares. He can't believe there's suddenly a hand reaching into the tunnel, can't believe someone has come back for him. Gratitude swells in his throat.

But it's not until he hears "It's all over, son," in a voice much too deep to be his father's, that he starts crying.

Myung-gi's feet are lifting off the ground. He's being plucked out of the maw of hell.

And soon he will be set down in the right place—at home, in Busan, where he will hug Uhma tight and thank her for being both mother and father. Where he will tell his artist sister how proud he is of her and then gaze upon her portrait of their father. Where he will go to Sora, the girl he will always love, and finally say he is sorry. Where he will find the humpbacked halmoni and make sure she has enough water to drink. Where he will dig up that book from Teacher Chun and read it from beginning to end. Where he will take that entrance exam and hope for the best. Where he will write their history, his family's, the one he already started. Where he will finally do as his father said and not be afraid to go on without him.

The sun is beating down on Myung-gi's face, warm and tingly. So much to do, so much to say, so much to write. He closes his eyes because the brightness is too much for him.

But even then, he can see a pink new world glowing on the inside of his eyelids.

THE END

EPILOGUE

35 Years Later in the North

It arrives inside a crate, underneath a sack of rice, beside a bag of seeds, among some counterfeit clothing.

There, like a baby swaddled in smuggled goods, it stares up at him: a memoir, the face of his son on the cover. Except the photo looks more like himself—from nearly forty years ago, when he was a principal at the boys' school in Chagang Province—than the son he remembers, whose dark eyes, magnified behind his glasses, were always staring into a book.

Myung-gi's father looks around before lifting the book from the crate, even though he is in the far corner of his bedroom, with the door shut, inside his own thatched-roof house, deep in the countryside where there is nothing but mountains and a view of the Yalu River. Even so, someone could peek in through a window or the crack in the wall, he thinks. Gone are the courageous speeches of his younger days, beaten thoroughly out of him. Old age has turned him weary and soft. Fanning through the pages, arthritic pain stabs his joints, but he is used to that by now. He flips through the book again—this time to breathe in that musty paper scent.

He brings the book close and then farther away, trying to focus the words; the cataracts in his eyes have worsened over the last ten years. The jacket says it's based on the author's life and family. There is mention of being a soldier and fighting in the Korean War, of being stuck in a tunnel. This last part frightens him, and he's not sure he is ready to read it all just yet.

So, instead, he keeps turning the book over to look at the author photo: Myung-gi Kim. Squinting, he tries reading the bio under the picture, which mentions something about living in the United States.

But it's not enough; he wants to know more. Turning to the back pages, he searches for the acknowledgments and finds it, because he knows his way around a book. Here, it's as if his son is talking directly to him, and his hands start to tremble. He can make out a few words here and there, but those cataracts blur everything—it's like looking through smudged glass.

It says he wants to thank so many people; but who are these names? Skimming further down the page, he sees more names and more of them, and he marvels at all the friends his son has made. And then he sees it—a name he knows:

To Yoomee, my amazing little sis, who always found time to read my manuscript while managing her art gallery; thanks for feeding me every time I came to NYC.

Yoomee-ya! His beautiful little girl, all grown up! This makes his face crumple. He pauses and wipes his eyes, but then he smiles, thinking of all those drawings she used to make. He continues reading.

And Uhma, my guardian angel in Heaven...

At this, he stops and clutches the book close to his chest.

A small groan escapes him. His lovely, dear wife, already passed on from this world? How can that be? *Will you forgive me, yeobo, for marrying again? I missed you so...*

Though an ache burns like napalm inside him, he must read on:

To my beautiful wife who has always shared my love of books...

He wipes his cloudy eyes and hopes that his son married that girl, the love of his life.

And my three children...

Three! Oh, how he wishes he could meet them—his grandchildren.

Now the decades start rolling in waves upon him—his children going off to college, falling in love, pursuing their dreams, becoming parents, and growing old—all stolen and lost. But if there is any bitterness left in him, it is no longer biting.

What if you get caught for smuggling that book? What if it ends up bruising your heart? his wife had asked. *Ah, but sometimes it feels good to press that bruise, like pushing hard into knotted muscle,* he told her.

Looking back, he sees that he was selfish to ask her to risk it: this book endangers her life, their family, everything they've built together. And all the sacrifices she made to save enough to pay the smuggler! Eating only twice a day, gathering edible tree bark, making "meat" with the leftover residues from soybean oil. He never wanted to hurt his good, kind wife who saved him after the war when he was alone, on the run, and hopeless. The first time he saw her, fleeing over the misty hills, beside her son and daughter, US fighter jets roaring across the sky, he called out, "Yeobo, my dear, it's me! Children, it's your father!" And though it wasn't them, they eventually became the family he would love.

From the other side of the sliding rice-paper door, voices float inside.

What time is it? We shouldn't have stayed so long at the women's league meeting. Now I hardly have time to soak the beans for dinner.

Uhma, what were we supposed to do? Leave? And have Comrade Kwa put us on the watch list?

Aigoo, my daughter, you know I'm just venting in private. Help me with dinner before your brother and his family come. And do me a favor; go find your father.

Music from the radio flicks on. Pots and pans clank in the kitchen. Someone knocks on the door.

Oh, you're here already! Come in, come in! Let me see my beautiful grandchildren!

There are squeals and laughter and greetings.

Ahpa, where are you? Everyone's here!

Sounds of a past life, of something familiar, of second chances. He puts the book back in the crate. The autumn sun streams in through the window. Its rays are not as warm as during the summer, but he angles his face toward it.

Ahpa, are you home?

ACKNOWLEDGMENTS

This book would not have been possible without the love and support of so many people. First, I want to thank my incredibly kind and astute agent, Michael Bourret, who always looks out for me with such care and attentiveness. I am so grateful to have you in my life.

Many thanks to my amazing and talented editor, Mora Couch, who nurtured not only *In the Tunnel* but also *Brother's Keeper* and became a Korean history expert along the way. Your insights elevated this story to another level. To the entire Holiday House team, including Terry Borzumato-Greenberg, Sara DiSalvo, Michelle Montague, Hannah Finne, Miriam Miller, Della Farrell, Rebecca Godan, K Dishmon, Kerry Martin, and George Newman, thank you for reigning in my words and bringing greater clarity to this story.

To Stephanie Son, the talented artist responsible for the cover art of *In the Tunnel* as well as *Brother's Keeper*, thank you for perfectly capturing the essence of these stories. I couldn't be happier with both covers.

I also want to thank Kyung-Lin Bae, my accomplished translator, who not only worked on the Korean translation for *Brother's Keeper* but also helped me research *In the Tunnel* by translating critical documents available only in Korean. Without your skilled translations, I would not have been able to write this book.

Special thanks to Varian Johnson for taking time to read my entire rough draft and offering your insightful critique—something you did not have to do but you so generously did. I also want to thank Martine Leavitt, An Na, and Deb Noyes for sharing your writerly wisdom. I am so grateful to have had all of you as my advisors while at VCFA.

To Linda Sue Park, thank you for lifting up Korean voices through your Kibooka site which celebrates kids' books by Korean

Americans and Korean diaspora (www.kibooka.com). You and all my fellow Korean American writers are such an inspiration to me.

I also want to thank all the people in my life who are always rooting for my stories: Sohee, Gloria, Judy, Jungmi, Caroline, Cathy, Heidi, Ann, Lori, Mary, Susan, Michelle, and Jungyoon. Your friendship keeps me afloat. Special thanks to my friend Jo Ann for allowing me to interview her about her experience of meeting her grandmother in North Korea during the 1980s and about her father's experiences during the war. To my fellow VCFA writers, it gives me great comfort to know that you write alongside me, putting your own much needed stories out into the world; thank you for your support.

Special thanks to my sisters Helen, Gloria, and Joyce who teach me so much about life and writing. I am also eternally grateful to my mother for sharing her stories, and to my father, whose scholarly nature formed the basis of Myung-gi's personality. I also want to thank my late uncle, Dr. Luke Kim, whose memoir, *Beyond the Battle Line: The Korean War and My Life*, was invaluable to my research. Thank you for so bravely writing about your mother's abduction in North Korea and speaking candidly about your belief as a young man that in joining the ROK Intelligence Unit, you could also perhaps find news on your kidnapped mother—a hope that became Myung-gi's motive for enlisting as well.

I couldn't have written this book without my husband's support and encouragement. Thank you, Chris, for being my greatest cheerleader and for allowing me to indulge myself in doing what I love. And to my daughters, Laura, Abby, and Emily, thank you for always reading my stories and for giving me a reason to write.

Finally, I want to express my deepest gratitude to the Korean War generation of my parents who have shown us not only how to survive, but how to live. And thank you, dear readers, for fulfilling the final and most important leg of this writing journey by letting these stories into your hearts and minds.

AUTHOR'S NOTE

After *Brother's Keeper*, I didn't think I would write another story set during the Korean War. But while researching that novel, I kept coming across new refugee accounts from archives across the ocean, from stacks of obscure documents, from pages of old newspaper interviews. While their stories, like Myung-gi's, seemed unlikely and unbelievable, I discovered they were, in fact, commonplace. There were thousands of others like him—children who were never reunited with family members separated across the border, refugees who experienced war crimes barely acknowledged in official war history, child soldiers who were unjustly used in a war that later only forgot them. I wanted to finally acknowledge this last category—these boys from the Korean War—and the unredressed injustices they faced. But I wondered how I could write a story for young readers in which wrongs inflicted upon the characters were never righted. In confronting this question, I knew I had no choice but to write about this history, because sometimes life is terribly unfair, and I needed to figure out a way to reconcile this reality with being able to move on and be happy—for my sake and my readers.

An astounding ten million Koreans were permanently separated from their immediate family after the Korean War.[1] They searched and waited for loved ones trapped across the border—a few, like Myung-gi, even enlisting in the ROK Army as a means of somehow finding them, but often to no avail. Though there have been several reunion programs over the decades bringing together a few lucky families from the north and south for a supervised visit, most Koreans hoping to see long-lost family members have never been able to meet. Just as Myung-gi must learn to live with this lack of closure—by choosing to love and embrace family, friends, and the life he must still lead—so must millions of Koreans who have suffered this same loss.

But it is not only through love, but also forgiveness, that so many Korean War survivors I encountered were able to move on with their lives. Because of this, I knew I had to let Myung-gi forgive himself and even the enemy he comes upon in the tunnel during the Battle of Triangle Hill which took place from October 14 through November 25, 1952, in the Osong Mountain region by the North-South Korean border. Although peace talks were already under way, and only a few months later an armistice agreement would be signed, the Battle of Triangle Hill was one of the bloodiest of the conflict, as both sides tried to make territorial and political advances before the war's end.[2] During the day, US and ROKA soldiers would make gains and force the Chinese to hide in the tunnels they had built, while at night, Chinese forces would attack and recover their losses, resulting in a back-and-forth effect that reflected the overall stalemate of the Korean War.[3] While writing this story, I imagined that Myung-gi would have been rescued during one of those brief periods when US and ROKA forces took control of the ridge. And I imagined the enemy would have been just as human as him.

It should be noted, for Myung-gi, forgiveness does not mean forgetting or diminishing wrongs or foregoing justice. In fact, Myung-gi's act of writing his life story is the opposite of these things, as is my act of writing this book. Acknowledgement of people and their experiences is as important as love and forgiveness in establishing peace. Which is why I based Myung-gi's character on the actual child soldiers of the Korean War, to finally acknowledge their sacrifices. Their names include Park Tae-seung[4], Hyung Kyu Shin[5], Kim In-Sun, Kim Sang-gi, Park Im-Jo, Yang Jong-Taek, Jo Woo-Hyun, Park Yoon-Pyo, Kim In-Seon, Song Doo-Bin, and Kim Nam-Hoon.[6] All their lives, most child soldiers struggled to be recognized but were rarely heard. Known as sonyeonbyong (child soldiers under the age of seventeen), these boys were among the most forgotten casualties of war. More than 30,000 boys ages fourteen to seventeen were conscripted into the Korean War by the

South Korean government, and approximately 3,000 of them died as a result, according to NPR News.[7] Additionally, many more boys, like Myung-gi, were allowed to enlist voluntarily. While the North Korean military also conscripted child soldiers during the war, exact figures are more difficult to find.

During the UN-South Korean retreat, the sonyeonbyong often lagged and faltered, unable to keep pace with their older cohort, yet their contribution was significant, according to Lee Sang Ho, a historian at the South Korean Ministry of National Defense Institute for Military History.[8] When North Korean forces captured approximately ninety percent of the entire peninsula and continued pushing toward Busan—the last unconquered foothold in the south—it was the boy soldiers who helped keep the Busan Perimeter from falling, according to General Paik Sun-yup, as noted in Lee's research.[9] Sadly, they never received recognition as veterans, as many were not officially registered as part of the military due to their underaged status. Traumatized and neglected after the war, many of these boy soldiers struggled to finish their education and maintain employment and ended up in the lowest social classes.[10]

As part of Myung-gi's story, I also wanted to acknowledge the bombing of the bridge at Waegwan by the Nakdong River, which for many years was considered an event that never officially occurred. The overpass was filled with refugees—including many women and children—when US commanders gave the order to detonate it to prevent the enemy from crossing over. I placed Myung-gi here to highlight this relatively unknown tragedy which was not reported until 1960 when the 1st Cavalry Division's Maj. Gen. Hobert R. Gay briefly acknowledged it in an official war history.[11]

While I tried to maintain accuracy in the historical timeline of events, I did alter the chronology of Myung-gi's military training and service near the end of the war. Instead of depicting a longer, more thorough training to reflect the final two years of the conflict when a stalemate allowed the ROKA more time to sufficiently prepare its soldiers, I had Myung-gi experience the same hurried training that young recruits received earlier in the war when the North Korean army was advancing quickly and time was short. During this early period, it was not uncommon for recruits to train for only ten days and fire their M1 rifles only eight or nine times; the result was heavy casualties among South Korean soldiers.[12] Having Myung-gi experience the inadequate training seen in the earlier part of the war allowed me to show the dire straits many child soldiers faced.

At the start of writing *In the Tunnel*, I had no idea how to reconcile unredressed injustices with finding peace within oneself. I kept wondering how Myung-gi, and so many others like him, could ever return to any semblance of normalcy knowing their loved one could be alive on the other side of a border. But as the story progressed, Myung-gi showed me the importance of love, forgiveness, and acknowledgment in being able to move on and be happy. He reminded me of the importance of books as instruments for such healing. For these insights, I am grateful to the elucidative aspect of the writing process and, more importantly, to the generation of Korean War survivors who have since lived and flourished despite having experienced so much undeserved hardship. Their stories, as told through Myung-gi and Sora, are now yours to share and consider. Thank you for reading.

1. *Encouraging Reunions of Divided Korean-American Families*. 2020, https://www.congress.gov/116/crec/2020/03/09/modified/CREC-2020-03-09-ptl-PgH1545.htm
2. Peters, Richard A., and Xiaobing Li. *Voices from the Korean War: Personal Stories of American, Korean, and Chinese Soldiers*. University Press of Kentucky, 2005.
3. Peters, Richard A., and Xiaobing Li. *Voices from the Korean War: Personal Stories of American, Korean, and Chinese Soldiers*. University Press of Kentucky, 2005.
4. Kuhn, Anthony. "Thousands of Child Soldiers Died in the Korean War. Survivors Want More Recognition." NPR, 25 June 2020.
5. Shin, HK. *Remembering Korea 1950 A Boy Soldier's Story*, University of Nevada Press, 2001.

6. Lee, SangHo, and Young-Sil Park. *A Study of the Korean War Boy Soldiers*. Institute for Military History, Ministry of National Defense, 2011.
7. Kuhn, Anthony. "Thousands of Child Soldiers Died in the Korean War. Survivors Want More Recognition." NPR, 25 June 2020.
8. Kuhn, Anthony. "Thousands of Child Soldiers Died in the Korean War. Survivors Want More Recognition." NPR, 25 June 2020.
9. Kuhn, Anthony. "Thousands of Child Soldiers Died in the Korean War. Survivors Want More Recognition." NPR, 25 June 2020.
10. Kuhn, Anthony. "Thousands of Child Soldiers Died in the Korean War. Survivors Want More Recognition." NPR, 25 June 2020.
11. Choe, Sang-Hun, et al. "Ex-GIs Tell of More Korean Civilian Deaths." *Los Angeles Times*, 14 Oct. 1999, https://www.latimes.com/archives/la-xpm-1999-oct-14-mn-22195-story.html.
12. Sawyer, Robert K. *Military Advisors in Korea: KMAG in Peace and War.* Center of Military History United States Army, Washington, D.C., 1988.